W9-CAB-734

THE WRITING ON THE WALL

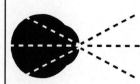

This Large Print Book carries the
Seal of Approval of N.A.V.H.

THE WRITING ON THE WALL

ELIZABETH MATTOX

THORNDIKE PRESS
A part of Gale, Cengage Learning

GALE
CENGAGE Learning·

Farmington Hills, Mich • San Francisco • New York • Waterville, Maine
Meriden, Conn • Mason, Ohio • Chicago

GALE
CENGAGE Learning®

LIBRARY OF CONGRESS CATALOGING-IN-PUBLICATION DATA

Mattox, Elizabeth.
    The writing on the wall / by Elizabeth Mattox. — Large print edition.
      pages ; cm. — (Thorndike Press large print Christian mystery) (Secrets of Mary's bookshop)
    ISBN-13: 978-1-4104-6745-4 (hardcover)
    ISBN-10: 1-4104-6745-7 (hardcover)
    1. Large type books. I. Title.
PS3613.A8595W75 2014
    813'.6—dc23
                                      2013047776

Published in 2014 by arrangement with Guideposts, a Church Corporation

Printed in Mexico
1 2 3 4 5 6 7 18 17 16 15 14

Dear Reader,

Writing a volume in the Secrets of Mary's Bookshop series has been as fun as I imagine living in Ivy Bay would be. I loved exploring Mary's new hometown — visiting Bailey's Ice Cream Shop (and picking Mary's flavor of the month!) and the local library, and running into Mary's many friends and neighbors around town. But I think what I enjoyed most about writing this novel was exploring the history of the lighthouse. Behind every buried treasure, there is always a family story, usually from generations past. And the role of family is reflected in Mary's personal journey with her beloved sister, her children, and grandkids. This book is particularly dedicated to the gift of motherhood, in all its tenderness and fierceness.

Sincerely yours,
Elizabeth Mattox

ONE

Mary was deep in the forests of Brazil with Detective Andrew Jones, trying to discover the real reason Dame Judith Harring had gone missing while on an Amazon cruise, when the chimes on the front door of Mary's Mystery Bookshop rang. Mary jumped, the book nearly flying out of her hands. Her friend Henry Woodrow grinned as he walked into the sun-drenched store. "Sorry to interrupt," he said.

Mary smiled sheepishly. "I must have lost track of the time," she said, closing her book and smoothing the cover.

"That happens when you get lost in a mystery," Henry said with a grin. "I think there could be a tornado approaching, and you'd be too busy figuring out who did it to notice." Her old friend knew her well. Back when they were children, when Mary and her sister spent summers in Ivy Bay, Cape Cod, with their grandparents, Mary always had a mystery tucked into her back pocket for long days on the beach or out on the water in Henry's dad's boat. Both she and Henry had changed a lot since those days, but some things, like good mysteries, shared faith, and good friends, stayed the same.

"I was just putting away a new shipment of books." Mary noticed Henry exchange an amused look with Rebecca, her assistant at the store. "Well, maybe I was doing a bit more reading than shelving," Mary admitted with a smile.

"Why own a bookstore if you can't enjoy the books?" Henry asked.

Mary cast an affectionate glance around the store that had become a second home to her. After raising her family in Boston, the recently widowed Mary had chosen to retire in her childhood haven of Ivy Bay, moving in with her sister Betty. But Mary, who had become a librarian when her own children started school, also planned to fulfill a lifelong dream: to open her own bookshop. Mary's Mystery Bookshop was everything she'd hoped, set up in a beautiful historic storefront now complete with shelves and shelves of her favorite authors. Light streamed in through the big windows on the west side of the store, making the smooth pinewood floors gleam. Ladders allowed customers to access the highest shelves, and two soft chairs, with sea-colored throw pillows, sat at the back of the store by the fieldstone hearth, giving customers a place to browse in comfort. That area was also where Mary served free tea and coffee.

"I do enjoy it," Mary said.

"And you're not the only one," Henry said. It was true that business had been good. Mary had a steady stream of customers, a mix of local mystery lovers and tourists looking for a satisfying beach read. Mary had hired Rebecca shortly after she opened, and now Rebecca, a warm woman in her thirties, was at the register. She was ringing up a stack of books for a young couple in flip-flops and sweatshirts: typical attire for one of Ivy Bay's beautiful fall days. Rebecca's daughter Ashley loved spending time in the store and was sometimes allowed to ring up sales on the old cash register, a job she took utterly seriously. She was Mary's top adviser on the children's book section of the bookshop, and she spent many quiet hours reading in the softly upholstered bathtub, the crown jewel of the kids' reading area. Mary missed having her around as often now that school had started.

"Everyone loves a good mystery," Rebecca

said, closing the drawer of the antique cash register that sat next to Mary's computer atop the marble top. Inside the bookshop, Mary displayed rare first-edition books — which she enjoyed hunting down at estate sales and online — and also books featuring Cape Cod and those penned by local authors.

"That they do," Henry said. He turned to Mary. "So are you about ready?" he asked cheerfully. Henry was also recently widowed, and he and Mary had reconnected when she'd come back to town.

"I am," Mary said, standing up and stretching her legs. She'd been sitting for longer than she'd intended and felt a bit stiff. She started toward the door, then glanced at Rebecca. "That is, if you're sure you don't mind holding down the fort on your own for the afternoon."

Rebecca's face lit up with a smile. "Of course not," she said. "You've been sorting that shipment for hours. Go get some sun!"

"It is a beauty out there," Henry said, absently picking up a Tom Clancy sitting on a table of staff favorites. "Perfect day for a visit to the lighthouse."

"Yes, so you get to it," Rebecca said.

Mary glanced at the big bay window at the front of the bookshop. Sunlight streamed in, and she could see a patch of clear blue sky. It was indeed a perfect day, though Mary relished most days in Ivy Bay. Sunny days meant walks on the beach, the waves lapping the shore softly as gulls glided above on the sea winds. But rain meant cozy afternoons reading mysteries wrapped in her favorite afghan. The soft patter of rain on the roof was the ideal backdrop to a good whodunit. And then, overcast days were just right for spending time in Betty's lush backyard garden. After spending most of her life in Boston, coming back to her childhood summer haven on Cape Cod really was a blessing.

Mary turned to Henry, who was now reading the back of the Tom Clancy in earnest.

"Is this a good one?" he asked.

"Absolutely," Mary said, having read and reread most of the staff favorites several times.

"Then I think I'll need to take it," Henry said with a grin, pulling his old leather wallet out of his pocket.

Rebecca rang up the book while Mary grabbed her floppy straw hat to protect her face from the sun. Moments later, she and Henry joined the tourists and locals meandering down Meeting House Road, Henry with a Mary's Mystery Bookshop bag tucked under one arm. As they passed the quaint buildings, many of them historic landmarks, Mary breathed in the fresh sea air blowing in gently off the bay nearby. She and Henry turned down Liberty Road, where Henry had parked his car. Sitting in the front seat was Mary's sister, Betty.

"I hope we didn't keep you waiting too long," Mary said as Henry held open the door for her and she slid into the backseat.

"Not at all," Betty said. "I got supplies." She held up three water bottles, their sides slick with condensation.

"Buckle up and let's get this show on the road," Henry said as he settled into the driver's seat.

Mary leaned back contentedly as the car started and Henry pulled onto Main Street.

"So, Mary, have you ever been to the lighthouse?" Henry asked. A number of Cape Cod lighthouses had been renovated, but the lighthouse outside Ivy Bay, in an unpopulated bit of land on the bay, was just far enough out of town that it hadn't become a destination for visitors. In fact, many locals didn't know of its existence, tucked away at the end of a windy road on a rocky strip of beach.

"Not that I remember," Mary said, thinking back. Most of her Ivy Bay memories consisted of long days at the beach, fresh fish and clams, and boat rides.

"It's a great spot," Henry said as the car crested a curve, leaving the town center behind. "Though a bit run-down. Chipped paint everywhere, and dusty enough to bring on a sneezing attack. But the structure is sound, and the view is still wonderful."

"How did you discover it?" Betty asked.

Mary bit back a grin. If Betty had spent as much time with Henry as she had, she'd know what an explorer he was. Mary was sure he'd investigated every inch of the Cape, not to mention the nearby ocean on his boat. But his answer surprised her.

"I have a bit of family history at the lighthouse," he said. "My great-grandfather was appointed the first keeper when they built the lighthouse in 1869."

"That must have been an honor," Betty said.

"That and a lot of hard work, from what I understand," Henry said. "The keepers lived in a house right off the lighthouse. They took breaks, of course, but the responsibility of the lighthouse rested on their shoulders."

"What a big job," Betty said. "The Cape was such an important fishing center."

"Exactly," Henry said as he turned the car down a narrow road that passed the marsh, its thick beach grass shimmery in the afternoon sun. The smell of salt and rose hips perfumed the air. "There are treacherous rocks here, and ships got blown off course during storms. The lighthouse let them know how far away the rocks were and that help was nearby, if they needed it."

"It was like a candle in the window, giving people guidance," Betty said.

"It does sound like an important job," Mary said. She couldn't help think it would be the perfect place to write mysteries, alone in a tower, the solitary beam of light washing over the dark water.

"Yes, for a long time," Henry said. "Though now ships have computers and such. The need for lighthouses isn't what it was."

"Things do change," Mary said wistfully.

Henry pulled the car into a small parking lot. The three of them got out, and Mary felt her heart quicken at the sound of the gentle bay waves lapping ashore. The sight of the ocean spread out in front of her, vast and rippling its way to the horizon, never ceased to move her. She closed her eyes for a moment, giving thanks to God for the beauty of His creation.

"Let's see this lighthouse," Betty said, leading the way. They walked slowly, careful to step around the numerous potholes and cracks in the old parking lot.

The lighthouse was atop one of the low-standing dunes. A small white house was attached to the thick tower, its big window covered by a black roof trimmed with red paint. Over the years, the harsh weather of the Cape had dulled the white to a dingy gray and the red paint had faded. The glass in the windows was covered with a muddy film, and the path leading to the stairs was overgrown.

"Let me give you a hand," Henry said, stopping to help Betty and then Mary over the first step, which had rotted out. But the top two stairs were firm, and the inside of the lighthouse was clearly intact, save for the paint peeling off the walls. They were in a small lobby area that had a staircase at the back, which Mary assumed led to the lighthouse, and a dark hallway off to the left, in the opposite direction of the water.

"Let's see the house first," Mary said.

"Sounds good," Henry said, leading the way down the hall. The floors were scratched wood, and the walls had probably once been white but were now a dingy gray, chipping and streaked with the dust of many years. The hallway opened into a room with windows at the back. The furniture was long gone, though Mary could see scuff marks from where a table and chairs might have been, back when a keeper lived here with his family. There was a small closet, but Mary found nothing inside but a bit of sand.

"This was the living and dining room," Henry said, walking toward the back of the house. "And the kitchen was over here."

Mary and Betty followed him to the tiny room that had piles of dust where a fridge and stove had probably once been. The tops of the walls were stained with years of grease. The room smelled musty, with no traces of the meals that had once been prepared in the small space.

"There's one more room downstairs," Henry said. He walked out of the kitchen, through the living room and into a room that had one small window facing the dunes. It was covered with sand, but the sun still sparkled through on the dingy paint and scuffed floor.

"Was this a bedroom?" Betty asked.

"I believe it was the keeper's study," Henry said. "There are two bedrooms upstairs, but a hurricane about ten years ago created a leak that damaged the stairs. I'm afraid we can't go up there."

"It's wonderful to be able to see this part of the house," Mary said, imagining the keeper with a desk facing out toward the dunes while he updated his log and did other paperwork during the daylight hours on calm days. She noticed another closet and went over to investigate, fully expecting it to be empty like the one in the living room. But to her delight, there was a battered metal file cabinet sitting on the floor.

She turned to share her find with Henry and Betty. "Look at this," she said.

"Right," Henry said. "Last time I checked, there were some old papers inside."

"Do you think it would be okay if I took a peek?" Mary asked.

"I don't see why not," Henry said.

Mary wrestled the top drawer of the cabinet open. There were stacks of brittle yellowed paper. She lifted the papers out and found a black hardcover book with "Log" printed on the front. When she took it out, a wave of dust flew into the air, making her eyes water. Betty leaned over her shoulder, and the sisters looked at the list of boat sightings, visitors, and storms, all neatly dated and recorded. The last entry was listed in 1935.

"Was the lighthouse decommissioned in 1935?" Mary asked.

"Yes, I believe so," Henry said. "How did you know?"

Mary smiled. "That's the last date listed."

Henry smiled back. "Always the detective," he said.

Mary set the log back and pulled at the second drawer of the file cabinet. It came open with a loud squeak. There were a few papers at the bottom, including a list of supplies the keeper had ordered. Mary noticed there was a large amount of coffee on the list, which was probably necessary when one had to be alert through the night.

The bottom drawer was empty.

"Ready to see the lighthouse?" Henry asked.

"Definitely," Mary said, following him and Betty back through the dark hall to the lobby and then to the staircase in the back, where the air was laced with the salty smell of the ocean.

"My, that is a lot of stairs," Betty said, gazing up at the narrow stairs that twisted up toward the tower.

"Do you feel up to it?" Mary asked, instantly concerned. Betty had rheumatoid arthritis, and strenuous exercise sometimes caused her pain.

Betty smiled. "As long as we take it slow."

"That we can do," Henry said, starting up

the first step. Betty followed, with Mary behind. Betty kept one hand on the thick wooden banister as they made their way up. The narrow walls made the space feel small, but light came down from the glass room above. Paint chips crunched under their shoes as they climbed. As Mary turned the corner on the landing halfway up, she brushed against a wall, and a sprinkle of paint strips rained down.

"It could definitely use a new coat of paint," she said.

Above her, Betty agreed. Henry was already walking through the door that led into the top of the lighthouse, and moments later, Betty and Mary joined him. All three headed eagerly to the railing that looked out over the ocean, and the sight made Mary's breath catch in her throat.

From up here, the sand sparkled with sunlight, and the tops of the dunes, crowned with gently blowing beach grass, were majestic. But most breathtaking was the sea itself, the waves calm as they moved rhythmically toward the shore, peaked with frothy whitecaps that splashed softly to the beach, then slid back again. Toward the horizon, a sailboat, framed by the blue, cloudless sky, moved slowly past. Seagulls called to one another, occasionally dipping down into the water for fish.

"A seal," Henry said, pointing. Mary looked, and sure enough, the little creature raised its head for a moment, snout pointed to the sky, then back down it went.

"Just gorgeous," Betty murmured. "The Lord's work shines in this little corner of the world."

"Yes," Mary agreed, her voice tempered with the peace that flowed through her as she looked out at the seascape. Then she smiled at Henry. "I can see why you come here."

He smiled and laid an affectionate hand on hers for a moment. It warmed Mary, who smiled back. She heard a soft click and turned, her hand falling away from Henry's. Betty had taken a small digital camera out of her purse and was snapping photos of the view.

"In case I don't make it up here again for a while," she said when she noticed Mary's gaze.

They lingered a moment longer, drinking in the beauty of the panorama before them, and then headed back down.

Mary was last again, and this time, as she turned on the landing of the halfway point, her water bottle, which was still slippery, slid out of her hands, right into the nest of paint chips she'd knocked down earlier. As she bent to get it, she slipped on a pile of loose chips and fell firmly on her backside. Laughing at herself, she brushed off her hands, preparing to stand up. But then she noticed something. The paint was a faded white, but some of the chips had blue marks on them. Puzzled, Mary looked at the chips, then at the wall they'd once covered. And then she sucked in her breath. The paint had been covering some kind of drawing. Mary grabbed another loose edge of paint, pulling a thick strip off the wall and revealing even more lines and markings.

"Are you all right?" Betty called from below.

"I'm more than all right," Mary called back excitedly. "Come see what I've found."

TWO

"Well, what is it?" Betty asked, walking back to the landing. She raised her eyebrows when she saw her sister standing in a pile of paint chips.

"I think it's a map," Mary said, gesturing to the wall. Her voice gave away her pleasure at the find. Now that she had pulled away more strips, it was clear that the crisscrossed lines were in mostly a grid formation and looked like the streets of a town. There were a few squares, which looked like they were supposed to represent buildings. At the top, there were triangles, symbolizing dunes, right before a big expanse simply labeled "sea."

Henry had come up behind Betty, and they both bent down to get a good look at the markings.

"What do you think it could be a map of?" Mary asked. Her imagination was beginning to roam, picturing a lonely lighthouse keeper drawing the way to the place where his beloved awaited him.

Betty narrowed her eyes, studying the lines, squares, and triangles. "It could be one of the towns nearby, since it's obviously a beach town."

Mary nodded, pulling off another strip of paint. This one revealed a single red star. "This spot must be important to whoever drew the map," she said.

Behind her, Henry sucked in his breath. "I wonder," he said so quietly she almost missed the words.

"Wonder what?" she asked.

Henry stared at the map, lost in thought. "Annie did always say David loved the lighthouse," he said, more to himself than to Mary and Betty.

Mary was intrigued. "Do you mean your cousin Annie?" she asked. When they were kids, Henry's cousin Annie, who was a worldly four years older, had visited several times, and unlike a lot of the older kids, Annie went out of her way to be kind to her younger cousins. Henry had mentioned that she lived in Wellfleet now, and Mary knew they were still close.

"Yes," he said. "But it's probably nothing."

The long glance he gave to the map told

Mary he wasn't so sure. "Will you tell us anyway?" she asked gently.

Henry nodded, his eyes still on the map. "Well, I told you how my great-grandfather was the first keeper of the lighthouse," he began. Mary nodded. "He had his family late in life, in part because of the nature of his work. My grandmother and her two younger brothers were very young when he died."

"How sad," Mary said, her heart going out to those three children and the widow who had been on her own.

"Yes, I think it was tough for them," Henry said. "Though it doesn't excuse what happened."

Mary's curiosity was lit by Henry's words and the sharp look in his eyes.

"As Annie tells it, the youngest brother, my great-uncle David, became a real troublemaker," Henry went on. "He started out with smaller stuff, getting suspended from school and such, and then moved on to shoplifting and stealing from neighbors."

"How awful," Betty said sympathetically. She took a sip of water from her bottle, but like Mary, her eyes stayed on Henry.

"Yes, and it got even worse," Henry said. "Soon, David was committing more serious theft. And he could never hold down a job

— he was always getting fired. Annie told me that the job David held the longest was at a hardware store, and it lasted only a few months. It was terrible for my grandmother. For all of them, really." Henry paused for a moment, his face solemn. "And the story doesn't end well. David stole a large sum of money. The police were onto him, and he skipped town before they could arrest him."

"Did he ever come back?" Betty asked.

Henry shook his head. "There was a warrant out for his arrest, and he disappeared for good."

Mary drew in her breath. To think of anyone in Henry's family fleeing the law was shocking. Henry's family had been in Ivy Bay for generations, highly respected as hardworking, law-abiding members of the church and community. It was hard to imagine one of his family members committing such crimes. Though she supposed even Scripture was full of black sheep, even in families as faithful as Henry's.

"Goodness," Betty said.

Henry nodded. "Yes, apparently it was quite a scandal. But here's the interesting thing. Family legend says that he left the money behind, hidden somewhere."

The mystery lover in Mary perked up at these words. "He left behind a buried treasure?" she asked.

"Of sorts," Henry said, smiling at her enthusiasm. "Of course, it's probably not true. If he had stolen the money, why wouldn't he have taken it with him?"

"Perhaps he saw the error of his ways," Betty said. Mary tensed at her sister's tone, which was a shade too close to smug. After all, Jesus preached compassion for all.

"Perhaps," Henry said easily. "Though I doubt it."

Mary noticed he was looking at the map again, his gaze resting on the star. She realized she'd been so swept up in the tale from Henry's past that she'd completely forgotten how the conversation had begun. "Henry, do you think this map might really have something to do with your family's story?"

Henry waved the thought away. "Oh, probably not. Although David did have a strong connection to the lighthouse. According to Annie's mother, it was the one place that seemed to calm him, and he visited regularly."

"Annie's mother?" Mary asked.

Henry smiled. "She was a bit of a family historian in her day," he said. "She passed all the family lore down to Annie, and Annie told me. Though to be honest, there's a lot I don't remember. Annie would, though."

Mary turned back to the map. "So according to what you do remember, it is possible he's the one who drew this," she said, her thoughts racing ahead. "But why would he need to draw a map?"

"Maybe he just enjoyed drawing maps of places he'd been," Betty said. "When he was out here relaxing."

"He did get around the Cape," Henry agreed.

That made sense, and yet Mary couldn't help thinking it was more than that. After all, if it was just a hobby, why do it on a wall? The place represented on this map was obviously important to the person who drew it, important enough to make it permanent. "I don't know. I suppose whoever drew it had a good reason to make this map and put it where he did," Mary said.

Betty was smiling fondly at her sister. "Such as?"

Mary considered. "Well, obviously people use maps to help them find a place. This place on the map must have been important to David, if he was the artist." She tapped her finger on the star. "This spot in particular." She shook her head. It sounded crazy, but it could be true, couldn't it? "Henry, do you think there's any chance this could lead to the money David stole?"

THREE

Henry nodded slowly. "I . . . I suppose it's possible."

"You think he drew the map so he could come back and find it one day?" Betty asked, sounding a bit skeptical.

"Maybe," Mary said. "That would certainly be a good reason." It didn't quite add up for Mary, though. There were too many missing pieces to the story.

"If it was even David who drew it," Henry said. "Really, it could have been anyone. This lighthouse has been here a long time. It could just be some graffiti some kids left."

Of course that was true, but Mary couldn't help but think that this all seemed too coincidental. And she didn't believe in coincidences. If Henry's great-uncle had indeed left behind stolen money, and if he had had a strong connection to the lighthouse, then it was plausible that he had drawn this map. And something in her gut told her that Henry's first reaction, seeing a connection between David and this map, was spot-on. "But it could have been David," Mary said firmly. "And if he never came back, that money could still be there."

Betty's eyebrows lifted. "Do you really think the money might still be there after all this time?" She seemed to think this was highly unlikely.

"There's only one way to find out," Mary said.

Henry grinned. "You want to see where this map leads?" he asked.

She smiled. "I do if you do."

Henry's eyes lit up. "You bet," he said.

Mary clapped her hands together. "Okay, first we have to figure out what town this is," she said. "If it's a small town off the coast of Ireland, we may not be able to visit so easily." She was mostly joking — Mary had a hunch this map was local and that it was indeed David who had left it. The pieces just seemed to fit, and she was excited to see where they might lead.

But Henry was checking his watch. "Unfortunately, as intrigued as I am, I need to get in a little fishing today."

"And I should really get to the market," Betty added.

Disappointed, Mary glanced at the time

and realized she should get back to the store too. But she wasn't ready to leave the map behind. She pulled her phone out of her bag and turned on the camera function, then snapped a shot of the map.

Henry was looking at the map as well. "You know, I would like to tell Annie about this," he said. "I'm going to give her a call and see if she can come over for dinner. If she can, would you both like to join us and tell her about our find?"

"Yes," Mary said, delighted by the idea. She looked forward to seeing Annie again after all these years and learning more about David.

"Thanks, but I'm afraid I can't if it's tonight," Betty said. "I'm meeting Eleanor at the club for an early dinner," she said, almost apologetically. Eleanor was Betty's sister-in-law, who took her status as part of Ivy Bay's upper crust a bit too seriously for Mary's taste.

"Ready now?" Betty asked Mary.

Mary made sure the pictures she had taken were clear on the screen. Then she tucked her phone back into her purse. "Yep," she said. She'd stop by the drugstore on the way home to get a print of the map, and then she could start to figure out where it was. And who knew where it might lead from there?

Later that afternoon, Mary waved good-bye
to Rebecca and headed to her car. Henry
had called to say that Annie couldn't come
to Ivy Bay for a visit, but had invited them
up to her home in Wellfleet, a picturesque
town about fifty minutes away. Rebecca was
happy to close up the store, so Mary agreed
to the trip. On the way back from the
lighthouse this afternoon, Mary had gone
to the drugstore to get a print of the photo
she'd taken at the lighthouse. They'd promised they'd have it printed out by evening,
so she stopped to pick the printout up on
her way. Then she headed to the marina,
where Henry docked his boat, and parked
in the small lot.

Henry was standing by his car, his face
bright from a few hours in the sun. He
waved in greeting, and Mary walked over
and got in his car, and then they headed to
Route 6 for the drive up the Cape.

As they sped down the Mid-Cape Highway, she thought more about the mysterious map. If David — or anyone else, for that
matter — had hidden something he wanted
someone else to find, why leave something
so cryptic? Why not just spell it out? And
why leave it there, on the wall, in any case?

Mary turned it around in her mind, but it didn't make sense. Was she seeing a mystery where none existed? It was possible it was just some graffiti left by local kids. Mary shook her head. There was more to it than that; she was sure of it.

"What are you thinking about?" Henry asked.

Mary told him her suspicion that the map was put there for a reason, and then the conversation drifted. Mary told him about an upcoming visit from her grandchildren, and Henry told her a story about his grandson's recent soccer game. Before she knew it, they had pulled off the main highway and were winding through the narrow streets of downtown Wellfleet.

Annie's home was right outside Wellfleet on a curving side road that was tree-lined and dotted with quaint Cape Cod–style houses. Henry parked in the driveway of number fifteen, a weathered gray house with red shutters and trim. There were carefully cultivated flower beds on either side of the brick walkway leading up to the house.

Annie must have heard the car because she opened the door before they knocked. She hugged her cousin, then turned to Mary with a warm smile.

"Mary, how wonderful to see you again

after all these years," Annie said. She had silver hair held back in a French twist and the same kind, green eyes as Henry. Mary could see traces of the spunky little girl she had been in her smile, but there was also a sadness that made her wonder if perhaps Annie had suffered some disappointments in her life.

"So nice to see you too," Mary said. "You look wonderful."

Annie smiled. "That's nice of you to say, but the years take their toll, don't they? I'd like to come see the lighthouse, but my knees have just enough arthritis that stairs are a real chore."

Mary nodded sympathetically. "Well, you don't have to go to the lighthouse to see the map," she said. "I just picked up a printout from the drugstore, and it's pretty clear."

"Excellent," Annie said. She linked her arm through Mary's, as if no time had passed, and took her into the house.

They walked through a small entryway, which had a coatrack and a polished cherrywood dresser with a vase of fresh lilies on top, and into the living room with gleaming wood floors spotted with maroon and tan throw rugs.

"What a beautiful home you have," Mary said as she settled on the wine-colored sofa next to Annie. Henry folded his tall frame into the armchair across from them.

"Thank you," Annie said. "It's small, but it was always enough room." The whistle of a teakettle sounded from the kitchen, and Annie popped up. "I'll be just a moment," she said.

A few minutes later, she was back with a steaming pot of tea and a bowl of grapes. She passed teacups to both Henry and Mary. Mary added a bit of honey to hers and took a small handful of grapes.

"So shall we tell you what we saw at the lighthouse?" Henry asked his cousin.

"Yes, but first I want to catch up just a bit with Mary," Annie said with a smile. "A lot has happened since I saw you last," she added with a laugh.

Mary laughed too. She gave Annie a short version of the decades that had passed, and Annie listened attentively.

"I'm sorry about the loss of your husband," Annie said when Mary had finished, giving Mary's arm a gentle squeeze. "I know the pain of that. I lost my husband almost thirty years ago now, and I still miss him."

Mary touched Annie's hand. "Henry told me," she said sympathetically. "I'm so sorry you were widowed so young."

Annie nodded, and Mary could see that

this was the source of sadness in Annie's eyes.

"It was a hard time," Annie said. "But God got me through. God and my new baby girl. We'd tried for years to have a baby, and it still brings me joy to know that Carson got to see her before he passed. God gave me that gift, and I've always been thankful for it."

"My faith has helped me through hard times as well," Mary said. "God is there when we need Him."

"That's the truth," Henry agreed.

Annie grinned. "My cousin helped me out as well," she said warmly. Mary had no trouble imagining that Henry had done all he could for Annie.

"That's what family's for," Henry said.

"Yes," Annie agreed. "And I guess it's family that's brought us together today. If you don't mind, I'd love to see that map now."

Mary pulled the map out of her purse and handed it to Annie, who adjusted her glasses before peering at it. Henry leaned over her shoulder, taking in the quick lines, squares, and star again. "What do you think?" he asked Annie after a moment.

Annie passed the map back to Mary, who put it in her purse. "It sure could have been drawn by David," she said. "My mother spoke of David's love of the lighthouse, and he enjoyed sketching. Though why he would have drawn it is another question entirely."

"Henry said something about money David might have left behind," Mary said.

"Yes, there is that story," Annie said. "Henry may have told you that my mother was a bit of a family historian. Nothing too detailed or high-tech; it was more that she stored many of my grandmother's keepsakes and knew her stories backward and forward. She had a notebook with a big family tree and information about every last second cousin twice removed. It all meant a great deal to her." Annie smiled at the memory.

"It sounds like she did a wonderful job of preserving your family history," Mary said.

Annie nodded.

"Did they know where David got the money?" Henry asked.

"Yes, apparently he stole it from his boss at the hardware store. There was a fire at the store, and the money went missing right after that. David was the top suspect, with the police looking to arrest him, so he skipped town and never came home. And the twist to the story is that apparently he didn't take the money with him, though my mother was never sure if that was proven or just a theory. But if he left the money behind, it's possible he drew the map to point to where it was."

"That's what we were thinking," Mary said.

"I hope you're planning to follow it and see just what that red star marks," Annie said with a spark in her eye.

"We definitely were. And it would be wonderful if you wanted to come," Mary said.

Annie patted her hand. "Thank you, but I think I'll leave the treasure hunting to you," she said, her eyes twinkling. "But please tell me what you find."

"That we'll do," Henry promised. Mary could hear in his voice how much he cared for his cousin.

"You know, it's funny, I was just thinking about David this past week," Annie mused. "I was going through a box my mother left me, just some drawings and keepsakes that her mother kept. I was looking to see if there might be anything about the ring, though of course my grandmother and mother both went through it a thousand times and never found anything about it. And I didn't either."

Henry's brow crinkled. "What ring?" he asked.

"You don't remember?" Annie asked, surprised.

Henry shook his head. "I can't say I do," he said.

"It's a sad story, and it really broke our grandmother's heart," Annie said. "There was a sapphire ring in the family, an heirloom given to our several times great-grandmother who married an earl. The ring came with a letter of authentication that we still have."

"But the ring is gone?" Mary asked.

Annie nodded. "David stole it. David's mother discovered it was missing a few months before David left town for good, in 1925. When she confronted him, he admitted to selling it. She begged him to get it back, offering to pay anything for it. It meant the world to her, and my mom said she'd have sold the house to get it returned to the family."

"But David never got it back?" Mary asked, saddened by the stark story. What a terrible thing to lose something so precious to the family history, especially since Annie's mother was such a family history buff.

Annie shook her head. "He never did. I've told you how much family history meant to my mother, and she cried the day I told her I was engaged. She wanted so much for me

39

to have that ring."

"The tears were just for the ring," Henry said lightly, though Mary noticed him pat Annie's arm comfortingly. "She was happy Annie had found a great fellow to settle down with."

Annie squeezed Henry's arm. "Yes, she did dote on Carson those last few months of her life."

"She died young?" Mary asked. Annie had truly lost a lot in her life.

"Yes," Annie said. "Both she and my father took ill when I was in college."

"Annie dropped out to take care of them," Henry said.

"I never did make it back," Annie said. "But it was a gift to be able to spend those final years helping them, after all they had given me."

Mary admired Annie's generous outlook on her life's story. She had suffered a great deal, yet her spirit was strong, thanks in no small part to her strong faith. She was truly living her faith, and it was inspiring to see. Mary felt a deep warmth for Henry's cousin and felt blessed to reunite with her.

"So why were you thinking of the ring just now?" Henry asked. His brows drew together. "Could this have anything to do with my niece?"

Annie's face broke into a delighted grin. "Oh, I was supposed to keep it a secret," Annie said. "She'll be cross with me for letting it slip, but I'm just so happy. Kate is getting married."

"Congratulations," Henry said joyfully, hugging Annie. "I had a hunch the last time I saw Kate that they were getting ready to take the next step."

Annie was beaming and she turned her bright face to Mary. "Kate is my baby girl, though not so much a baby anymore," she said affectionately. "She's thirty, and I worried she'd never settle down, so you can imagine how happy I was to get her call."

"How wonderful," Mary said.

"Yes," Annie said with a mischievous smile. "I want some grandbabies!"

Mary and Henry laughed.

But then a cloud seemed to pass over Annie's face. "After I spoke to Kate, I remembered when I told my own mother about my engagement, and her tears over the ring," Annie said. "And I truly understood how she felt. That's why I got out the box. It would have been such a beautiful thing to be able to pass that ring to Kate."

Henry looked solemn, and Mary's heart ached for both of them. It would have been profoundly meaningful to have passed such a proud family heirloom down, especially one that marked the growing of family. It was indeed a loss.

"Ah, but what's lost is lost," Annie said philosophically as she stood up. "And if you'll forgive me for ending this lovely visit, I have to meet Kate for dinner. We have a wedding to begin planning."

"And what fun that will be," Mary said, remembering her happiness in helping Elizabeth plan her special day. Lizzie and Chad had chosen the date and the music, but Mary had been her dress consultant, going to several stores before Lizzie found a dress that she loved. Mary had teared up, seeing her daughter in her wedding dress for the first time. Even under the harsh fluorescent lights of the dress shop, Lizzie looked beautiful. They had also had fun visiting the florist to choose bouquets and centerpieces. Lizzie had ultimately selected wild roses that grew along the dunes and marshes of the Cape.

"I'm quite looking forward to it," Annie said with a smile, standing up.

As she and Henry followed Annie to the front door, Mary thought back to the box Annie had mentioned. "Annie, do you think I might be able to take a look at that box of your great-grandmother's things sometime?" she asked. "I know you need to get going now, but another time?"

"Sure, anytime," Annie said easily. "It's a small chest, and it's mostly empty. I'm not sure you'll find anything useful in it, but it's kind of fun to see relics from the past."

"Yes, I'd like that," Mary said. "Thank you."

Once they were back at the car, Annie hugged Henry, and then Mary. "Happy treasure hunting to you," she said gaily. "I look forward to hearing all about it."

As Mary got into Henry's car, she said a silent prayer that the map might yield something from the past to share with Annie.

FOUR

"So tonight is the big debut," Betty said. She had arrived home early from her dinner with Eleanor and had sat with Mary while she finished her meal of leftover potpie. It was one of those dishes that was almost better the second day.

Mary grinned. "I'm excited about this one," she said, rinsing off her plate and setting it in the dishwasher. Every month, Bailey's Ice Cream Shop featured a flavor that Mary came up with, and tonight was the first night of her latest creation. Mary had been inventing ice-cream flavors since her children were young and very enthusiastic tasters, and it was a thrill to see her flavors at Bailey's.

"You're excited about every one," Betty teased. "As you should be. So we better get to Bailey's before they run out."

There was a nip in the air, and Mary pulled her cardigan tighter around her as they walked into town. They passed Cape Cod houses with gray wood walls, cheerful white shutters, and driveways covered with crushed clamshells. There was a big weeping willow tree in the Rawlings's front yard, and they stopped to smell the roses Cathy Danes cultivated into frothy bushes bursting with red, pink, and gold.

"I think your new flavor is going to be especially popular," Betty said as they turned onto Main Street. The sun was setting, so the streetlights had gone on, bathing the street in a soft yellow glow. The storefronts twinkled with lights, and the sound of laughter floated through the air. Families meandered along the slate sidewalks of Main Street, stopping into the shops and restaurants, and of course, Bailey's. "Who doesn't love strawberries, almonds, and fudge, especially mixed together?"

"I hope you're right," Mary said. She didn't like to admit it, but she was always slightly nervous when a new flavor went on sale. What if customers didn't want to try it, or worse, didn't like it? She knew that was silly, but she couldn't help feeling a little anxious.

"It's delicious," Betty said. "And I would know," she added with a smile. Betty was

Mary's official taster, helping out with the early stages of a new flavor and offering feedback with every change and new addition. Having a sister, especially one as supportive as Betty, was a true blessing, and Mary was feeling thankful for this as they headed into Bailey's.

The shop was crisp and clean, with bubblegum-pink-and-white-striped walls and matching pink padded stools that lined the old-fashioned counter at the front of the store. Scattered throughout the homey space were small round wrought-iron tables painted a cheerful white. And there in the cooler, under a sign that said Mary Fisher's Flavor of the Month, was a tub of scrumptious-looking pink ice cream dotted with almonds and fudge and little chunks of strawberry. There was a long line of customers, and Mary noted with pride that a number of patrons seated at the tables were eating her flavor. Mary waved at Jeremy and Kaley Court, who ran Meeting House Grocers, and Johanna Montgomery, who was a reporter for the *Ivy Bay Bugle.*

"You've outdone yourself, Mary," Johanna called, and flashed Mary a thumbs-up.

"You're pretty popular around here," Betty said, beaming and patting her arm.

"Well, hello there, Betty and Mary." A tall

woman with a neat French twist stopped on her way out the door, and Mary recognized Cynthia McArthur Jones, sister of Police Chief McArthur. She was wearing a flowing gray dress with a red sweater and matching flats, a smile on her face as she greeted them.

"I got your ice cream," Cynthia said to Mary, patting the bag with a Bailey's insignia on it. "Nick is picking me up, and we'll enjoy it at home."

"I hope you like it," Mary said.

Cynthia grinned. "I had them give me a sample, so I already know it's delicious. What's your secret?"

"My lips are sealed," Mary said, glowing at Cynthia's compliment. She wanted to answer that the secret was plenty of cream and sugar, but suspected Cynthia wouldn't want to hear that. And each flavor did have its own secret ingredient, one thing that pulled everything together and fused the flavors. For the strawberry almond fudge, that secret ingredient was a small sprinkle of coarse sea salt that heightened the sweet of the berries and chocolate.

Mary and Betty stepped forward as the line moved up, and Cynthia moved with them.

"Just what I thought you'd say," Cynthia

said. "Whatever it is, the flavors just explode in your mouth. And after the long town hall meeting I just sat through, this" — she patted the bag — "is just what I need."

"What's new at Town Hall?" Betty asked. She always liked to stay on top of local happenings.

"Oh, you know, budget cuts and zoning disputes," Cynthia said with a sigh. "Zeke Hanson is trying to sneak a fast-food franchise onto Main Street. Again."

Betty shook her head. "He's been trying to do that for the past fifteen years," she said.

"You'd think fifteen years of being told no would get to him, but he just keeps at it," Cynthia said, smiling the tiniest bit at Zeke's tenacity.

"I hope he heard a no again tonight," Mary said. It wasn't that she wouldn't want Zeke to get his business, but the magic of Main Street was in its small mom-and-pop businesses. A fast-food restaurant would not only change the feeling of Ivy Bay, but also threaten the small eateries owned by locals.

"He was told what he's always told," Cynthia said. "That he's welcome to buy property outside of town to open whatever he wants."

"That's good, then," Betty said.

"I hope Nick gets here before this melts," Cynthia said, glancing out the big glass windows of the store. "He was finding out when the next zoning board meeting is, and I hadn't expected it to take so long."

"Already planning for the next meeting, huh?" Betty said with a smile.

"Well, actually I have a personal interest this time. I've been working on a project for years," Cynthia said. "And after all the work I've put in, it looks like it's finally going to come together."

"What is it?" Mary asked, curious.

"You know our old family building on Meeting House Road, the one the Crenshaws are renting for Cape Cod Togs?" Cynthia said, naming a store that sold country-club casual clothes.

Betty was nodding, but Mary hadn't realized that the pretty old Colonial building was owned by the McArthurs. "It's a beautiful building," Mary said.

Cynthia smiled proudly. "It's been in our family since the 1920s, but it was built in 1875, and I decided to start the process of getting it named as a historic landmark."

"Wonderful," Betty said.

"Yes, and after more than two years, it's finally going to happen," Cynthia said, smiling with delight. "Oh, here's Nick." Her eyes were on the black sedan that pulled up out front. "If you ladies will excuse me, I have to get home before I have a container of ice-cream soup." She headed out of the store with a wave.

Mary and Betty were next in line. When Tess Bailey asked what they'd like, Betty loyally ordered the strawberry almond fudge. Mary had had her fill of the flavor, having tested it multiple times, and ordered one of her favorites of Bailey's flavors, caramel chocolate swirl. After they paid, they took their treat to a table outside under the cheerful green awning.

"You didn't have to get that," Mary said, gesturing to Betty's bowl.

Her sister smiled. "But it was the flavor I wanted." She took a bite and closed her eyes for a moment. "And it is good."

Betty took another bite, then pointed her spoon at Mary. "So are you ready for the big visit?"

Mary grinned at the reminder of the pending visit from her daughter Lizzie, who would be bringing her two children, Luke and Emma, during a vacation from school. Unfortunately, Lizzie's husband wouldn't be able to come, as he had to work, but it would be a joy to have her daughter and grandchildren around for a whole ten days.

"Yes. We are going to have a very full house."

Betty nodded contentedly. "That sounds just lovely."

Mary thought of energetic little Luke, rushing about the house and yard with his newest LEGO creation, and thoughtful young Emma, who always enjoyed telling Mary about the latest book she was reading. She couldn't believe how quickly they were growing up. It seemed like just last week that she was pinching Emma's chubby little baby thighs and rejoicing with Lizzie over Luke's first steps. She could still remember how excited she had been when Lizzie had first told her she was going to be a grandma, and she could still feel the rush of anticipation she had experienced waiting for that tiny newborn to make her appearance. She still felt that same anticipation every time she was going to see her precious grandchildren. Of course, the kids brought chaos and messes along with them, but Mary didn't mind that a bit. Cleaning up a little mess seemed a small sacrifice for the joy she got from seeing those sweet little faces smiling at her. Lizzie and the kids were set to arrive in six days. She couldn't wait.

When they got home from the ice-cream shop, Betty went to bed, but Mary wanted a cup of tea to settle herself before sleeping. It had been a long day, and her mind was still buzzing from the discovery at the lighthouse and the visit with Annie. She put on the kettle and then sat down to wait for the water to heat, the photo of the map on the table in front of her.

She looked at the crudely drawn streets, the little squares — which were probably buildings in town — and, of course, the red star.

The kettle whistled, a cheerful chirp in the quiet kitchen. Mary stood up and readied her cup of peppermint tea. Once it was set, cooling in front of her, Mary went back to the map. But as she rested her hand on it, her attention was drawn to the pearl ring John had given her on their tenth anniversary. Mary touched the pearl lightly, thinking that one day she would pass it along to Emma. With a pang, she thought of Annie, and what it would have meant to her to be able to give Kate the family ring.

Then she looked down at the map, her eyes once again drawn to the red star as something occurred to her. What if David had drawn the map, and what if he had hidden more than the money there? Was it possible he had also buried the family ring there?

FIVE

The next morning, Mary went down to the kitchen and was surprised to see that it was empty. Usually, Betty was up with the sun, brewing coffee and baking muffins or scones to start the day. But today, the stove was cold and the coffeemaker dry, which could only mean one thing. Mary headed to the back of the house where Betty had moved her bedroom so as to avoid going up and down stairs, and knocked. "How are you?" she asked softly as she opened the door.

Betty smiled at her sister, but Mary could see the tightness in her face: Betty was in pain. "Let me get your medicine," she said and hurried to the bathroom. When Betty's rheumatoid arthritis flared up, it not only swelled her joints, making movement difficult, but also hurt.

Mary brought her sister her prescription painkiller, a heating pad, and a glass of water, which Betty accepted gratefully.

53

"Can I bring you breakfast?" Mary asked.

"If it's not too much trouble," Betty said.

"Of course not," Mary said, heading back to the kitchen. Gus, her little gray cat, twined around her ankles, mewing musically, which was his way of saying it was time for his breakfast. Gus had arrived in Mary's life when her husband was in the hospital, and he had been a sweet source of comfort during that hard time, purring on her lap on late nights when Mary was unable to sleep and greeting her happily when she came home from long days at John's bedside. Mary rubbed his furry head in greeting, then scooped some wet food into his dish while Betty's bread toasted. Ten minutes later, she was back in Betty's room with a tray containing toast and a bowl of yogurt mixed with fresh blueberries, as well as a steaming mug of coffee with half-and-half and sugar, just how Betty liked it.

"That smells wonderful," Betty said, taking the coffee before Mary had even set down the tray. As Betty drank, Mary put the tray across her lap, checking to be sure it was secure. "Between this and my medicine, I'll be feeling better in no time," Betty said.

Mary hoped this was true, though of course when these flare-ups happened,

Betty was confined to her bed until the swelling in her joints eased. "Can I get you anything else?" she asked, reaching down to smooth the light quilt over Betty's legs.

"No, this is perfect," Betty said. "You go eat something. I know you're meeting Henry this morning."

Mary hesitated. "I can call him and re-schedule," she said. She and Henry were planning to do some map research at the library, hoping to figure out what town the lighthouse map showed. Mary had some old decorative maps of Ivy Bay in her store, but she had a feeling they would need real atlases of the entire Cape, and maybe beyond. Mary was eager to get started, but of course Betty came first.

"Nonsense," Betty said, waving a hand. "All I need is a bit of rest."

After a few more reassurances, Mary finally agreed to leave, though she left a sandwich in the fridge for her sister and the phone right by her bed so that she could call if she needed anything.

"I know what this really is," Betty said teasingly, gesturing to the phone. "This means you'll be calling to check on me all day."

"Perhaps a few times," Mary admitted.

"Go, I'm fine," Betty said with a smile.

Mary was happy to note it had lost its tightness. Clearly, the medicine and food had done her sister some good.

"Okay, but remember I'm just a phone call away," Mary said, pulling on a light cardigan.

"How could I forget?" Betty asked fondly.

Before Mary headed out the door, still feeling anxious about her sister, a thought occurred to her. She found Gus curled up on one of the antique wing chairs in the living room, one of his favorite spots, and lifted him gently over her shoulder. "Mind staying home today, Gus?" Mary whispered to the cat. Moments later, she deposited him on Betty's bed, where he immediately sat down and began grooming.

"How about some company?" Mary said with a smile. When Mary had first moved in with Betty, Betty had been uneasy about a cat in her immaculate home. But Gus had won her over, and she was now well on the road to becoming a bona fide cat lover.

"Some company that rascal is," Betty said, already reaching out to pet him. "All he does is sleep." Gus gave her hand a delicate sniff and then settled in to be petted.

Mary couldn't help grinning at the relaxed look on Betty's face as Gus rolled over for a good belly rub. She was a firm believer in the healing company of a cat.

The Ivy Bay library was housed in a red-brick building with white doors and windows. It was spacious and light, with skylights in the high, vaulted ceiling that allowed sunbeams to sparkle over the blond-oak bookcases and furniture. Tables and chairs were arranged in cozy nooks and reading areas, and there was a computer room, with free Internet service, in the back. Henry was already there, waiting for Mary at the circulation desk piled high with books and papers.

"Good morning," he said, walking up to meet her. "How are you?"

"I'm doing well, though Betty is having one of her bad days," Mary said. She unconsciously ran a hand through her hair that she'd barely had time to brush.

Henry's face was instantly concerned. "Oh, that's a shame."

Mary nodded. "I know. She always claims to be fine, but it was definitely getting to her today."

"I know it's a real comfort to her that you're there," Henry said.

Some of the tightness she'd felt in her chest since the morning loosened at Henry's words. "I hope so," she said. The door behind her opened, and two children ran in, trailed by a weary-looking woman. Mary smiled. She remembered those days. "Shall we get started?" she asked.

"Yes, let's see if we can find out what town that map shows," Henry said. "And then, maybe, we can figure out where it leads."

They had been walking toward the front of the circulation desk, but Mary stopped. "Something occurred to me last night," she said. "If David did draw the map, and he left the money at the star, it's possible he also buried the ring there."

Henry sucked in a breath. "Do you really think it's possible?"

Mary could hear in his voice how much this would mean to him. "Why not?" she said. "Your great-uncle David's father was the keeper of the lighthouse, and David historically found solitude there. He stole a large sum of money and a family heirloom. Legend has it that he left the money behind, and if he had second thoughts about that, why not the ring too? And now, there's this map, which we found at the lighthouse. Hard to deny the connection." As she was recapping what they knew, she thought of the one piece of the story that hadn't quite fit for her: the reason that David had drawn the map. "What I haven't seemed to figure out is why he drew the map in the first place."

"*Hmm,*" Henry said, an encouraged look on his face. "What if David left the money and the ring and drew the map so that his mother could find it?"

Mary considered it. "That would make sense," she said.

"Though, of course, that raises about a thousand other questions," Henry said. "Like why didn't he just tell her where to find them, and why did he decide not to take either of them with him?"

Mary grinned. "I suspect we'll find our answers right here." She pointed to the star. "And, maybe, we'll even find that ring in time for your niece's wedding."

Henry beamed at the thought. "Boy, finding that ring would mean so much to Annie. It would be such a huge surprise."

Henry's words inspired Mary. A buried treasure was fun to search for, but to uncover a long-lost family heirloom and return it to one of her dearest friends and his cousin was more than fun. That was righting a wrong, and the thought of returning the ring to Annie, who had lost so much, made Mary's determination soar. "Let's get started," she said, leading the way to the circulation desk. This was a mystery she was resolved to see through.

"Morning, Henry and Mary." Mary turned to see librarian Victoria Pickerton approaching with her arms full of books. She set them on the circulation desk with a thud. The librarian was a trim woman in her midforties, and today, as always, she was wearing one of her trademark pairs of cat's-eye glasses. "Phew, those were heavy," she said with an exaggerated exhale.

"Who knew working in the library could be such a workout?" Mary asked with a smile.

"Yes, between the carrying and the shelving, I'll never need a gym membership," Victoria said. Her words were light, but Mary thought she noticed an anxious look in her eyes.

"How are things going?" Mary asked gently.

Victoria sighed, and now her anxiety was evident. "There was just a meeting at Town Hall last night," she said. "Our budget is being cut again. We'll probably have to cut our hours and get rid of a couple of programs."

"That's terrible," Mary said. Mary had been a librarian herself for many years, and she knew how vital libraries were. She also knew how much heart Victoria had poured into developing programs at the Ivy Bay library.

Henry shook his head ruefully. "I know a lot of people count on the classes you have. I hate to think of cutting any of them."

"Yes, me too," Victoria said, shaking her head. "How can I give up reading hour when we get over fifteen kids every Monday afternoon? Or the computer classes for retired folks?"

"That is hard," Mary said. Inwardly, she said a quick prayer, asking for guidance for Victoria with the challenges she was facing.

"I guess I'll find a way," Victoria said. She took a deep breath and then forced a smile for Mary. "And now, what can I do for you both today?"

"We're looking for maps," Henry said.

Victoria's brow wrinkled. "Maps of what?"

Henry turned to Mary.

"Maps of local towns," Mary said. She thought it made sense to start on the Cape, since David had lived there his whole life up until his disappearance. It was also the easiest place to start.

"That I can help you with," Victoria said, walking purposefully toward the side wall of the room.

Henry gestured for Mary to go first, and he followed. Victoria's low heels clicked on the polished wooden floor as she led them to a shelf holding a row of oversize books. "Here we go," she said. "We have atlases of the Cape going back a good twenty years."

"Thanks," Mary said, getting ready to take out the first atlas. But then something occurred to her. "And if we wanted to look at anything older, where might we find it?"

Victoria pointed at the back wall, where the shelves were lined with thick books of maps. "Those go back to the eighteen hundreds."

"Perfect, thank you," Mary said. Now that they knew where to look, she was ready to dig in.

Victoria left them, and Mary sat down at the table next to the shelves while Henry grabbed the atlas dated two years back. "Let's start here," he said.

The towns of the Cape were organized alphabetically, and Henry flipped to Ivy Bay. "Might as well start at home," he said. Mary pulled out the printout of the map, unfolding it and placing it above the atlas.

"Not a fit," she said after a moment. There were some similarities in the layouts, but on the lighthouse map, the main road curved around as it wound through the town, and the streets in the town intersected it at an angle. There were also many more side streets marked on the lighthouse map than existed in Ivy Bay. "I suppose that would have been too easy." She turned back to the beginning of the book so that they could go through town by town.

She flipped through the book carefully, studying each page. She loved looking at the colors and shadings on each page. It was almost like art, and she would love to spend hours studying the lines and shading. It was also interesting how little you could actually tell about a place by seeing its roads all laid out like this. You could see the logic — or lack thereof — of how a town was organized, but not what it was like in person. Looking at a map was so different from actually walking the streets and seeing the shops and homes and people that brought them to life. After twenty minutes, they'd covered all of Cape Cod and nothing looked similar to their map. Mary closed the heavy book, and the sound echoed in the quiet corner.

"Shall we start looking at maps from towns off the Cape?" Henry asked. He leaned back in his chair and eyed the shelf of books skeptically. There were so many possibilities.

"Actually," Mary said, eyeing the shelf of atlases from the past, "I wonder if we should stick with the Cape." The map showed a town by the sea. Technically, there were nothing called a sea nearby — just Cape Cod Bay on the north, the Atlantic Ocean on the east, and Nantucket Sound on the south — but David, or whoever had drawn the map, was depicting a town with close proximity to water. And that described most of Cape Cod. She got up and walked to the shelf and carried back a stack of heavy atlases. She dropped them on the table, and they landed with a thud.

"Let's see what these towns looked like when David was around," Mary said, reaching for the top book in the stack. "So if David did draw that map, it would have been right around the time he disappeared," Mary said. "And Annie said that was 1925." She saw that the book she'd picked up was from the 1960s, and she longed to flip through and study how the cartographer had drawn the towns fifty years ago, but she had to focus, and she set it aside sadly.

"You do have a good memory," Henry said. He scanned the spines in the stack on the table and reached for one near the bottom, labeled 1923. He flipped it open carefully, and the divine scent of old paper wafted up. Mary inhaled deeply.

"Where do we look first?" he asked.

"Let's start close to the lighthouse," Mary said. It made the most sense for the map to show someplace local, and the town in David's map did share a lot of similarities with Ivy Bay. She flipped gently through the yellowed pages and stopped on the map of old Ivy Bay.

They both gazed at it. This map was drawn at a slightly different scale than the more recent map, and it had the curve of Route 6A coming in at a different angle. Mary knew that Route 6A was the original road that had stretched from the mainland to the eastern shore. Years ago, before the modern highway known as Route 6 was built, it was the main thoroughfare but now was considered to be the scenic route around the Cape. It was only two lanes wide, and it meandered across cranberry bogs and curved around homes and trees as it snaked its way east. Mary had always assumed that it followed the same route it always had, but was it possible that the course of the road had changed over time?

"It looks like it *could* be Ivy Bay," Henry said, turning the map to study it from another angle. Mary nodded. If 6A had been rerouted to come into town more from the south, it was definitely possible. But what about all the extra streets on David's map?

Mary leaned in closer. There were streets here she didn't recognize. There was a narrow little road, unnamed, that ran behind Meeting House Road, and another that ran behind the stores along Main Street.

"These are alleys," Mary said, running her finger along the thin black line. There was still a narrow alleyway behind her store's back garden, where she put out the trash. She turned back to the contemporary map. The alleys weren't marked on the map today, but they had been in David's time. She looked back at the map David had drawn. Sure enough, the maps matched up.

David had drawn a map of Ivy Bay.

"Well, I'll be," Henry said. "It *is* Ivy Bay." Then he glanced at the clock and stood up.

It made sense, Mary thought. And that meant that the lighthouse was . . . She ran her finger along the printout and tapped the spot where she thought the lighthouse would be. The red star was not far off, just down the beach.

"Should we go see what we find out by the lighthouse?" Mary asked.

"I would love to," Henry said, narrowing his eyes at the printout, "but I'm afraid I'm taking a tour out in a little while," he said.

"I have to get to the marina."

Mary glanced up at the clock and was surprised to see that it was almost ten thirty. She was supposed to have opened the shop a half hour ago.

"Oh dear, I need to run too," she said, hopping out of her chair. Henry carried the old atlases back to the shelf, and the two of them walked out, waving to Victoria as they went.

Mary blinked against the bright morning sun as they stepped out onto Liberty Road. Henry turned to Mary, a frown on his face. "Here's what I don't get about all of this," he said. "Why did David need to draw a map of the town right next to the lighthouse?"

"That is just what we're going to find out," Mary said determinedly.

Six

When Mary got to the store, she called to check in with Betty, who reported she was indeed feeling better, and then she began shelving books. The shop was busy, and she and Rebecca helped several customers pick the perfect mystery. It was a satisfying day, and on her walk home, she noticed that the leaves on the trees were just starting to turn. She looked forward to the gorgeous fall foliage she knew would soon appear. She opened the front door after the walk home and found Betty sitting on the sofa, an afghan covering her legs.

"Glad to see you up," Mary said, taking off the light cardigan she had worn to ward off the nip of the fall air.

Betty smiled, the tension almost completely gone from her face. "Yes," she said. "Well enough to get a change of scenery. And, of course, this rascal came along."

Mary hadn't even noticed Gus, tucked so

deeply into the afghan, his tail curled around his body. "Yes, he does love a warm blanket," she said affectionately, walking over and giving the cat a rub on his soft head. "How does a simple roast chicken with baked potatoes sound for dinner?" she asked Betty.

"Just perfect," Betty said. "I can help, if you'd like."

Mary frowned at her sister. "You'll do no such thing," she scolded. "You will sit here and rest."

Betty laughed as Mary headed to the kitchen. She had just taken the roasting pan out of the cabinet when the phone rang.

"Hi, Mom." Lizzie's cheerful voice greeted Mary, who tucked the phone against her shoulder so that she could start with dinner preparations while talking to her daughter.

"Hello, love," Mary said. "How are you?"

Lizzie let out a breath. "A little over-whelmed," she said, though Mary could hear the joy in her voice. Ever since she was a little girl, when her games all centered on playing house and caring for her baby dolls, Lizzie had been looking forward to starting a family. And she couldn't have done any better, Mary thought proudly, thinking of Lizzie's hardworking husband Chad, who had changed diapers like a pro. Mary's grandson Luke was a sunny seven-year-old with explosive energy, and Emma, who had just turned twelve, was quiet and thoughtful. As always, Mary's heart swelled when she thought of her grandchildren. "Between Luke's soccer games and Emma's active social life, I feel more like a chauffeur than a mom."

Mary chuckled as she rubbed olive oil into the chicken, then sprinkled on rosemary. "I remember those days," she said. "Carting you and Jack to cross-country and band and then sitting in the stands for those football games." Mary's son Jack was a doctor who lived with his family in Chicago. He was busy with a thriving practice and Mary's other granddaughter Daisy.

"I did love being a cheerleader," Lizzie said. "I don't think that's the route Emma will take, though."

"No?" Mary asked. Was twelve the age when kids started trying on different interests and clothes, seeing what felt right? Funny how it was so important at the time, but now the years blurred together into a mass of happy memories. Well, mostly happy. Senior year, Jack had broken his ankle before the homecoming game, and Lizzie's boyfriend had broken up with her right before prom. But God had helped them through the tough times, and each child emerged stronger. "So what is Emma up to?"

She could almost hear Lizzie's smile on the other end of the phone. "I'm going to let her surprise you this weekend," she said. "But I can tell you that she's joined the church choir."

"That's wonderful news," Mary said. She'd gotten great joy out of seeing both her children be a part of her church community. "It's a wonderful way for her to participate in the church community."

"Yes," Lizzie said. "You should see her in her robes. She looks so grown up."

Mary could hear the pang in her voice. "She'll always be your little girl," Mary reassured her daughter.

"A girl does always need her mother," Lizzie said affectionately. "And we're all looking forward to seeing you and Aunt Betty this weekend."

"We can't wait," Mary said, setting the roasting pan in the oven. "I got the Clue game set out, as well as the art supplies and some books."

"Perfect," Lizzie said. Mary heard a crash in the background.

"Mom, I have to go," Lizzie said quickly. "We'll see you on Saturday." As she was hanging up, Mary heard her say, "Luke, what's the rule about using your remote control car in the kitchen?"

Mary was grinning, her mind filled with memories of little ones running around. She couldn't wait until they got here.

The next morning, Henry rang the doorbell just as Mary was placing the last plate in the dishwasher. Betty, who was feeling much better, had surprised her with a breakfast of blueberry pancakes, and their scent was still perfuming the air as Mary hurried to open the door. "Come in," she said.

"Henry, can I interest you in a few pancakes?" Betty asked, walking into the front hall.

Henry shook his head regretfully. "I stopped by the Black & White Diner on my way over, and I'm stuffed."

"Another time, then," Betty said.

"Watch out," Henry said, "because I'll definitely take you up on that."

Betty laughed, and Mary gave a quick prayer of thanks to God for helping Betty through her pain yesterday.

"So you're off to see where the map leads?" Betty asked.

Henry nodded. "Yep, and it's the perfect

fall day to be out on a treasure hunt. A little dreary, a little windy . . ."

"It's the stuff great adventure movies are made of," Mary said with a chuckle.

"Shall we?" Henry asked, opening the door for Mary.

"Have fun, you two," Betty said.

Mary waved to her sister, then followed Henry out into the cool fall morning, a copy of the map clenched in her hand.

According to the map, the red star was south of Ivy Bay, near the lighthouse, but first Mary wanted to stop in at the store to make sure Rebecca had everything under control. Henry drove slowly down Main Street, where people were already bustling about, starting their day. Tourists, looking sleepy, walked more slowly, taking in the charming stores and restaurants. A family in Cape Cod sweatshirts walked into Sweet Susan's Bakery, no doubt lured by the smell of freshly baked bread that wafted out from the shop every morning. Kaley Court was setting up a display of fresh fruit by the door of Meeting House Grocers. Outside the Tea Shoppe, Mary saw Lynn Teagarden and Amy Stebble from her prayer group and waved. The group was meeting in a few days, and it was something Mary looked forward to. Sharing her faith with members of her church community was one of her most treasured ways to stay close to God, and their prayers never ceased to lift her spirits to the sky.

Henry parked in front of Mary's shop, and she went in to find Rebecca counting out money in the cash register, getting the shop ready to open.

"You're sure you've got it under control?" Mary asked. Rebecca waved her concerns away.

"Opening the shop is easy. You have nothing to worry about."

Mary smiled, thankful to have such reliable help, and then headed back out to the car. She buckled herself in, and then Henry turned down Meeting House Road, then made a left onto Liberty Road, which led out to the main highway.

"You have some visitors coming your way, don't you?" Henry asked casually as the car pulled off Route 6A and onto the windy road that led to the lighthouse. The smell of salt water was rich in the air as the car sped past the low pines and dune grass next to the road.

"Yes," Mary said, unable to keep the smile from her face. "For a whole week. There's some kind of district-wide teacher training, and Lizzie thought it would be a good time for a visit."

"And you agreed," Henry said. "Would I be wrong to think that their beds are already made and cookies are in the cookie jar?"

Mary laughed, her cheeks turning slightly pink. "The games and kids' books are set out too," she confessed.

Henry smiled good-naturedly. "Misty was the same way when our grandkids came. And I might even admit to setting out some games a few days early myself."

Mary knew Henry was a doting grand-father whose eyes shone when he was accompanying his grandkids around Ivy Bay. "When will you get to see them next?" she asked as Henry pulled the car into the lot at the lighthouse.

"Actually, I'm going to Boston for Thanksgiving," Henry said, smiling at the thought.

"That will be great," Mary said, getting out of the car. She shut the door and held up the map. "Shall we get started?"

They headed into the lighthouse and took another look at the map drawn on the wall, but Mary didn't see anything she hadn't noticed before, so they went back outside and studied the printout. Henry peered at the map, his arm brushing lightly against Mary's. "Let's start at the lighthouse and follow that path there." He pointed to the thin line that appeared to go along the dunes and ended at the red star. Based on the distance from town, they could surmise that the red star was about a quarter of a mile from the lighthouse, by the base of a dune.

"Have you ever been to this stretch of beach?" Mary asked as they made their way across the cracked parking lot. She noticed a dandelion growing through one of the cracks and admired its determination.

Henry looked around when they reached the dune. "Years ago, I'm sure," he said. "I've walked pretty much every inch of beach on the Cape at some point. I don't recall there being anything special on this stretch, but then again, I wasn't looking for anything."

They stepped onto the sand, and Mary paused to regain her balance on the unsteady footing. Henry reached out and deftly tucked her arm under his. His steps were sure as he led them both on the uphill path through the dunes. They paused at the top, looking out over the beach, and the water spread to the horizon and beyond. Whitecaps danced lightly in the wind, and seagulls flew overhead, squawking to one another.

For a moment, Mary just gazed at it, taking in the beauty of God's landscape. Then she held up the map and studied it for a moment. "It looks like we should go left."

They started off, Mary's hand still resting gently in the crook of Henry's arm. The lighthouse was now behind them, but when Mary glanced back, it looked majestic on top of the dune. The beaches of Cape Cod were all gorgeous, but there was something especially lovely about a beach like this, with no lifeguard chairs or stray sandwich wrappers, where the two of them were the only people as far as the eye could see. It was just sand, driftwood, and lapping waves. "This is stunning," she said with a happy sigh.

Henry squeezed her arm lightly. "Of course, I love Little Neck Beach," Henry said, referring to the public beach in Ivy Bay, where Mary and Betty lived. "But a beach like this makes you feel like you're the first person to ever lay eyes on it."

Mary was surprised at how perfectly Henry had put her feelings into words. "Yes, exactly."

A gull flew low above them and then sailed over the water and dove in.

"So what are we looking for here?" Henry asked.

Mary held out the map. "It seems like the

path goes around a curve and the star is right there."

Henry looked at the map, then at the beach. And then he frowned. "Obviously David was in a hurry when he drew this," he said. "But now that we're out here, it looks like he has the outline of the shore all wrong."

Mary looked at the map, and after a moment, she could see that he was right. There should have been a big curve coming up, but instead the beach lay before them, straight and spread out, with not even the slightest deviation.

"That's strange," Mary murmured, looking back toward the lighthouse. "We should be facing a curve right here, and we aren't. We can't even see one from here."

Henry looked at the map and nodded in agreement.

"Perhaps there's something tucked in by one of the dunes," Mary said. "After all, the shoreline changes over time. Maybe some land got covered in a hurricane, straightening out this stretch of beach."

Henry looked doubtful. "I think something that extreme would take a pretty long time," he said. "But there could still be something by the dunes, I guess."

"Let's check," Mary said, trying to stay upbeat.

They walked to the spot marked by the red star, or where it would have been had the beach curved, then looked around. There were no nooks or tiny spaces between the dunes. There were just mounds of golden sand topped off by beach grass that blew in the cool breeze off the water.

"I don't know," Henry said, turning in a slow circle. "I don't see anything here."

Mary and Henry exchanged a look, then began to bend down and start digging in the sand. Mary suspected it was a futile effort; it didn't seem likely that someone would bury a treasure in such a shifting foundation. But it was worth a shot.

Soon enough, their hands and arms were covered in sand up to their elbows, and they both began to slow their pace. Mary slumped into her knees and looked at Henry, who had now also stopped digging.

"Could we have missed something or taken a wrong turn?" Mary checked the map, but even leaving room for error, the distance was right.

They both bent over the map again. Mary retraced every step they had taken with her finger, and there was no getting around it: This was the spot marked by the star, and there was nothing there.

They had come to a dead end.

SEVEN

It had been a busy day at the bookstore. A bus of tourists from Providence came in for the day, and they were all apparently mystery lovers. Mary had greatly enjoyed helping people pick out books they would like; she had a few key questions that quickly told her whether a reader would enjoy an action-packed Sue Grafton, a rich Tana French, or something by the master herself, Agatha Christie. The group had gone back to Providence with bags from Mary's bookshop.

But despite her pleasure, disappointment sat in her belly like a stone. She had known it was a long shot, but the fact that the map had not led to the ring was still disappointing. Worse was the letdown she could see in Henry's eyes.

"Mary, do you mind if I leave now?" Rebecca asked, interrupting Mary's thoughts. Ashley stood next to Rebecca, her backpack hitched up on her shoulder. Rebecca's husband had a dentist appointment that afternoon, so Ashley had come to the shop when school let out and had been very helpful with the tourists, pointing a couple of gray-haired women to children's books she thought their grandkids might enjoy. The elderly women had found the precocious girl winsome, and Mary was certain that having Ashley here had increased the store's sales for the day. Sometimes Ashley seemed much more mature than her seven years.

Rebecca had mentioned wanting to get home a bit early today because Ashley needed to do some baking for a school celebration the next day.

"No, that's fine," Mary said. "Have a great time baking. What are you making?"

"Oatmeal chocolate-chip cookies," Ashley said, grinning, and suddenly she seemed like a child again. "With walnuts."

"Those sound delicious," Mary said and smiled as Ashley nodded vigorously. "You'll have to save one for me."

"We will," Rebecca said, laughing, as they turned to go. The phone rang just as the door closed behind them.

"Mary's Mystery Bookshop," Mary said after picking it up.

"Mary, hello, it's Annie."

Mary's spirits sank even further. She had assumed Henry would break the news to Annie about the map and did not relish the thought of doing it now, over the phone. But then Annie went on.

"Henry told me about the map," Annie said. "And I wanted to thank you for taking the time to see if it led anywhere."

"It was my pleasure," Mary said, touched by Annie's thoughtfulness.

"And I wondered . . . ," Annie said. "I'm in Ivy Bay to see a friend, and I brought that box, the one I told you about that has some of David's old things in it. I'm not sure if you're still interested, but I'd be happy to drop by your store and go through it with you."

As soon as Annie mentioned the box, Mary had felt a prickle of excitement. Just because the map had been a dead end did not mean she was ready to let go of the mystery of David and what had become of the ring. And perhaps there was something in the box that would lead her one step closer. "I'd love to see it, if it's not too much trouble."

Mary could hear the smile in Annie's voice as she replied. "Not at all. I packed it hoping I'd have some extra time and you'd be free. And both of those things have happened, so I'll be there in about five minutes."

Mary was smiling too as she hung up the phone.

It was five minutes on the dot when Annie walked in, a wooden box the size of a shoe box in her hand. She set it down on the counter to hug Mary and then looked around Mary's store.

"What a beautiful space, and you've set it up so nicely," she said. "Can you give me the tour?"

Mary felt a flush of pride as she took Annie around the store. Annie cooed over the bathtub in the children's section, admired the first editions that were displayed in the glass case under the register, and gladly accepted a warm cup of tea in the back reading area.

"You have quite a selection," Annie said, glancing around the shelves of books. "You're going to have to tell me where to start. I'm afraid my mystery reading is confined to a few Agatha Christies and some Sue Graftons."

Mary smiled. "Choosing inventory is one of my favorite parts of the job," she said. "And it's always exciting to find a new author. I can definitely make some recommendations for you."

"I'd love that," Annie said. "But first let me show you the box."

"I'm so sorry the map was a dead end," Mary said as Annie went up to the counter for the box and then came back and sat down.

"It is disappointing, though I suppose not a surprise after all these years," Annie said.

"Once Henry told me about David, I felt sure he'd drawn the map and that it would lead us somewhere," Mary said.

Annie was nodding. "Yes, it does seem likely that David drew it," she said. "I have to admit that ever since I saw that picture of the map, I've been thinking about the unanswered questions about David."

"Just because the map didn't turn up anything doesn't mean there wouldn't be other traces that he left," Mary said.

"It sounds like you're not ready to give up yet," Annie said with a smile.

Mary laughed. "I can get a bit single-minded when it comes to mysteries," she said. "And this one is very intriguing."

"Then let's get to it," Annie said. "Maybe you'll see some clues in here that the rest of us missed."

Mary felt her conviction deepen at Annie's words. If there was even the slightest chance that she could find something that would be meaningful to Annie, Mary was going to try.

Annie moved the wooden box between them and lifted the solid wood lid that was carved with leaves. Then she took out a packet of papers. "As I said, there isn't much here," she said, passing the pile to Mary.

On top was a black-and-white photograph. "That's my grandmother," Annie said, pointing to a solemn and well-dressed girl. "And that's David." The small boy had a mischievous grin on his face. "He was a cutie, wasn't he?"

"Indeed," Mary said. "And your grandmother was a beauty."

Annie smiled, then moved the picture so Mary could look at the rest of the papers. There was a yellowed church bulletin announcing David's baptism on June 7, 1901.

"Have you ever been to First Congregational Church?" Mary asked Annie, noting the name of the church where David's baptism had taken place.

"No," Annie said. "My parents moved to Boston before I was born, and then when I came back to the Cape, after Carson died, I settled in Wellfleet, near my sister and her family. My grandmother was a real church-goer, though. My mother said she belonged to every committee there was and never missed a service."

"Do you know if David went to church?" Mary asked.

Annie thought for a moment. "Well, he must have gone when he was young, because my mother said her grandmother took them every week, no matter what. But I'm not sure if David continued his relationship with the church after he turned to crime."

Mary made a mental note to visit First Congregational Church, then continued through the stack of papers, seeing announcements for plays David had participated in, as well as some of his early drawings and schoolwork. The last thing in the box was the ring authentication, written on stiff paper, with an official-looking seal.

"What an honor," Mary said, running a finger down the old document.

"And such a loss," Annie said sadly.

Again, Mary felt another surge of conviction that she should look for the ring. "Thank you for showing these things to me," Mary said.

"My pleasure," Annie said. "It was my mother's passion to share family history, so I appreciate the chance to look through these things. And I must say, I'm thinking about my mother more now that we've started planning Kate's wedding."

"The same thing happened to me when we planned Liz's," Mary said. "It truly is special to see your daughter prepare for marriage."

Annie nodded with a smile.

"How is the planning going?" Mary asked.

"Well, we have a date," Annie said. "June 8. It's my anniversary with Carson, and next year, it just happens to fall on a Saturday."

"How meaningful," Mary said.

Annie smiled, though her eyes were tinged with sadness. "Of course, Carson's spirit would be with us whatever day it was, but I do feel like it's a nice connection for Kate to have with her father."

Mary reached out and squeezed Annie's hand. "It will be a beautiful day," she said. She remembered her own wedding, how her stomach had been filled with butterflies as she got ready, and how she'd felt like her knees were going to give out as she walked toward the sanctuary doors. But then she had suddenly felt miraculously calm when she saw John waiting for her at the front of the church. She had walked toward him, holding on to her father's arm, and their eyes locked on each other as the music swelled. Mary still choked up thinking about how happy she had been at the moment, how she'd felt like she had everything she'd ever wanted right in front of her.

Annie nodded, then put the papers back in the box and stood up. "I should get going, but thank you for indulging my trip down memory lane," Annie said.

Mary stood and walked Annie to the door of the shop. "I enjoyed it," she said. "And it did give me a few ideas for ways I might try and track down a bit more information about David."

"Keep me posted," Annie said. "And I'll have to come back soon since I didn't have a chance to get those book recommendations from you."

"You're welcome back anytime," Mary said.

"Then I'll see you soon," Annie said, and with one last smile, she headed out.

On the short drive home, Mary thought about her pleasant visit with Annie, and her spirits were light as she pulled into her driveway. As she walked up the steps of the cheerful light green house, she recalled the determined dandelion in the lighthouse parking lot. It was an unlikely spot for it to grow, but it was tenacious enough to thrive. She decided she, too, would stick things out until the end. Just because the map had somehow led them astray didn't mean she was ready to give up, especially if there was the smallest chance she could find that ring for Annie. All she needed was a good lead and God's guidance.

She opened the door and was met with the fragrant scent of Betty's special marinara sauce. She found Betty in the kitchen, stirring a bubbling pot of spaghetti. "Breakfast *and* dinner?" Mary asked. "I could get used to this."

Betty grinned. "We have so many ripe tomatoes. They were just falling off the vine," Betty said. "I did some canning, and then since I was already in here, I whipped up this sauce for us. And I made a bit of extra to freeze for when Lizzie and the kids are here."

"Wonderful," Mary said, peeking in the oven, where a loaf of garlic bread was nestled in a wrapping of tinfoil. "It's always good to have a quick dinner ready after a day out with the kids. And they do love your sauce."

Betty's eyes shone at the compliment. Her mother-in-law had taught Betty how to make the sauce when she was a new bride, and when Mary and John came to visit when the kids were young, they'd enjoyed the big family dinners over steaming plates of Betty's spaghetti.

Mary set the table, and soon they were both sitting down to the mouthwatering meal.

"So how did the treasure hunt go?" Betty asked, twining strands of spaghetti around her fork.

Mary filled her in on the morning's adventure, as well as her visit with Annie.

"That is too bad," Betty said. "Though, of course, not really surprising. The map was so old, and who knows what the star might have meant. I hope Henry wasn't too disappointed, though. Or Annie."

Mary paused. "I know it would mean the world to Annie to give that ring to her daughter, and Henry would love to see that happen. Of course, the possibility of retrieving that ring would have never occurred to him had we not found that map."

Betty broke off a piece of garlic bread, then passed the basket to Mary, who helped herself to a buttery slice. "The whole story is really something," she said after a moment. "Stolen money, a missing ring, a young man disappearing . . ."

Mary nodded. "And not knowing where he went or if he was okay. . . . That must have just eaten at his mother, no matter how disappointed in him she was."

"It's a sad story," Betty said, taking another piece of garlic bread. "So there was no trace of David after the night he disappeared?"

"None that Annie or Henry knows of. But I was thinking I might poke around and see if there's any other information on him I might be able to turn up," Mary said.

Betty grinned. "I suppose I should have guessed that."

"Do you think Eleanor might know anything about David?" Mary asked. Eleanor's family had a long and proud history in Ivy Bay.

"It would be worth asking," Betty said. "You could give her a call. Though, actually, our book club is meeting tomorrow morning right here at the house. You could just ask her then." Eleanor had started the exclusive book club and made such a fuss about the pedigree of the members that Betty was a bit sheepish about her own membership. She did enjoy the book discussion, though.

"That's a great idea," Mary said. "If you don't mind me taking up a bit of her time at book club."

"Not at all," Betty said, standing up and beginning to clear the table.

"No, let me do that," Mary scolded. "You

did all the cooking, so you get a night off from cleaning."

"Thank you," Betty said with a smile. "I wouldn't mind doing a bit of reading."

She left, and Mary cleared the table, then began loading the dishwasher. Where should she start looking for more information about David? He must have lived nearby if he visited the lighthouse often. Maybe she could find out where. If the house was still around, it was possible there was still some remnants of his there. She could also look into the records of the First Congregational Church, where David had gone as a child, to see if there was anything there. Though her first stop would be the Ivy Bay Public Library, she decided as she arranged the glasses on the rack. David's story might have made the newspaper. It was worth looking through the library's archives to see if she could find anything there.

As she set the last pieces of silverware in the basket, she realized that her disappointment of the morning had transformed into hope. The map had been a dead end, but Mary's investigation was just beginning.

EIGHT

The next morning, Mary helped Betty set out freshly baked muffins, a fruit salad, and chocolate croissants from the Tea Shoppe for Betty's book club. A big pot of coffee was brewing in the kitchen, and Mary set out cream and sugar. The doorbell rang at ten o'clock on the dot, and Mary heard the voice of Virginia Livingston when Betty opened the door. Virginia's family was one of the founding families of Ivy Bay, and Mary realized she would be a good person to ask about David as well.

"Hello, Mary," Virginia said pleasantly as she walked into the living room.

The doorbell rang again, and Betty went to answer it.

"Good morning, Virginia," Mary said with a smile. "Let me take you in to get some coffee."

She led the way to the sunny kitchen and passed Virginia a mug. Moments later, Betty came in, with Eleanor and Frances Curran, a retired literature professor, right behind her.

Mary greeted everyone and helped make sure everyone was set with coffee. And then she put a hand on Eleanor's arm. "I have an Ivy Bay history question for you," she said. "And, Virginia, perhaps you could help me with it as well."

Eleanor nodded in her knowing way, and Virginia smiled. "I'd be happy to help, if I can."

The doorbell rang again, and Betty left to answer it, but Frances lingered, clearly curious about Mary's question.

"Well, I'm doing a bit of research on Henry Woodrow's great-uncle, a man named David Woodrow," Mary said. "He stole a large sum of money and disappeared."

"That sounds like something out of a novel," Frances said.

"It does, doesn't it?" Mary agreed. She was looking at Eleanor and Virginia, but neither seemed familiar with David or his story.

"I'm sorry, Mary, but that name doesn't ring a bell for me," Virginia said.

"Me neither," Eleanor said. "I'm afraid I'm more familiar with the proud history of

Ivy Bay, not the unseemly underbelly."

Mary hid her grin at those words. "Well, thank you, anyway," she said.

Betty walked in with Madeline Dinsdale, the last member of the club.

"I need to get to the store," Mary said, after greeting Madeline. "Enjoy your meeting."

She walked out into the sunny morning, thinking about the one other person she knew who was well versed in the history of Ivy Bay: Leroy Steckler, a colorful old-timer who was not particular about what side of Ivy Bay history he was familiar with.

But when Mary called him from the store fifteen minutes later, she was disappointed to learn that Leroy was also unfamiliar with David's story.

Mary spent the next hour unpacking boxes while Rebecca manned the register. As she worked, she thought over what to do next. She was already planning to go to the library later to see if Victoria had any resources that might help. And while she was there, she would look up old newspaper articles about David. His story had to have made the papers back then, and perhaps she'd find a lead there.

At noon, Mary walked over to the public library. It was another gorgeous fall day, the air crisp and the sun bright. She breathed in the scent of fall leaves as she walked down Meeting House Road, lively as always. A family of five walked by, the kids bickering cheerfully about where the best place to buy T-shirts was, their parents holding hands as they strolled behind. Mary walked down the stone path to the Ivy Bay library.

Victoria was sitting at the circulation desk when Mary came in. She was scanning in a big pile of books.

"Good morning," Mary said.

"Good morning," Victoria said cheerfully. "How are you today, Mary?"

"With this perfect weather and my grandkids coming to town, I couldn't be better," Mary said.

"How nice that they're visiting," Victoria said as she closed the cover of a book and reached for the next.

"Yes, I've been looking forward to it for weeks," Mary said with a grin.

"So what can I do for you today?" Victoria asked. "More maps?"

Mary shook her head. "This time I'm here to look at old newspapers," she said.

Victoria cocked her head. "Are you looking for anything in particular?"

Mary nodded. "I'm doing some research on a man named David Woodrow who committed a crime in 1925 that was never solved." She had planned to explain more but noticed Victoria's eyes widen.

"It's the funniest thing," Victoria said. "There was a young man in here just last week researching the same thing. He's a graduate student up in Boston, but apparently there was a case in Ivy Bay he wanted to get some more information on. I bet he'd be a great person to talk to about this."

"That would be great," Mary said. A graduate student might have found information she wouldn't have even thought to look for. "Do you know where I could find him?"

Victoria frowned. "You know, I'm not even sure if he mentioned the name of his university."

Mary's heart sank. There were over fifty colleges in Boston.

"He did say he'd be back again in the next few weeks to do more research," Victoria said. "I can let him know you'd like to talk when I see him."

"Thanks," Mary said. She hated the idea of waiting weeks to speak to him, though. "What was his name? Maybe I can track him down."

"Connor Briggs," Victoria said.

"Great, thanks," Mary said as a young woman came up to apply for a library card.

Mary walked to the back of the library where the computer room was. She had the space to herself as she logged on and did her first search, this one for Connor Briggs. There were a surprising number of men with the unusual name, so Mary did the search again with the city of Boston attached. The search turned up several Connors on Facebook, as well as a group of articles about a Connor Briggs who was a high school football star. But on the second page, she saw a listing for a Connor Briggs who was a teaching assistant for a class at Boston College. The class was on the history of Prohibition and had been taught the past spring. This had to be the Connor she was searching for. And best of all, the Web site had contact information that students could use to get in touch with him.

Mary opened up her e-mail account and wrote a quick note to Connor, explaining how Victoria had told her about him and asking if he might be willing to talk about some of his research. And then she turned her attention to David Woodrow.

Mary spent the next half hour researching David on the library's microfilm archives. She had used the machines many times, so she knew exactly how to look through the shallow drawers where the spools of film were kept. She found the roll of the *Ivy Bay Bugle* that would include the time he disappeared and sat down in front of one of the big microfilm readers. In her time as a librarian, Mary had shown hundreds of reluctant students how to use the old machines. Students today were usually unfamiliar with the older system of locating information, and she'd had to explain to more than a few incredulous faces that Google hadn't always been the primary way to do research. She knew many libraries had digitized their holdings, making them easier to search, but she didn't mind the old-fashioned way of searching.

She carefully threaded the thin film through the machine and scanned the tiny print. She advanced the film to January 1925, the month of David's disappearance. There was a front-page article about the big fire at the hardware store where David worked. Apparently it had taken the volunteer fire brigade several hours to get the blaze out, partly because they'd had to bring water all the way from the pond by the gristmill to spray on the blaze. There were a couple of follow-up stories in the following days, none of which offered anything new, until the announcement a few days later that a large sum of money had disappeared from the hardware store shortly before the fire broke out.

Mary scrolled through the pages, passing by the lovely old advertisements and the news stories about local happenings. Old newspapers were a treasure trove of information about what life was like when they were published, and Mary could spend hours poring over them, but she willed herself to concentrate on the task at hand.

The next paper had what she was looking for. Local Man Disappears in Wake of Fire and Theft, the headline read. Then, in smaller type, David Woodrow Presumed Guilty of Crimes. Mary scanned the article. The article was slanted, to be sure, and made no effort to hide that the paper believed David was guilty, but Mary had to admit, reading the story, that it made a pretty convincing case. The article didn't tell her anything she didn't already know, but she could see why everyone believed David had stolen the money and run.

She continued to scan through the paper, though, and didn't find any mention of David leaving the money behind. If he had buried the money or hidden it somewhere, the local paper hadn't gotten wind of it. She turned the knob and advanced the screen, searching all the way through the end of the year, and then let out a sigh. She stretched her tired neck muscles and tried to relax her shoulders, which had become tight as she stared at the screen. There was nothing more. Another dead end.

Mary walked back to the bookshop slowly, trying to rid herself of the disappointment of her fruitless search. She tried to focus on the beauty of the gold, orange, and ocher leaves against the soft gray sky and the quaint charm of her small town. She waved at Kaley Court, who was out for an afternoon stroll with her dog Pipp, and by the time she entered her shop again, she was feeling much more optimistic. The bell over the door tinkled as she stepped inside, and she took a deep breath, appreciating, as she always did, the rich scent of paper and ink and the sweet smell of freshly baked treats that wafted in from the bakery next door. Mary waved to Rebecca, who was helping a customer, and sat down at the counter. She checked her e-mail, hoping for a message from Connor Briggs, but he had not written her back. She returned a few e-mails, then straightened up the store and helped customers until it was time to close for the day.

She sent Rebecca home, saying she'd finish up closing the shop, and checked her e-mail one last time, but there were no new messages, so she powered down the computer. She locked up the store and headed for home. It had rained in the late afternoon, and the evening air still held a bit of mist. As she walked down Main Street, she noticed Chief McArthur walking toward her, away from the city's municipal buildings. She waved and waited for him to get closer. It was a long shot, but Chief McArthur had helped her with some crazy requests before, and his family had been around town a long time. It was at least worth asking if he knew anything about David.

She waited under a streetlamp, which had just turned on for the evening. It gave off a warm light, and droplets from the afternoon's shower sparkled in its glow.

"Out patrolling?" she asked with a smile as he got close.

"I was just leaving a meeting," he said. "A meeting that ran quite late."

"Meetings tend to do that," Mary said.

"Did you just close up shop?" he asked, nodding at the door of her bookshop.

"Sure did. It was a good afternoon too. Nothing like a stormy fall afternoon to get people in the mood for curling up with a good book."

He nodded. It had started to drizzle again, and Mary could see he was in a hurry, so she decided to get to the point. "I was wondering," Mary said, "if you might know anything about an unsolved crime in Ivy Bay, something that took place in 1925."

Chief McArthur's mouth pursed slightly in curiosity. "Which case in particular?" he asked.

"In 1925, a man named David Woodrow stole some money from his employer and then disappeared."

Chief McArthur began shaking his head before Mary had even finished her sentence. "Sorry, I don't know anything about it," he said. But were his eyes clouded with what looked like worry, or had Mary just imagined it? Was the edge in his voice really there? Was he being truthful with her?

"Would you mind looking at the station to see if there are any old records from that time? They might —"

"Sorry, we don't have them." Chief McArthur tipped his hat.

"Is there any way you could look to be sure?" He had found older records than that for her in the past, so his quick dismissal was a surprise.

Chief McArthur eyed her, and Mary smiled, trying to understand what was going through his mind. "I'll look," he finally said, then started to brush past her. "I'll let you get going so you can stay dry," he said, turning on his heel and heading to his car.

Mary watched him go, trying to make sense of his reaction. Maybe he'd had other things on his mind, she decided. He'd said he'd just come out of a long meeting. She'd no doubt interrupted him while he was thinking about something else. Finally, she turned and started for home, glad she had tucked an umbrella in her bag. But she couldn't stop thinking about the strange interaction with Chief McArthur. The moment she had said David's name, his face had registered recognition. Clearly, he had heard the name before. And his refusal to look for records made her suspect that he knew more than he was letting on. By the time she'd turned onto Shore Drive, she was *sure* that Chief McArthur knew more than he was letting on. For some reason, this was one crime that Chief McArthur did not want to talk about.

NINE

The next morning, Ivy Bay sparkled, as though last night's rain had given it a good scrub down. Drops of water hung on branches, reflecting sunlight and dew spread like jewels across the lawn of Mary and Betty's house. Betty had been out first thing to check that her beloved hydrangeas had survived unscathed, and she had come back with the happy report that they had. Mary had made them both a simple breakfast of oatmeal sprinkled with fresh blueberries, and then Betty had headed out to spend the day in her garden.

Mary was planning to spend the day at the bookshop, but she had one quick stop to make first. Better to leave Gus here, in that case. "You get to stay here with Betty today," she said, patting Gus's head. Then she headed to the door.

She pulled out of the driveway and threaded through the charming streets of

Ivy Bay. The leaves on the trees were even more beautiful this morning, set against a clear blue sky, and she thanked God for the beauty in the everyday world. A few minutes later, she turned onto Cook Street and drove slowly, looking at the house numbers. She found it toward the end of the block. David's childhood home.

A surprising number of cars were parked on the street, so Mary had to park a few houses down. She walked back to the house, noting the two tricycles and a big plastic play car in the driveway. Whoever lived here now clearly had young children.

So Mary was surprised when the woman who opened the door was older, probably in her late fifties, with mostly gray hair pulled back in a ponytail at the nape of her neck and lines etched around her eyes.

"Good morning," she said cheerfully to Mary, then glanced past her.

Mary looked to see if there was something in the yard that had caught this woman's attention, but there didn't seem to be anything. When she turned back, the woman appeared puzzled. "Can I help you?" she asked Mary.

"I hope so," Mary said with a friendly grin. "My name is Mary Fisher, Betty Emerson's sister. I live with Betty over on Shore

Drive." She stuck out her hand, and the woman hesitated, then reached out and shook it.

"Deborah Taylor," she said.

"It's nice to meet you," Mary said. "And I hope you don't mind me just knocking on your door, but I have a bit of an odd request." She smiled, expecting Deborah to smile back, but Deborah's face had gone taut, as though she expected Mary to give her bad news. "Would it be alright if I came in?"

Deborah now looked positively suspicious. "I'm quite busy right now," she said shortly.

There was the sound of a crash, and Deborah glanced behind her.

"Is everything okay?" Mary asked, concerned. There came a low wail from inside, and Mary walked up the steps. "Is there something I could do to help?"

"No," Deborah snapped. She looked at Mary, her eyes hard. "I know what you're really here looking for," she said, stepping back and quickly closing the door in Mary's face.

Mary pulled back, reeling as though she had been slapped. She had been unsure what to expect when she knocked on the door of David's former home, but it was certainly not this. Realizing she was standing on a porch where she was not wanted, Mary quickly walked down the steps toward the sidewalk. Her cheeks felt warm from the unpleasantness of the conversation, and she hurried toward the safety of her car.

Once she was sitting in the front seat of her car, she let out a long breath. She was puzzled by the encounter. The moment Mary had mentioned the house, Deborah had gone from friendly to hostile. And why had she repeatedly gazed over Mary's shoulder? What had she been looking for?

The sound of laughter brought Mary back to where she was. A mother and little girl were walking past Mary's car, and Mary gave them a quick wave, then slipped the key in the ignition and started down Cook Street, back toward her bookshop.

But as she drove, she couldn't shake the uncomfortable feeling that Deborah Taylor was hiding something, and Mary couldn't help but wonder, did that mean that Deborah herself had found something David had left behind?

When she got to the store, Rebecca had already opened the doors, and two customers were browsing in the stacks.

"Good morning," Mary said to Rebecca, who was sitting behind the register.

Just then, the chimes on the door rang out and Joe, the UPS guy, came in, wheeling two boxes on a cart. "Hello, Mary and Rebecca," he said. "Who wants to sign for these?"

"I've got it," Rebecca said, sliding off the stool and coming around the counter.

"Thanks," Mary said.

She took Rebecca's place on the stool while Rebecca signed and then led Joe to the rear of the store. He deposited the boxes in the back room and then held up the receipt for Rebecca to sign. Once he was done, he walked briskly to the front of the store.

"See you later," Joe said as he headed out with a wave.

"Have a good one," Mary called after him. Then she turned to Rebecca. "Are you okay opening those and getting started shelving them? I just want to check my e-mail, and then I'll come help."

"Absolutely," Rebecca said. "Take your time." She disappeared into the back room.

Mary checked that the customers were happily browsing and then logged into her e-mail. She was excited to see she had one new message. Sure enough, it was from Connor Briggs. She opened it up and read eagerly.

Happy to talk anytime. Call or stop by. I'm in my office Tuesday and Thursday afternoons and all day Friday.

There was an address and a phone number at the bottom. Mary sat back and considered. Today was Friday, and while it was short notice, it was the last chance Mary would have to drive to Boston before Lizzie and her family arrived. And she really did want to see if Connor could give her any good leads. Decided, Mary picked up the phone and dialed.

"Connor here," a pleasant voice said after the first ring.

"Hello, Connor, this is Mary Fisher from Ivy Bay," Mary said. "I sent you the e-mail about discussing your research."

"Right," Connor said easily.

"I know it doesn't give you much time to prepare, but I wondered if this afternoon might be a good time for me to stop by." Mary could see one of the customers heading to the register, a book in hand, and she hoped to wrap up the call quickly.

"Sure, that's fine," Connor said. "I'll be here all afternoon."

"Great," Mary said. "I'll try to get there around three."

"See you then," Connor said.

Mary hung up the phone, pleased to have

made the appointment. "Are you all set?" she asked the young woman who had arrived at the counter, a Sara Paretsky book in hand.

"Yes, thanks," the woman said, passing her the book. Mary rang it up and then tucked it into a paper bag with a Mary's Mystery Bookshop sticker at the center. She straightened the handles of the bag and passed it to the customer, and then went to the back to help Rebecca with shelving and to let her know that she would be heading out later that afternoon.

When she got to Boston College, Mary stopped by the administration building and talked to a bubbly undergraduate who gave her careful directions to Maloney Hall, where the history faculty had their offices. Mary crossed the pretty campus, where students walked briskly to and from class, and then entered the large, stately building. She took the stairs to the fourth floor and walked down the hall until she found the office with a list of four graduate assistants on the door. The last name was Connor Briggs. She knocked and then waited.

A moment later, the door opened, and a young man with shaggy black curls and blue eyes opened the door. "You must be Mary," he said, reaching out to shake her hand. "Come on in."

Mary followed him into the room and looked around. There were four desks, each on a different wall, each piled high with books and papers. All the available wall space was covered by bookshelves that were crammed with books.

Connor sat at the desk on the wall opposite the door and waved an arm at the bookcase next to it. "This is all my research," he said. He took the desk chair from the desk next to his. "You can sit here. Haley's away for the weekend and she won't mind."

"Thanks," Mary said, sitting down. "And thank you for being willing to talk."

"That part is easy," Connor said with a grin. "It's getting me to stop talking about my research that's hard."

Mary laughed. "I want to hear it all," she said. "What is your dissertation topic, and how did you choose it?"

Connor sat up just the tiniest bit straighter. "Well, my dad is a cop so I grew up pretty interested in crime. And my mom is into antiques, so with all the museums and antique shops she dragged me to, I also developed an interest in history. This project merges both of those interests. I'm writing about unsolved crimes in New England during Prohibition. That's what you're hoping to find out more about, isn't it?"

"Yes," Mary said. "One case in particular."

A strange expression passed over Connor's face, and for a moment, he looked almost hostile. But it passed so fast Mary wasn't sure if she'd misread it. "What's the case?" he asked, his voice as friendly as ever.

"A man named David Woodrow," Mary said. "Have you heard of him?"

Connor nodded. "Yes, I'm familiar with his case," he said. "I'm actually hoping to include it in my dissertation."

Mary was thrilled to hear that Connor knew something about David. "How did you get interested in the case?" she asked.

"Well, there were a lot of unsolved crimes back then," Connor said. "Forensics and such not being what they are now. And because of government corruption on the town level, a lot of crimes went unpunished if the culprit had enough to pay off the cops."

"So you have a lot of cases to write about for your dissertation," Mary said, curious as to why David's case stuck out to Connor.

"Yes, but David's case is different," he said. "From the little I've been able to dig up on him, he doesn't seem like your average run-of-the-mill criminal."

"Oh? What makes him different?" Mary asked.

Connor paused, as if considering how much to say. "For one, he had a strong family and community network," he said. "What's your interest in the case?" His gaze was keen.

"Well, David's great-nephew Henry is a close friend of mine," Mary said, deciding to tell just the bare details since it wasn't really her story to tell. "It would mean a lot to him to know more about the case. There are so many unanswered questions."

If this sounded a bit weak to Connor, he didn't show it. In fact, he smiled. "There *are* a lot of questions about the case," he agreed. "That's part of what intrigues me about it. Though there won't be much to include in my dissertation if I can't find any answers." His voice was glum.

"How did you first learn about David?" Mary asked.

"I started off wanting to focus just on Massachusetts, so I did an extensive search on unsolved crimes between 1920 and 1930. There were a number that interested me, but a few of them just had no record, nothing written about them other than a brief write-up in the paper."

Mary felt a mounting excitement at his words. If Connor had dismissed those cases for lack of research material, that meant that there were resources beyond the newspaper articles about David.

"What other sources have you found?" Mary asked.

"Oh, you know." He waved his hand dismissively. "Books, police records — you'd be surprised how few of those there are. A lot of them went missing or just got lost in the shuffle back then," he said. He tapped his fingers on the desk. There was something decidedly less relaxed in his manner than there had been when Mary first came in.

Mary noticed a small stack of books next to his computer and looked at the top title, which was *New England Crimes in Prohibition: The Unsolved Cases of an Era.* "Are those books that mention David?" she asked.

Connor suddenly sat up straight and reached for the books. "Not David in particular, no," he said quickly. "But they might be worth glancing through, just to give you an idea of the times. Here, you can take a look."

He slid the books to Mary, but she noticed that he had left out the bottom book on the pile. She was about to mention it when he slipped the book hastily into his bag. Was he hiding it from her?

"Thanks," Mary said, looking at his bag for a second longer, and then she accepted the pile of books. The one he had hidden was bound in deep red, but she hadn't been able to read the title. She flipped through the books he'd shared with her for a few minutes while Connor typed, and then she passed them back to him. "Did you have any other resources on David?" she asked, hoping she wasn't being too pushy.

But Connor shook his head. "Not yet," he said. Mary was surprised. He had claimed to have chosen the case in part because of the resources available, yet now claimed there weren't any. "I'm still looking into that case," he added. "In fact, do you have any other leads I could follow up on?" he asked.

Mary hesitated, unsure if she should tell him about the map and the dead end. "I'm still looking for them," she finally said.

Connor watched her, like he was trying to read her. Mary didn't say anything more, and after a moment's pause, he looked at the clock on the back wall and stood up. "You know, I hate to ask you to leave, but I need to get back to work," he said.

Mary stood up quickly. "Well, it was nice to meet you," she said. "Thank you for taking the time to talk."

"Anytime," Connor said. "I'll probably see you around the library in Ivy Bay. I'm planning to be there a few times in the next couple of weeks, to see what I might turn up." Then he looked keenly at Mary. "And be sure to tell me what you uncover."

As she drove home in the fading light of the day, Mary thought over her meeting with Connor. Really, there was nothing so unusual about Connor needing to hold on to one of the titles and to his quick end to the meeting. Young people were often scattered like that, and Connor probably had a lot on his plate. But as she took the turn for Route 6 that would lead her home, Mary couldn't shake the feeling that Connor had been displeased to learn he had company in his research about David.

TEN

By five o'clock Saturday evening, the hamburger patties were stacked up next to the grill, with buns next to them. Lettuce, tomatoes, pickles, and onion were sliced in bowls and set out on the deck table, next to the ketchup and mustard. A big salad with the last of Betty's lettuce from the garden was in the wooden salad bowl at the center of the table, which had place settings for five. Mary was just setting a frosty pitcher of lemonade on the table when she heard a car pull into the drive. She took off her apron and rushed toward the front yard.

"Grandma, Grandma!" Luke shot out of the car as though he'd been sitting for days and bounded over to her, wrapping his arms tight around her. She knelt down to squeeze him tight, his soft cheek pressing against hers. There was nothing in the world better than hugging your grandchild.

"Hello, my boy," Mary said. Luke let go,

and Mary leaned back and whistled. "You sure have gotten tall," she said.

Luke grinned proudly. "I'm big and strong because I eat my vegetables," he announced. And then he was racing off toward the backyard, where Mary had set out balls, a Frisbee, and the croquet set.

"He has a lot of energy, doesn't he?" Mary said to Lizzie, who had come up to hug her.

Lizzie groaned affectionately. "He's like that wind-up bunny from the minute he wakes up until the minute he conks out at night." She leaned in for a hug of her own, and Mary pulled her daughter close. After a moment, Lizzie pulled back, and Mary gave her a quick once-over. Lizzie looked tired, as all mothers with young children did, but her cheeks were a healthy pink and there was a spark of happiness in her eyes that warmed Mary's heart.

Mary looked around and saw Emma standing shyly at the car, her arms folded.

"And who is this beautiful young woman?" Mary asked, and her granddaughter's face lit up. With a pang, Mary remembered how much Lizzie had loved to be called a grown-up at that age. "Let me look at you, darling," Mary said, reaching out her hands. Emma ducked her head but walked forward, wrapping her hands around Mary's and smiling.

"I love your hairstyle," Mary said, noting the careful French braid. "And that shirt is so pretty. Pink is your color."

Emma dropped her grandmother's hands and wrapped her arms around Mary, who squeezed her tight. She remembered Lizzie mentioning that her granddaughter had a new interest, and Mary was excited to hear all about it. But she didn't want to rush Emma, so she simply kissed the crown of her head and patted her cheek.

There came a yowl from the doorway, where Gus was standing, his front paws anchored in the screen door. Mary laughed. "Someone else is greeting you too," she said. Both Emma and Luke were gentle with Gus, who always loved the extra attention.

"Who's hungry for burgers?" Betty called from the backyard.

Lizzie hurried to hug her aunt while Emma stayed close to Mary. In the backyard, Luke had the Frisbee on his head and was tossing a ball at the same time he was trying to climb the sturdy crab apple tree. Lizzie was already helping set burgers on the grill while Betty came over to hug Emma. Mary's heart swelled at the sight of some of the most precious people in her life, gathered together at her home. She closed her eyes and gave thanks to God for the safe arrival of Lizzie, Emma, and Luke, for Betty's health, and for the time they would be able to spend together. It was a true gift.

A little while later, they were all gathered around the table. They joined hands, and Mary lowered her head and closed her eyes, ready for Betty's grace.

"Lord, we thank You for the delicious food," Betty said, her voice low and calm. "We are grateful for each person sitting at this table, and grateful that You have brought us together this night. Thank You for seeing Lizzie, Emma, and Luke here safely, and thank You for this time we have together. Amen."

Mary was touched by Betty's simple but profound words that said everything she was feeling in her heart.

"Let's eat," Betty said, starting the platter of burgers going around the table. Soon, everyone had a bun filled with Mary's special hamburgers and topped with the vegetables from Betty's garden. Mary had noticed Luke try to pass the salad bowl without taking any for himself, but Lizzie had quickly served him a healthy portion of greens.

"Those vegetables will make you big and strong, right?" Mary said with a wink.

Luke nodded seriously, then began stuffing the leaves into his mouth as fast as he could. Lizzie sent an amused look toward her mother, who well remembered the voracious appetite of an energetic child.

The sun was low in the sky, sending rays of lavender and pink overhead, and casting a glow over the flowers and vegetables of Betty's garden. The air was crisp and laced with the scent of barbecue and salt water, a mouthwatering combination.

The children finished eating quickly and went inside to rediscover the book and game supply and to play with Gus.

The adults savored the food and the company in the fading light.

"So what have you been up to, Mom?" Lizzie asked. She was now working on her second burger. She had been so busy helping Luke and being sure that Emma had enough that she had barely been able to eat her own dinner.

"Your mother has found herself another mystery," Betty said affectionately.

Lizzie turned to her mother, her eyebrows raised in question.

"We made a bit of a discovery at the old lighthouse," Mary said. She filled her daughter in on the details of the map, as well as David and the ring.

Lizzie sighed. "How disappointing the map was a dead end. I wonder where it is." She paused, then said, "And how sad for Henry's family to have lost something so precious."

"Yes, I think so," Mary said. "It seems especially hard for Henry's cousin Annie. Her mother was the family historian, and she grew up hearing about the ring. Now her daughter is engaged, and I know she'd love more than anything to have that ring to pass on."

Lizzie smiled warmly at her mother. "I'm sure she's passing on advice on marriage and children and all the things a new bride needs to know," she said. "I know my mother did that for me, and it meant more than any ring ever could have."

Mary reached over and patted Lizzie's cheek. "You are such a sweet one."

"Yes, you got lucky with me," Lizzie said playfully.

The back door slammed. "So when do we get ice cream?" Luke shouted.

Lizzie admonished him for the outburst, but Mary and Betty just laughed quietly.

Betty stood up to clear the table, and Mary headed into the house. After getting a nod from Lizzie, Mary put her arm around Luke. "Want to be my helper?" she asked. "There's a big carton of ice cream in the freezer, and I may need some help getting bowls out to everyone."

"I can help. I'm a big help!" Luke said, beaming. He scurried into the warmly lit house, and Mary followed contentedly behind.

But at the back of her mind, she couldn't stop thinking about that ring. She hoped the next few days would bring her one step closer to knowing what David had done in those final days and where he had left the Woodrow family ring.

ELEVEN

The next morning, Mary was bursting with familial pride as she walked up the steps of Grace Church, Lizzie on one side and Luke clinging to her hand and skipping along on the other. Grace Church was a picture-perfect New England church, complete with a tall spire that could be seen for miles, and Mary took a moment to admire it as they approached. But of course what made the church truly special was how the community gathered together to worship, hearing the sermons of Pastor Miles, singing along with the choir, and praying together each week. The community had welcomed her from the moment she arrived in Ivy Bay, bereft and on unsure footing as she set about establishing her new life. God had guided her into the loving embrace of Grace Church, and Mary would always be grateful for that.

"Good morning, Mary," Jayne Tucker said

as they walked in, Jayne's husband Rich right behind her. "This must be your family."

"This is my daughter, Lizzie," Mary said as Lizzie stepped forward with a friendly smile to shake Jayne's and Rich's hands. "And these are my grandchildren, Luke and Emma."

Luke stepped forward and said seriously, "Pleased to meet me."

Emma rolled her eyes at her brother, but Jayne grinned. "Indeed we are," she said.

"How long are you here for?" Rich asked Lizzie.

"A week," Lizzie said.

"Wonderful," he said as a few more people gathered around to be introduced to Mary's family. Luke was bubbling over with joy at the attention, and Emma was smiling quietly. She was a young lady now, not the gangly girl she had been on her last visit. Mary was very much looking forward to spending time with the sweet girl.

Pastor Miles's sermon on compassion was both inspired and thought-provoking, and Mary couldn't help reflect on David as the pastor talked about knowing that all humans are flawed, but that Jesus' love is both accepting and fully healing, making us whole once more. David must have heard this lesson himself growing up: What had happened that he had turned his back to its message? Or was there more to the story, some event or consideration that explained his crime? She was determined to find out.

Mary found her spirits lifted, as they always were during a sermon, as Pastor Miles closed by giving real-life examples of compassion changing lives. It was always invigorating to hear of God's work being done.

The children, who had gone for Sunday school, returned for the final hymn, and Luke snuggled happily against his grandmother. Mary found her voice ringing out, joining in with her community as they praised the Lord through song.

The congregation filed out slowly, most heading to the back room for coffee hour.

"Mary," a voice called as Mary came into the bustling room that smelled of hot coffee and Pam Singleton's famous apple turnovers.

Mary turned to see Cynthia McArthur Jones standing with her husband Nick. They were next to the back window, close to the refreshment table, and Mary headed over, Lizzie and her family close behind. Betty had stopped to chat with Cathy Danes, no doubt exchanging gardening tips, but Mary knew her sister well enough to know she'd be over before all the turnovers disappeared.

"Hello," Mary said, introducing Lizzie and her children.

"I made an angel," Luke announced, lifting up his paper-plate creation from Sunday school.

"Isn't that something?" Nick asked, bending down to get a better look.

"And how old are you, sweetie?" Cynthia asked Emma.

"Twelve," Emma said, ducking her head shyly.

"And already a beauty like your mom," Cynthia said, earning smiles from both Lizzie and Emma. "Not to mention your grandmother."

Cynthia really was a charmer, Mary thought, but she was genuine. Emma walked over to the refreshment table for turnovers, and Mary saw Luke disappear into the backyard with some of the local boys, Lizzie in his wake.

"So how is your project coming?" Mary asked.

Cynthia's eyes lit up. "We're in the homestretch," she said excitedly. "The final visit from the landmarks committee is this week, but it's really just a formality."

"That's great," Mary said.

"It is." Mary turned and saw that Chief McArthur had come up behind them. He started when he saw who his sister was talking to, but it passed so quickly that Mary couldn't be sure she had really seen it at all.

Cynthia leaned over to give her brother a quick hug, but then her eyes darted to the refreshment table. "Mary and Benjamin, if you'll excuse me, I need to corral my husband before he eats every last one of those turnovers."

Indeed, Nick had migrated slowly over to the platter of pastries and was just taking a big bite of a flaky triangle of turnover. Chief McArthur chuckled as Cynthia flew in and pulled her husband toward the door, where Pastor Miles was saying good-bye to members of the congregation as they left.

Mary turned to the police chief, and he shifted uncomfortably.

"How are you, Chief?" Mary asked. He smiled, but Mary could see it was forced. "Wasn't that a lovely sermon today?"

"Yes, Pastor Miles did a nice job," he agreed. His voice was friendly, but there was something distant in his eyes. "If you'll excuse me —"

"Have you had any luck with that police report?" Mary asked before he could sneak away. "The one for the David Woodrow case

I was telling you about?"

"I'm sorry, I didn't find anything," the police chief said.

"Oh." Mary wasn't sure he was telling her the whole truth, and she wasn't going to give up that easily.

"Could I come down to the police station and take a look?" Mary said. "If we could find it, there might be information in there that could help me."

The chief's face visibly tensed up. "Well, I'm not so sure about that, Mary," he said slowly. "There might be sensitive information in there that I couldn't allow access to."

Mary was taken aback by this. Why would the chief expect there to be sensitive information in such an old file?

The chief now looked at her carefully. "Did you say you knew a lot about the Woodrow case?" he asked. "I mean, any of the details and such?" His voice sounded strained.

Mary shook her head, wondering what kind of information he was looking for. "Almost nothing," she said. "That's why I'd appreciate getting to see that file. I'd be happy to come down to the station and put in a request if you think that might be the better way to go."

His face seemed to tighten at her words. "How about this?" he asked quickly. "I'll look again for the file, and if I can locate it, I'll let you know what I find out."

"That would be great, thank you," Mary said. All the time she had spent thinking about David had her excited about not only solving the mystery but also better understanding David, who was his own mystery. Why had he turned to crime, and what had provoked him to leave behind the money and ring, if he had indeed done so? She was of course most interested in finding the ring, but somewhere along the way, good old-fashioned curiosity had gotten ahold of her, and Mary was interested in any insight she could get into this complicated history. And she knew his police file would be a good starting point.

Mary could see Lizzie and Luke heading back in, Emma right behind them. "Would you be able to look at it sometime this week?" Mary continued.

"How about tomorrow?" Chief McArthur asked, sighing. "I'll check it out in the morning and come by the store on my lunch break and tell you if I found anything."

"Perfect," Mary said. "I'll see you then." She gave him a smile, and he nodded, then turned and quickly headed for the door.

Mary watched him go until Lizzie came up beside her. There was a crease in her forehead, a sure sign she was annoyed about something, and one glance at Luke told Mary exactly what it was: Both knees of his crisp blue dress pants were covered in mud.

"I have some stain remover that should do just the trick," she said, squeezing Lizzie's arm.

"You're a lifesaver, Mom," Lizzie said.

Betty came up. "Are we ready?" she asked.

They joined the short line at the door to say good-bye to Pastor Miles. He smiled when he saw them. "Mary, Betty, wonderful to see you both as always," he said, taking the time to shake each of their hands. "And, Lizzie, those children of yours get bigger and more beautiful each time I see them."

"Thank you," Lizzie said, shaking the pastor's hand.

He turned his attention to Luke and Emma. "I hope you both do your best to mind your mother and work hard in school." His kind eyes took in each child, and even Luke seemed soothed by his calm presence.

"Yes, sir," Emma said.

"Yes, sir," Luke mimicked seriously.

"I'm glad to hear it," the pastor said. "And, Mary, will I still see you at the church tomorrow?"

When Mary moved to town, she had started a prayer group among the women of the church. They sometimes met at different members' houses, but Mary had reserved the church's chapel for tomorrow's meeting.

"I'll be there," Mary said. She and Lizzie had already laid out plans for the week, and tomorrow Lizzie was going to take the kids on a hike around Salt Water Pond in Orleans before meeting Mary to go apple picking in the afternoon.

"I'll see you then," Pastor Miles said.

"Grandma, I like your church," Luke said as they headed out into the late morning sun. "But next time, you should have chocolate doughnuts like we have at our church."

Mary tousled her grandson's hair. "I'll see what I can do about that," she said.

Betty led the way to the car, with Emma and Lizzie chatting behind her. What a good morning it had been: a stirring sermon, a beautiful service, and her family all together. Mary was smiling with contentment as she headed across the parking lot, ready to go home and start a Sunday evening feast.

That evening after a dinner of black bean soup, ham, mashed potatoes, green beans, and Betty's fresh biscuits, Lizzie announced that it was time for Luke's bath.

"No," Luke whined.

Mary looked affectionately at Luke, whose eyes were glazed with the fatigue from a day of hard play, and whose face and arms had traces of the dirt he'd been digging out in the yard. She set down the pile of dishes she had been clearing and smiled at Luke.

"Don't you want to be a pirate of the bath, darling?" Mary asked.

Luke scrunched his brows together. "There are no pirates of the bath," he said, but his tone was doubting.

Mary gave Lizzie a quick glance, and her daughter grinned. Clearly, she remembered Mary using this technique with her brother back when they were kids.

"There most certainly are pirates of the bath," Mary said. "Let me show you their ship." She stood up, then stopped and dramatically slapped her hand to her forehead. "Oh, but I can't show you the ship unless you're in the bath. Those are the strict pirate rules."

"I'll get in the bath. I'm getting in right now," Luke yelled, racing for the stairs and trying to pull his shirt over his head as he went. Lizzie followed, making sure he didn't trip as he went up the stairs.

"He'll believe anything," Emma said, rolling her eyes.

Mary bit back a smile. "I remember a girl who once spent all day in the back garden searching for fairies."

Emma shrugged. "I was little then," she said dismissively, as though it had been decades ago.

And perhaps to her it had been, though to Mary it felt like just yesterday.

Emma stood up and picked up the stack of plates Mary had piled up. "I'll take these in for you, Grandma," she said with a smile. "I know you have to get that boat for Luke."

Mary paused to kiss Emma on the head, then she went up the stairs and into her closet where she stored the box that still held just a few of her children's most sacred toys. She emerged moments later with a wooden ship that she carried into the bathroom.

Luke was already in the tub, surrounded by bubbles. She could tell Lizzie had clearly already scrubbed his face, because his cheeks were wet.

"The pirate ship!" Luke squealed, reaching for it and causing a wave of water to come dangerously close to overflowing.

"Careful," Lizzie reminded him as Mary handed him the ship.

Luke set the boat on a mound of bubbles

and began to play.

"Thanks, Mom," Lizzie said with a smile.

Mary paused to watch her grandson for a moment, then headed back downstairs to help with after-dinner cleanup.

Mary and Emma finished clearing the table while Betty began loading the dishwasher. When the plates, cups, and silverware had been loaded and the machine started, Betty filled the sink and began scrubbing pots. Mary grabbed a dish towel printed with a large chicken and was surprised to see Emma do the same. She had expected Emma to head upstairs to read or into the living room for some TV. But clearly her granddaughter was the kind of girl who saw a job all the way through, a sight that pleased Mary.

Emma was carefully drying out the roasting pan. "Grandma, where does this go?" she asked.

Mary took it from her. "Cabinet over the sink," she said, reaching around Betty to set the heavy pan in its place.

"Maybe you can dry and your grandma can put the pots away," Betty suggested.

"Good idea," Mary said.

Betty, her hands encased in dripping yellow rubber gloves, handed a fry pan to Emma.

They worked together in companionable silence until each pot was in its place and the kitchen was spick-and-span.

"That does go faster with extra help," Mary said. "Thank you, Emma."

Her granddaughter flushed at the praise.

"I'm going to put on the kettle for some tea," Betty said. "Why don't you both go out and enjoy the last of this sunset?"

The sun had dipped below the horizon, but the sky was still bright with streaks of lavender and powder blue.

"Shall we?" Mary asked Emma, who nodded. They both grabbed sweatshirts and then headed outside.

Mary lit the citronella candle to keep mosquitoes away, then settled into an Adirondack chair next to Emma, both of them looking out at the beauty of the evening.

"It's so pretty here," Emma said.

"It is," Mary agreed. "I'm blessed to live in such a beautiful place."

"I can't wait to go apple picking tomorrow," Emma said. A farm a few miles away had a small orchard that they opened to visitors every autumn. For a small fee, you could pick apples right off the trees and then buy them by the bag. Mary was also looking forward to the trip.

"So how are you liking seventh grade so

far?" Mary asked.

"There's a lot of homework," Emma said. "Way too much math."

Mary chuckled. "That was never my strong suit, but your mom was a real math whiz."

"Yeah, she's pretty good at explaining stuff," Emma said, shifting slightly in her seat to get more comfortable. It was starting to get dark now, the sky a satiny dark blue.

"And what about your other classes?" Mary asked. The flame of the candle flickered in the slight wind that came from the ocean, casting soft shadows around them.

"I have a really cool English teacher this year," Emma said. "We're doing creative writing, and she said my first story showed real promise." It was clear from her tone that she had memorized the compliment and was repeating it exactly as her teacher had written it.

Mary could hear in her voice how much this had pleased Emma. "Wonderful," she said.

"Yeah, I was psyched about it," Emma said. "She said I should keep working at it, like start keeping a journal and writing short stories and stuff."

"That's a great idea," Mary said. "I bet

you have some terrific story ideas."

"It's really fun to come up with story ideas," Emma said. "Mom bought me a journal, and I already started a new story."

"I bet it's a good one," Mary said. It was so gratifying to hear Emma sound so happy and engaged in a project, especially something so close to Mary's heart. And she loved the mature tone Emma had acquired; she remembered Lizzie taking on adult airs around twelve, wanting nothing more than to leave childhood behind and be seen as a grown-up. "You know, I have my own book that I'm working on," she confided.

Emma turned to her. "Really? That's so cool."

"Well, sometimes I have my doubts," Mary said. "But I think most writers do. The most important thing is to keep at it."

"That's just what my teacher says," Emma said. "She also said it's really important to get feedback and revise."

"That's true," Mary said. "Some of my very favorite books went through more than ten drafts before they were published."

"Wow, that's a lot," Emma said.

"It is," Mary agreed. "But those authors cared enough about their work to want it to be as perfect as possible."

"I want mine to be good too," Emma said

thoughtfully. "So I guess I'll have to do that as well." Suddenly her eyes lit up. "Hey, maybe you could help me with my story! Like, be kind of an editor for me, with feedback and stuff, like real authors get."

"I'm not sure how good my feedback will be," Mary said. "But I'd love to see your story and tell you what I think."

"I'm almost done," Emma said. "I'll finish it while we're here, and then you can read it."

"I look forward to it," Mary said.

Emma got up and opened the door to the house.

"Where are you going?" Mary asked, surprised.

"I need to work on my story," Emma said with great resolve. She headed into the house before Mary could reply.

Mary smiled, already anticipating the joy of reading her granddaughter's work.

A few minutes later, Lizzie slipped into the yard, a mug of tea in her hand. She took a sip and sighed happily. "What a gorgeous night," she said.

The sky was a rich navy, and stars were starting to peek out.

"Yes," Mary agreed. "Is Luke asleep?"

"Yes," Lizzie said, stretching out comfortably in the chair. "He races through the day and then just conks out the second his head hits the pillow," she said affectionately. She took a sip of tea. "And I saw Emma heading upstairs for her writing journal, so I take it she told you about her new interest?"

"She did, indeed," Mary said. "You were right, it's a good one."

"I thought it would please my book-loving mother," Lizzie said, and Mary could hear the contentment in her voice.

"You know me well," Mary said, giving her daughter's hand a light squeeze. "She even agreed to let me read her story when she finishes it."

"Oh, that's something!" Lizzie exclaimed. "She never lets me read her writing. I think you'll be the first person to see it other than her teacher."

"I'm honored," Mary said, feeling both pleased by the trust her granddaughter had in her and concerned that Lizzie might be feeling miffed. "I think sometimes it's easier to show these things to a grandmother than a mother."

"Definitely," Lizzie said. Mary heard no trace of mixed feelings in her voice, only pleasure at what was best for her daughter.

What a joy it was to see her daughter turn into such a wonderful mother. The night was gentle around them, and Mary gave quick thanks to God for her many blessings.

She just hoped that when the time came, she would be able to offer her granddaughter the help she was hoping for.

TWELVE

Monday morning, after a breakfast of muffins with her energetic grandchildren, Mary walked into town for her prayer meeting. It was a beautiful, warm fall morning, and Mary enjoyed the short walk through town. Tables and chairs were already set up in a circle, and Jill Sanderson was setting out scones and making coffee for after the meeting. Jill and Mary chatted about how Jill's sons were faring in the new school year, and soon Lynn Teagarden and Amy Stebble arrived and dropped two plates of cookies on the table. The other women soon gathered, and Mary made a special point to say hello to Dorothy Johnson, with whom she sometimes had a hard time seeing eye to eye. They sat in the chairs and shared about their lives, and the time passed quickly. They prayed together, pouring out their hearts to God, and Mary ended by asking God to bless them all in the coming week. Soon,

Mary and Bernice Foster were cleaning up the room. They were putting the folding chairs away when she heard footsteps coming toward the room.

"We're just finishing up," she called, hoping they hadn't held up anyone who needed the room after them.

"It's just me," Pastor Miles said as he took the last chair from her and rested it on the stack in the closet. "I was on my way out for a meeting and heard you all in here, so I thought I'd come down and say hello. How did your meeting go?" he asked.

"It's always good to pray together with the other ladies," Mary said. She'd been more blessed than she ever could have imagined by the women she'd gotten to know through the group. In their meetings, they were able to open up to one another and share one another's burdens and triumphs.

The pastor smiled. "I'm glad to hear it." He leaned back on the counter. "How are those delightful grandkids of yours today?" he asked.

"Just great," she said. "They were going on a walk at Salt Water Pond."

"It's the perfect day for it," Pastor Miles said. "Will you join them later?"

Mary nodded. "I just need to drop in to

the bookshop for a bit first."

"And how are things down at the bookshop?" he asked. "I'm planning to stop by later this week for a new mystery."

"Come by anytime," Mary said. "We just got a new shipment of books, and there's a title by a new author in there that I think you'll love."

"Sounds too good to miss," he said with a smile. "I'd come now if I didn't have the monthly meeting of local pastors starting in a few minutes."

His remarks reminded Mary about her desire to visit First Congregational Church.

"Does Reverend Allen attend?" she asked. Mary had met Reverend Allen, the pastor of First Congregational Church, very early on when she moved to Ivy Bay. Betty had introduced them outside Bailey's Ice Cream Shop on a warm spring evening, and they had chatted.

Pastor Miles grinned. "He's always there," he said. "He's a real New Englander, gruff but with a heart of gold. You know him?"

"Yes, we met," Mary said. "And I know just what you mean."

"I think we're about set here," Bernice cut in. Mary realized that Bernice had done all the cleanup while she had been chatting. But when she apologized, Bernice waved it off. "It was just a bit of sweeping," she said. "You can do it next time, if that makes you feel better."

Mary promised herself to do just that as the three of them left the church together. The sun was bright in the sky, and for a moment, Mary squinted as her eyes adjusted. But the rays were warm on her shoulders, and the beauty of Main Street bathed in golden autumn sunlight was always a sight to behold.

"Thank you both for your hard work," Pastor Miles said. "I'll see you later." He waved and headed down Main Street.

"Want to grab a quick bite to eat?" Bernice asked.

Mary shook her head, thinking of all the work at the store and her meeting with Chief McArthur. "I'd love to, but I can't today," she said. "I'll take a rain check."

"Enjoy the rest of the day, then," Bernice said, heading down Main Street.

"Thanks," Mary said as she turned toward Mary's Mystery Bookshop. Her mind was running through the tasks that would be waiting for her at her business, but at the same time, a part of her was already anticipating the meeting with Chief McArthur. There was a good chance that something in David's police file could be a clue that would lead her closer to the ring. At least that was her hope.

Mary was busy ringing up a sale when the chimes on the door rang and Chief McArthur walked in, his police hat and crisp uniform making him look very official.

"Chief McArthur, hi," Mary said as she slipped the books into a bag for her customer and passed it to her with a smile. "How are you?"

He nodded. "Just fine, thanks. It's a beautiful day out there."

Mary glanced at the sun streaming through the bay windows of the store. "Another perfect fall day," she said. "And how is Claire? I missed her yesterday at church." Chief McArthur's wife was quiet, seeming to prefer her knitting to conversation, but she had a warm presence, and Mary was always happy to see her.

"She had to leave right after the service, to get to the yarn store in Hyannis, so we took separate cars to church," Chief McArthur said. "Some kind of knitting emergency." His voice was affectionate.

"Her knitting is exceptional," Mary said, thinking of the beautiful sweaters, hats, and scarves she produced.

"It is that," Chief McArthur agreed.

148

The store had emptied out, and Rebecca took over the register. Mary was glad to see that Chief McArthur seemed less on edge than he had yesterday.

"Let's head over to the reading area," Mary said, gesturing to the cozy chairs at the back of the store, in front of the fieldstone hearth. She led the way, then paused at the refreshment station. "Can I get you anything?" she asked.

"I'd love a cup of coffee," Chief McArthur said. He had removed his hat and was absently running his hand along the brim.

"You got it," Mary said as she filled a steaming cup full of fresh coffee. She handed him the cup. "Black, just as you like it."

"That I do," he said, and Mary laughed. She poured herself a cup and then settled on the chair across from Chief McArthur.

"So I looked around and dug up that file," he said. He took a sip of coffee. "On David Woodrow."

Mary waited eagerly, but he didn't seem to be in any hurry to share.

"Well, you must know he had a record," Chief McArthur said. "Mostly for theft and unpaid bills. He was never able to hold down a job either. His longest stint was at a local hardware store, and he was fired after only a few months, right after he got arrested for possession of alcohol."

"Right, it was Prohibition," Mary said.

Chief McArthur nodded. "Not that that stopped our friend David. But his biggest crime was the one he fled town to escape, though I think you already know that."

"Yes," Mary said. "He stole the money from his boss and then disappeared right afterward. But I don't know what became of him after he left, and that's what I'm hoping your file will show me."

"I'm sorry, Mary. I can't help you with that," Chief McArthur said. "The case was never closed because he disappeared, and there's no record of him ever returning."

"Did the police search for him?" Mary asked, although she noticed how he had sidestepped the mention of her seeing the file herself.

"Yes, they searched for him," Chief McArthur said. "But the trail was cold. There were no leads, at least none that came to fruition. Back then, the resources would have been pretty limited," he added. "No way to put out an APB."

"Right," Mary said.

The chimes on the door rang out, and Mary saw a small group of tourists being greeted warmly by Rebecca. She took a sip of coffee, considering what Chief McArthur had said. "So there was no recorded information about David's disappearance?" she asked.

Chief McArthur nodded. "That's right."

"Was there anything else in the file that might shed some light on David?" Mary asked.

The chief shook his head.

"What about the theft itself?" Mary asked. "I know that David stole the money from his boss, but what does the file say about when and how he took it?"

It felt to Mary like she was asking for something quite basic, so the chief's reaction took her by surprise. His body stiffened, and his fingers gripped the brim of his hat so tightly they turned white. "T-there aren't m-many details in the f-file," he said, his words choppy. "But he was the only suspect, and it's clear the police at that time knew he was the culprit. There was no doubt about that."

The chief's off-putting demeanor did not invite questions, but Mary couldn't help herself. "He was the main suspect, but there aren't details of the crime?" she asked.

"That's right," Benjamin said, standing up.

"Okay," Mary said, treading carefully. It

didn't seem possible to her that the file would not have the story of the stolen money in it. But the chief said it didn't, and she was certainly not willing to question him or his authority.

He gave a stiff wave to Rebecca and headed out.

Mary looked after him, unable to shake the feeling that there was something off about the story the chief had told her.

THIRTEEN

After an afternoon hauling bags of apples up and down the rows of the orchard, Mary, Lizzie, Emma, and Luke returned home tired, happy, and very hungry.

"Can I go take a shower?" Emma asked. Picking the apples had been good exercise, and they could all use some freshening up.

"Sure, sweetie," Lizzie said, after getting a nod from Mary. "Just help us bring these bags in first."

"Okay." Emma grabbed a paper bag loaded with apples from the trunk and carried it into the house. Luke picked up a smaller bag and followed after her.

Lizzie picked up the remaining sack. Mary closed the trunk and followed her daughter inside.

"Mother, what can I do to help with dinner?" Lizzie asked, setting the bag down on the counter.

"Not a thing," Betty said, coming in with

a smile. "It's just about ready."

Mary hadn't even thought about dinner, so this was welcome news indeed. "Thank you," she said to her sister.

"Don't you want to know what we're having?" Betty asked.

"If you're cooking, I know it's good," Lizzie said, leaning in to kiss her aunt's cheek before heading upstairs.

"She's a good one," Betty said fondly, watching her go.

"Yes," Mary said. Lizzie was a joy, and having her here made Mary's heart full of happiness, something she knew Betty completely understood. "And what can I do to help with dinner?"

"I think just set the table," Betty said. "I got a slew of clams over at the Seafood Market, and we're having those with biscuits and corn on the cob."

"That sounds scrumptious," Mary said. "I'll get the table ready now." She headed to the kitchen, grabbed a stack of the plastic plates they used for eating outside, each one printed with a different kind of flower, and walked out to the backyard. The kids' beach towels fluttered on the line as Mary set the table, bringing out silver, napkins, and a big pitcher of herbal sun tea that Betty had steeped that afternoon. By the time she was done, Emma and Luke were freshly showered and Lizzie and Betty were bringing out the food. Soon, they were all gathered around the table, the tasty smell of the food wafting in the air.

They held hands, and Betty said grace. When she was finished, she opened her eyes and smiled. "Let's eat!" She didn't have to say it twice; everyone dug in. The clams were fresh and full flavored and complemented by the fluffy biscuits and crisp corn on the cob.

"This is delicious," Lizzie said.

"Mm-hmm," Luke agreed, his mouth full. His mother shot him a look, and he looked down sheepishly, swallowed and then said, "It's yummy, Aunt Betty."

"I'm glad you like it," Betty said, grinning at the little boy.

Mary felt her heart swell as she looked around the table at those who were dearest to her. Luke was stuffing more clams into his mouth while Betty looked on with a grin, probably remembering her own son's table manners at age seven. Mary had to grin herself when she remembered Jack's. Crumbs and bits of food would litter the table and floor where he had inhaled his meal, often stuffing as much in as he could. He had believed that the faster he finished, the faster he would be able to return to playing. This was apparently Luke's strategy now.

"Slow down, little guy," Lizzie said affectionately.

"He's being gross," Emma said, one of her eyebrows raised as biscuit crumbs sprayed down Luke's shirt.

Lizzie raised an eyebrow right back. "I don't like to hear you use words like that when you talk about your brother," she said.

Emma made a huffing noise but cut it short when her mother glanced back her way.

"Can I get you another biscuit?" Mary asked Emma, hoping to distract her granddaughter, whose face looked like a storm cloud.

"Thanks, Grandma," Emma said, all sunshine once more. Mary thought back to Lizzie at that age, her moods blowing in and out without warning. Twelve was a time of such change.

"What's for dessert?" Luke asked. He had cleared his plate.

"Peach crumble," Betty said, and Luke clapped his hands. "Want to help me get it?"

Luke jumped up eagerly and returned a few minutes later carrying an ice cream container with an air of great earnestness. Betty followed with the dessert.

"That looks scrumptious," Lizzie said, standing up and gathering the plates. Mary helped her, and soon everyone was back at the cleared table, digging into the moist and rich crumble.

"The perfect end to the perfect meal," Lizzie said.

"And the perfect day," Mary said, thinking of the fun they'd had at the orchard.

Luke was reaching for his glass of milk, which was just out of his grasp.

"Here," Emma said, leaning across the table to help her brother.

Mary couldn't help smiling at the sweetness between Luke and Emma as Luke smiled his thanks, his eyes shining with love for his big sister. And Emma smiled back, clearly over her earlier huff. Mary could remember many a squabble between her own two kids, but there had always been love there too.

After everyone had helped clean up, Mary settled on the sofa in the living room, her Bible in hand. Gus padded over and settled into her lap. Mary ran a hand over his soft fur as she read. Betty was taking a bath, Lizzie was reading Luke his bedtime story, and Emma was working on her short story, all of which gave Mary some time to reflect on God's Word. She was reading the book of John, one of her favorites, when she heard light footsteps coming down the stairs. She turned and saw Emma, who walked over to her and sat next to her on the edge of the sofa.

"Can I ask you something, Grandma?" she asked.

"Of course," Mary said, putting the worn leather bookmark into her Bible and closing it gently.

Emma settled back fully on the sofa. "I'm having problems with my story," she said. "And I don't know what to do."

"Writer's block?" Mary asked sympathetically.

"Yes," Emma said. Mary could see in her eyes how much it meant that Mary was taking her writing seriously. "I can't figure out what should happen next."

"Do you want to tell me about the story up to this point?" Mary asked. She rubbed Gus's ears and was rewarded with his soft, rumbling purr.

Emma shook her head. "I want you to be surprised when you read it," she said.

"Okay, well, then, let me think of some of the tricks I've heard of to help with writer's block," Mary said.

Emma nodded expectantly, waiting as Mary thought for a moment. "What about research?" Mary asked. "Sometimes developing details of the setting and characters can inform the story."

"Like how?" Emma asked, her eyebrows scrunching together.

"Let's say your story is set in New York City," Mary said. "You can go online and read more about the city, and maybe you find out about a museum or an art gallery, and all of a sudden, you can imagine your characters going there, having a conversation. And then there it is, the next scene in your story."

"So they need to go somewhere?" Emma asked.

Mary shook her head, trying to think how to best explain. "Not necessarily," she said. "I mean that deepening your sense of the setting and then imagining your characters in it can lead you to seeing them doing new things. Like maybe your story is in Paris and you read about a café that has wonderful pastries and suddenly you can imagine your characters eating there, what they might order, and what they might talk about."

Emma was nodding thoughtfully. "That makes sense," she said. She smiled.

"Thanks, Grandma!" She jumped up, startling Gus. "I'm going to try that right now." She charged up the stairs, calling out to Lizzie to request the use of her laptop.

Mary soothed Gus, who settled back down with a soft meow. How satisfying it was to be able to offer advice to her granddaughter like this. Gus rolled over for a tummy rub, and as Mary stroked his silky fur, she realized that the advice she had given Emma was actually very good advice for herself and the story of David. What was the setting of his crime? What was going on in Ivy Bay at the time? Who were his neighbors? All these details would help her fill in gaps in the mystery and help her understand what had happened to David. And that insight could bring her closer to finding the ring.

Mary felt invigorated as she picked up her Bible to resume her reading. Yes, the answer she had found today wasn't what she had hoped, but she had two leads to investigate that might fill in the picture and give deeper answers to David's crime. And who knew what those might uncover?

Later that evening, the phone rang.

"Mary, it's for you," Betty called after a moment. "It's Henry."

After thanking her sister, Mary walked up the stairs to her bedroom and picked up her phone.

"Hi, Henry," she said as sat down on the velvet armchair next to a window with a view over the water. The sky was shrouded in clouds, and a light rain had started to fall.

"Mary, how are you?" His voice was cheerful.

"I'm enjoying the time with Lizzie and her family," Mary said.

"I'm sure you are," Henry said. "What did they get up to today?"

"A walk around Salt Water Pond, and an afternoon picking apples," Mary said.

"Wonderful," Henry said. "I'm glad they're having so much fun."

"Me too," Mary said. Gus poked his furry face through the doorway and spotted Mary. He trotted over and curled up in her lap. "How are you?"

"Well, I got a nice call today, from Annie," he said, and Mary could hear buoyancy in his voice. "From Annie and Kate both, actually. They had me on speakerphone. They kept talking over each other, and it was hard to hear anything."

He chuckled, and Mary smiled at the thought.

"And you'll never believe what they asked me," he said.

"What?" Mary asked, fully intrigued.

"To give Kate away at her wedding next summer," Henry said with a slight catch to his voice.

Mary almost welled up herself. Of course, Kate's wedding day would have an element of sadness, an emptiness where her father should have been. But Kate choosing Henry to give her away showed how much she loved her uncle, how important he had been to her in the years after she had lost her father. It was a joyful thing and a true honor for Henry.

"Oh, what a beautiful thing," Mary said softly.

"Well, unless I step on her train," Henry joked.

Mary laughed, but her thoughts went to the ring. This wedding was a celebration of triumph over loss, of the blessings of God for a new family, and of beginnings born of family heritage. For Kate to wear the ring that had been in her family for generations would be fitting and right. Of course, neither Annie nor Kate would ever expect it to be recovered, especially after all these years, but Mary believed in her heart that it was hidden somewhere, and that it was just waiting to be found. She closed her eyes and sent up a quick prayer asking for God's guidance in her search. She now wanted more than ever to find that ring.

"I spoke to Chief McArthur about the case," Mary said. "I thought it might be helpful to see if he knew some of the details of David's crime, especially the theft of the money."

"Good idea," Henry agreed. "Did Chief McArthur know anything about it?"

"Well, he said he hadn't heard of the case," Mary said, trying not to show her suspicions of Chief McArthur's strange behavior to Henry without anything substantial to back them up. "And at first, he said he couldn't find anything. But when I asked if I might look for the file on David, he offered to see if he could track it down and let me know what it said."

"That was nice of him," Henry said.

"Yes, and he was so eager to help that he looked it up this morning and already came over to tell me about it," Mary said, hoping her voice didn't expose how surprising she had found this. But her old friend knew her well, that or he himself was taken aback by it.

"Really?" he asked. "I'm surprised he'd move on it so fast."

"I was too," Mary said.

Henry chuckled softly. "Well, maybe there's such a dearth of crime in Ivy Bay that he welcomed the chance to research some action from the past."

"That's probably it," Mary said with a chuckle, though secretly she was not so sure. She laid a hand on Gus's soft back, the warmth of his fur soothing her. "Anyway, it turned out there wasn't much in the file. Nothing that would help us figure out where the ring is or what happened to David after he left Ivy Bay."

For a moment, they were both silent. Then Henry spoke. "Mary, it's so kind of you to be looking into all of this, but I worry that it's a waste of your time. You chased down this lead about the file, and it just ended up going nowhere. Chances are that ring is gone for good, and even if we do learn more about David, I'm not sure it will bring us any closer to the ring or the money."

"Like I said, Henry, I can't shy away from a good mystery, so I'm going to keep looking into this until all leads are dead," Mary said in a mock noir tone.

"Well, as long as you're sure it's worth it," Henry said.

"I am," Mary said with finality.

After they had hung up, she stared out at

the rain falling gently on the ocean outside her window, fervently hoping that the confidence she'd conveyed to Henry would turn out to be warranted.

FOURTEEN

The next morning, just moments after Mary's alarm went off, there was a knock on her bedroom door. She sat up in bed, rubbing sleep from her eyes, hearing the sound of giggles and shuffling. "Come in," she called.

The door burst open, and Luke bounded in, followed by Emma, who was carrying a wooden breakfast tray, and Lizzie, who leaned against the doorway with a smile.

"What's this?" Mary asked, a smile forming on her own face.

"Breakfast in bed!" Luke shouted.

Emma set the tray down carefully across the bed. "Muffins, juice, and coffee," she said proudly.

Mary surveyed the tray in front of her, seeing her favorite blueberry muffins, fresh-squeezed orange juice, a steaming mug of coffee and a sprig of rosemary from Betty's garden in a small vase.

"It's fall so there are no flowers," Emma said, noticing Mary looking at the vase. "But we thought this was pretty."

"It's beautiful and it smells divine," she told her grandkids. She was so touched she was close to tears. "But what did I do to deserve such a gesture?"

"Yesterday in the car, I told the kids how Jack and I used to bring you breakfast in bed on Mother's Day," Lizzie said.

Mary remembered bowls of soggy cereal and half-cooked oatmeal, prepared with such enthusiasm and love that she'd eaten every bite.

"So Luke said he wanted to do that for you too. And since we missed Grandparents' Day, we figured we'd just surprise you this morning," Emma said, looking pleased with herself.

"It's a wonderful surprise," Mary said. "And everything looks just delicious."

"Actually, Great-Aunt Betty made the muffins." Emma looked worried about getting too much credit.

Mary reached out and patted her hand. "My honest girl," she said. "And not to worry. You did the hard work of bringing them up here."

"Are you going to eat, Grandma?" Luke asked. "Because Mom said we have to clean up before we go to ride canoes."

Mary was laughing as she picked up a muffin.

Emma shot Luke a reproachful look. "Don't rush Grandma," she said protectively.

"That's right," Lizzie said. "You can go put on your water sandals, if you want to speed things along."

Luke bounded out with even more energy than he'd come in with, though he stopped first to give Mary a sloppy kiss. Mary finished up her breakfast, then wiped her mouth on the napkin that had been tucked under the vase. "*Mmm,* why is it that breakfast in bed tastes even better than when you eat it at the table?"

"It's the decadence," Lizzie said.

Emma picked up the tray, calling to Luke to help her as she headed for the door. But then she turned around. "Grandma, I'm just about done with my story," she said happily. "The research really helped. I think it will be ready to show you by tomorrow."

"I can't wait," Mary said.

Lizzie closed the door, leaving Mary alone to get ready for a day that had had a pretty perfect start.

Things were feeling decidedly less perfect

an hour later. There had been a leak in the store — luckily in the bathroom so no books were damaged — but Kip Hastings wouldn't be able to come take a look at it until the next day. Rebecca had positioned a bucket underneath, and the forecast didn't call for rain, but it still had Mary concerned. Mary had run out of the dry food she gave Gus at the shop, and when he made his indignation known, she had to run across the road to Meeting House Grocers to get more. And then Rebecca had gotten a phone call from Ashley's school. Ashley had a fever, and Rebecca would need to come to the school and get her. Rebecca had apologized profusely, but Mary waved her off, saying she understood.

The one piece of good news was she checked her e-mail and saw that she had a message from Connor, saying that he planned to stop by the Ivy Bay Public Library that day. Mary didn't want to leave the shop unattended but figured it would only be for a little while. What was the point of owning your own business if you couldn't do as you liked? She flipped the sign on the door to Shut, locked the door behind her, and headed to the library. Maybe this time, Connor would be a bit more forthcoming about his knowledge of David's case.

After greeting Victoria, Mary walked back to the computer room and was disappointed to see that it was empty, but she saw a coat hanging on the back of one of the chairs and a pile of books next to the computer terminal. She scanned the titles. *Rumrunners and Speakeasies: Prohibition in America* was on top of the pile. This had to be where Connor was sitting.

Mary set down her bag at the next terminal, hoping that Connor had just stepped out for a moment and that he'd be back soon. And then she looked back at the stack of books. He'd hidden one from her when they first met. Was it possible the book was still in his collection?

Library books were common property, after all. It wouldn't be dishonest to just look. Mary leaned over and looked at the spines of the books, reading each title. She saw a deep red spine and recognized the one she was seeking as soon as she saw it. It was called *Unsolved Crimes in New England, 1920–1930.* Gently, Mary eased the book from its spot in the pile and began to page through.

The book was part of a series that gave an overview of different types of crimes, and Mary gave a start when she saw David's name in the index.

His story was told on three pages, and Mary quickly turned to the first page. The section began in dramatic fashion, stating that the criminal had fled his hometown on January 20, 1925, a dark and snowy evening. Then the story went back a few days, to January 15, the day the money was reported stolen. There had been a fire in the hardware store, caused by an accident in the neighboring building, and when Mr. Fuller, the owner of the store, had arrived at his burntout business the next day, he discovered his safe, with all his money, had been cleared out. There was only one other person who knew the combination, and that was his former employee, David Woodrow, though it wasn't ruled out that he might have conspired with someone else. Once all this came together, the search to find and arrest David was on.

Mary sat back feeling the air drain from her lungs. Clearly, there was a great deal of information about the crime David had committed available at some point. If this author had been able to track it down, Mary was certain it had to be in the police file. Which could only mean one thing: Chief McArthur had lied to her.

There was no time to think about why the chief would have lied, not when there were still two more pages to read. So Mary bent back down over the book, reading quickly. What came next was an account of a sting operation, starting with the stolen money and the police setting up a net to catch David. They first tried to find him at home — something Mary imagined was extremely traumatic for his family. She shivered a bit at the thought of police lights shining, a harsh knock at the door, and officers pushing through the house.

But it was the next paragraph that made Mary gasp out loud. Apparently, there was a tip-off that David had gone to First Congregational Church. The cops followed, hoping to catch him there, but they were mere moments too late. They stuck around, hoping David might return, but it turned out that would be the very last Ivy Bay would see of David. He left town that night and never came back.

Mary sat back in her chair, her thoughts racing. Of all the places David could have gone in his last hours in Ivy Bay, he had chosen a church! It was not what she had expected, and she felt a burning curiosity to know why. Clearly, a trip to First Congregational Church was in order.

A footstep right outside the computer room brought Mary back to the present with a thud. She did not want Connor to find her reading a book he had clearly not wanted her to see. She quickly flipped to the back of the book to check one last thing, put it back exactly where she had found it, then grabbed her bag and headed out, waving to Victoria as she left.

As she walked through town, her mind ran through the information she had learned, trying to figure out what Connor had been hiding. She waved absently at her neighbor Sherry Walinski, who was walking to the bank, but her mind was on combing through the information. Many details of the crime were covered in the newspaper articles she had read so the answer clearly didn't lie there. In fact, the only new piece of information Mary had learned was the details of the sting operation. Was it possible that Connor didn't want her to know about David's trip to his church? It was the only thing that fit, yet it didn't make sense. At least not yet. It was entirely possible that if she went to the church herself, she would learn what it was that Connor had hoped to hide.

But the question that burned came from her final bit of research, the list of sources in the back of the book. The section about David's crime, including all the details of the fire and the safe, was endnote number twenty-five in chapter three. And in the back of the book, where all the endnote sources were listed, chapter three, number twenty-five was clearly listed as the police file stored at the Ivy Bay Police Department. The author of the article had pulled his information from that file. Which could only mean one thing: Chief McArthur had lied.

That afternoon, Mary had a hard time concentrating at the bookshop. She would find herself shelving books, but then stopping, her mind going over the chief's story. She had asked not once but twice, and each time he had said the same thing, that there were no details of the crime. Yet, obviously, there were. There was no getting around the fact that the chief had not wanted her to know the details of the crime, though for the life of her, Mary couldn't understand why.

"Mary, can I get that for you?" Bob Hiller's voice broke into Mary's reflection, and she realized she was standing on a ladder, books in hand but not moving, and must look quite strange indeed.

"I'm sorry," Mary said with a laugh, sliding the books in where they belonged. "I'm a bit distracted today," she said, stepping carefully back down the ladder.

The mailman looked relieved to have Mary herself once more. "That happens to me too," he said as he slid a stack of mail onto the counter. "Especially if I'm in the middle of a good mystery."

Mary knew he meant a mystery book, but his words were still exactly on target. "Yes," Mary said.

Bob left, and Mary rang up the one customer in the store, chatting briefly about who the best contemporary mystery writers were. When the woman had left, Mary grabbed a stack of Patricia Cornwell paperbacks and walked to the shelf where they belonged, her thoughts going back to the mystery at hand.

It was time to stop worrying about Chief McArthur, at least for the moment, and focus on moving forward.

She walked back to the box of newly arrived books, which she had finally emptied. She took the box to the back storage room, careful to leave the door open in case a customer came in, and broke it down, then set it in the large crate they had for recycling.

Her next step would be to go down to First Congregational Church. The other thing she'd like to follow up on was something that seemed impossible, and that was looking around David's old house. Mary sighed. It was such a shame she had gotten off to such a bad start with Deborah Taylor when she'd first visited the house. There would have to be some way to fix it, but she'd go to the church first before taking that on.

Now that she had a plan, Mary could fully focus on the store. But as she headed back up front to greet a customer, one thought still hovered at the back of her mind: Why had Chief McArthur lied to her?

FIFTEEN

"Grandma, Grandma!" Emma shouted, running out of the house as Mary walked up the path. She had clearly been sitting by the front window, watching for Mary's arrival home.

"Yes, darling?" Mary asked. She loved that her granddaughter was so animated and so happy to see her.

"I'm done with my story," Emma said, bubbling over with excitement. "Can you read it now?" She handed Mary her notebook eagerly.

Mary laughed. "I can't wait to read it, and I'll definitely read it tonight," she said. "But first, let me help your mom and great-aunt get dinner ready."

Emma's face fell. "Oh, okay," she said, sounding so dejected Mary reached out and patted her shoulder.

"I will read it the second we are done cleaning up dinner," she said. "But I can't let Aunt Betty and your mom do all the work, can I?"

"No," Emma agreed. "But you promise to read it tonight?"

"Cross my heart," Mary said. "I can give you my feedback before the evening news."

Emma's face was alive with joy once more. "I guess I can wait that long," she said, linking her arm over Mary's.

A cool breeze blew off the bay, and Mary glanced at the gorgeous view, taking in the rippling water shining under yet another beautiful sunset, before squeezing close to her granddaughter and walking into the house.

Luke was sitting on the living room floor playing with the box of LEGOs Mary had found for him at a yard sale. Unlike newer LEGOs, this set did not make a spaceship or Star Wars figure; it was just a collection of different-sized LEGO blocks that allowed Luke to create whatever he wanted. And tonight, that appeared to be an elaborate castle.

"My, that is quite an abode," Mary said, crouching down to admire his work while Emma headed upstairs.

"Is an abode a special kind of castle?" Luke asked with interest.

"It just means a living space," Mary

explained, taking in the careful towers Luke had created.

"Well, this is a pirate abode," Luke said. "I'm going to live there when I grow up, and I'm the ship's captain." He frowned. "I wanted to make a ship, but it was too hard."

"Maybe you could draw a picture of it," Mary suggested. "I got you some new markers and a big pad of paper. They're up on the bookshelf in your room."

"Yeah!" Luke said, jumping up. "I'll draw my ship."

He raced upstairs, and Mary walked toward the kitchen, which smelled of frying garlic and onion, one of Mary's favorite smells in the world. Inside, both Betty and Lizzie were bustling about in aprons.

"It looks like you're creating a feast," Mary said admiringly.

"Hi, Mom," Lizzie said, coming over to kiss her mother's cheek.

"We're making an Asian broccoli and chicken stir-fry with rice," Betty said. "Lizzie is the head chef; I'm just helping out." Mary knew her sister preferred classic dishes, like baked chicken, and was touched to see how gamely she was helping out Lizzie.

Mary went over to the pantry and grabbed an apron printed with roses. "What can I do to help?" she asked.

"If you could finish slicing up the broccoli, that would be super," Lizzie said.

Mary saw the cutting board and knife already out and went over to start chopping. Betty switched on the radio to a station that played hymns, and Mary found herself humming along as she fell into the rhythmic work of slicing the crisp vegetable. Next to her, Lizzie was chopping ginger, the smell pungent and pleasing. Lizzie, too, was humming along, and when the next song, "Joyful, Joyful We Adore Thee" came on, she began to sing. After a moment, Mary joined in and was surprised to hear even Betty raise her voice. They all smiled at one another as they sang and continued to cook and sing intermittently until the meal was set on the table. Then they sat and said grace, Mary's heart full with love for her family and her God who had brought them together.

"Grandma is going to read my story tonight," Emma said, taking a heaping portion of the stir-fry and setting it on the fluffy pile of rice on her plate.

The days were getting shorter, and for the first time, Betty had had to turn on the dining room chandelier while they ate. The chandelier, which Mary had always found to be a bit ostentatious, glittered overhead.

"Aren't you lucky to get feedback from someone who knows so much about books?" Betty said, taking the platter of meat and vegetables from Emma and helping herself to a somewhat smaller portion.

"I'm honored to be asked to read," Mary said. She served herself, then when everyone had full plates, picked up her fork and dug in. The chicken was soft and seasoned with the flavors of garlic, onion, and ginger, and complemented perfectly by the rice. "This is delicious," Mary told her daughter.

"It is," Betty said, a trace of surprise in her voice. "You'll have to give me the recipe."

"I'd be happy to," Lizzie said. The twinkle in her eye told Mary that Lizzie was well aware of her aunt's preference for more traditional food. It was flattering indeed that Betty was so taken with the dish, though, mother's bias aside, Lizzie was an exceptional cook.

Luke spent considerable time giving Mary and Betty a blow-by-blow account of their day at the aquarium that took them all the way through the caramel apple pudding Betty had prepared for dessert.

"I'm stuffed," Lizzie declared once her dessert plate had been cleaned.

"Me too," Mary agreed. "And what a delicious meal."

The whole family cleared the table, and then Mary headed for the sink to start rinsing dishes for the dishwasher. But Lizzie laid a gentle hand on her back. "Why don't you let me do that?"

Mary was about to protest that Lizzie had engineered the entire dinner and was due a rest, when Lizzie tipped her head slightly toward the doorway where Emma was standing, notebook in hand.

"If you're sure you don't mind doing all the cleanup," Mary said, glancing at Betty as she slowly took off her apron.

"Go read," Betty said, waving her hand toward the doorway. "We have this covered."

Mary followed her granddaughter out to the living room, sat down on one of the antique wing chairs, and accepted the notebook Emma proffered. She pulled her reading glasses out of a drawer in one of the end tables, then sat back to read. But after a moment, the burning intensity of Emma's gaze was too much. Mary looked up and almost laughed to see Emma sitting on the edge of the sofa, biting her lip, twining a lock of hair around one finger.

"You know what, darling?" Mary said, standing up. "I am going to read this in my room, just so I can focus on it fully."

Emma sat back on the sofa. "Okay," she said.

"It's just a lot of pressure to read with the author right here in front of me," Mary said.

Emma perked up when she heard herself referred to as an author. "I'll just wait for you down here, Grandma," she said.

"Perfect," Mary said, heading to the stairs. She walked into her own peaceful bedroom, closing the door so it remained open just a crack in case Gus wanted to join her. She settled down in her chair and began to read. After a few minutes, Gus came in and snuggled down on her lap, wrapping himself into a tight ball with the tip of his tail against his nose. Mary ran her hand over his soft fur as she read. Her window was cracked open, and she could hear waves lapping the shore, which provided a perfect backdrop to the story, which took place right in Ivy Bay. It was about a boy and a girl becoming friends while on summer vacation.

Mary finished the story and sat back with a grin. It was good. Really good. Emma had a gift for description that made the story come to life. Each character felt real, with strong points and flaws, and the dialogue was natural, not forced. Her granddaughter truly did have a knack for writing!

But Mary knew she needed to give Emma more than praise. She needed to help her budding author make the story stronger, so she settled in to read it again, this time with an editor's eye. She kept a pen in one hand, marking places that were particularly strong, and making two notes for places where Emma could still work on bettering the story.

After glancing over it a third time, Mary was satisfied that she had enough feedback to give her granddaughter. She gently set Gus on the bed, where he gave her an indignant look, then settled down with a sigh. Mary rubbed his neck until he purred happily, then headed downstairs.

Emma was sitting stiffly on the sofa, a book held in front of her. Lizzie was curled in the armchair knitting while Betty was settled on the love seat, her Bible in her hands.

"Grandma!" Emma shot up, the book almost tumbling from her hands before she grabbed it. "Are you done reading?"

"Yes," Mary said with a smile. She noticed that Betty had started a fire in the fireplace that crackled as sparks shot up with a burst, then fell back to earth as quiet cinders. Mary breathed in the smell of burning wood that called up thoughts of autumn days, wool sweaters, and hot cider.

Emma turned and stared at her mother, who got up obligingly. "I think that's my cue," she said wryly.

"We can go upstairs," Mary offered, not wanting to unsettle Betty and Lizzie.

"No," Betty said, standing up and stretching a little. "I want to take a bath to ease my joints anyway."

Mary shot her a look of concern that Betty brushed off. "I'm fine, just a tiny bit stiff. A bath will have me back in tip-top shape in no time."

"And I need to check on Luke," Lizzie said. "Things are a little too quiet up there."

They both headed out, leaving the living room to the writer and editor. Mary settled in the wing chair that was close to the fire. The warmth of the flames had an almost lulling effect on her. "What a lovely night for a fire," she remarked to Emma.

"Yeah," Emma said hurriedly. "But what did you think of my story?" She had her hands clenched and was rubbing one thumb against the other.

"I loved it," Mary said wholeheartedly.

"Really?" Emma asked, her hands loosening.

"Really," Mary said. "Let's see, I made

some notes." She got out the paper she'd scrawled her thoughts on, then slid her reading glasses across the bridge of her nose. "The beginning is wonderful," she said. "You start right at a point of action, which sucks the reader right in."

Emma nodded happily. "My teacher says that especially in a short story, you can't waste any words."

"Good advice," Mary said. "And you follow it well here. I also really like both your characters, Callie and Red. They feel like real people." She glanced up from her notes to see Emma beam. "And the ending is perfect. Happy without going over the top."

"I thought about having it that both their families move to Ivy Bay so that they can hang out all year," Emma said.

There was a particularly loud crackle from the fire as a log resettled.

"But choosing to have them agree to e-mail until they meet in Ivy Bay next summer is the more believable choice," Mary said. "You made a good writer's call with that."

"I'm so glad you like it," Emma said happily, starting to get up.

"I just had two quick things I think you could work on," Mary said, looking down at her notes again. "There are a few times when you tell us how they are feeling, instead of showing us. And I'm also wondering if the conflict between them needs to be just a bit bigger, to escalate the tension." Mary looked up, ready to discuss these points in more detail, but paused when she saw the tight look on Emma's face.

"I think the conflict is big," she said coolly.

"It's great how you have them argue about where to go for their last night together," Mary agreed. "I'm just wondering if we could make the stakes a bit higher."

Emma nodded stiffly. "I'll think about it," she said shortly, taking the notebook out of Mary's hands.

"We could talk about it more," Mary said, starting to feel distressed at her granddaughter's reaction.

"No, that's fine," Emma said, heading for the stairs, her back ramrod straight.

"I didn't mean any harm," Mary said. "You know how much I love the story overall. I just wanted to help you find ways to really polish it up, make it the best it could be."

"Right, I get it," Emma said coldly, not looking Mary in the eye as she spoke.

"Sweetie, I didn't mean to hurt your feelings," Mary said, bewildered at how things had gotten so bad so fast.

"You didn't," Emma snapped, but her feelings were obviously very hurt. She stalked up the stairs, two at a time, leaving Mary alone and dismayed.

SIXTEEN

Mary's heart was heavy the next morning as she was unlocking Mary's Mystery Bookshop. Emma had given her the cold shoulder at breakfast, and even Mary's attempt to offer her granddaughter her favorite waffles had gone unacknowledged. Emma was good and mad, and she was going to let Mary know it. As Mary twisted the key in the lock, she prayed silently. *God, please help Emma see past her anger and know that I only wanted to help. And please give me the strength to find the words and the actions to set this right.*

As always, reaching toward God gave Mary a sense of peace and strength, and she was able to breathe a bit more deeply. It had rained in the early morning hours, but the sun was shining now, making the droplets in the fiery autumn trees on Main Street glittery, something Mary took a moment to admire.

And then she saw a familiar sight: the chief of the Ivy Bay police stepping out of the Black & White Diner. When he saw Mary, he hesitated a moment, then crossed the street and ambled over.

"Morning, Mary," he said. "How's your research going?"

She didn't relish telling him what she knew; after all, calling the chief a liar was in very bad form. So she chose her words with care. "I have learned a bit more about David," she said. "I found a book that gave the details of the crime."

"Is that so?" Chief McArthur asked, his face reddening as he took a step back.

Chief McArthur cleared his throat loudly before she could go on. "That's some good work on your part," he said, the words coming out in a rush. He looked over at the clock on the Town Hall. "My goodness, I didn't realize how late it was. I'd better get to the office." He began to walk away, then turned back again. "Do keep me posted on what you find," he said. He walked away before waiting to hear Mary's reply.

For a moment, Mary just stared after him, too taken aback by the encounter to do much else. There had been guilt and discomfort in his eyes, confirming to Mary her earlier suspicions that he had fed her a story.

But for the life of her, she couldn't understand why. Equally confusing was his continued interest in the story, and wanting her to keep him updated.

A car drove by, and Mary gathered herself and unlocked her store, stepped inside, and smelled the comforting scent of the wooden bookcases, the books, and a hint of lemon from the cleaning solution they used to dust the furniture. As she began turning on lights and then her computer, she continued to mull over Chief McArthur's strange behavior in her mind. What was his connection to the case? Because there had to be something, some reason that he would both mislead Mary and want her to keep him in the loop. And the only conclusion Mary could come to was disturbing: Chief McArthur knew something about this case, something he did not want Mary to find.

It was a slow morning, so after asking Rebecca all about Ashley, who had fully recovered from her brief stomach bug, and helping a lone customer, Mary headed off to First Congregational Church. The weather had turned gray, with ominous clouds hanging thick and low in the sky. Mary was glad she had taken a white knit cardigan to protect against the chill.

The church was on the north side of town, and Mary had passed it many times, though this would be her first time inside. She admired it after she'd parked her car in the lot next to it. It was a large stone structure, with a red wooden door and high steeple. She grabbed her purse and an umbrella just in case, then opened the car door and headed for the stone steps. The door of the church was open, so she let herself inside.

The air was cool in the entryway, and Mary stepped through the cozy foyer into the sanctuary. The altar was simple but pretty, with a stained-glass window above it depicting the Virgin Mary holding baby Jesus. The wooden pews were solid and were marked with slight scratches and nicks, showing they'd stood the passing of time. Mary ran her hands over one, the wood smooth and soft from years of people's prayers. It was a peaceful space, and Mary took a moment to soak it in before turning back to find the pastor's office.

But he must have heard her come in, because she heard footsteps, muffled by the thick maroon carpet that covered the floor of the church, coming toward her.

"Hello," Mary called as she walked back to the foyer.

"Hello," Reverend Allen called, his voice a

mixture of welcome and what Pastor Miles had called his New England gruffness.

Reverend Allen was older than Pastor Miles, with short gray hair and a receding hairline. He wore wire-rimmed glasses over his blue eyes and a green button-down shirt with khaki pants. He looked at Mary for a moment before recognition dawned.

"How are you, Reverend?" Mary asked.

He nodded somewhat curtly. "I'm well, thank you. What brings you to our church today, Mrs. Fisher?" he said in a no-nonsense tone.

So much for small talk. Mary hid a grin at his New Englander ways. They actually made her feel right at home.

"I'm doing some research," Mary began.

"Oh?" Reverend Allen asked, his tone getting warmer.

"Well, research about a person who I believe attended First Congregational Church back in the 1920s," Mary said. "First Congregational was here then, wasn't it?"

"Yes, indeed," the pastor said, nodding. "We're one of the oldest churches in Ivy Bay." He smiled, pride shining in his face.

Mary nodded enthusiastically. "That's what I thought," she said. "And do you have any records that date back to that time? I'm looking into a man named David Woodrow, and I'm wondering if I could look through some of your old files."

Reverend Allen nodded. "We do have some old files you could look through," he said. "More than a few, actually. Come on back to my office, and we'll see what we can find."

And this was the other side to his New England demeanor, the side that wanted to help people and was willing to work to make it happen. She followed the pastor through a utility room parallel to the sanctuary where Mary imagined the congregation had coffee hour after services. The room was lined with windows, and Mary could see the gray day outside, plumes of fog hanging like spiderwebs across the graveyard in the back of the church. The pastor led the way down the hall to the middle of the church, flipping on a light as there were no windows in this part of the building. Halfway down, he opened a door. "This is my office, as well as the storage space for all papers since 1852, when the church was founded," he said, waving his hand to let Mary pass.

There were no windows in the office either; every wall was lined with floor-to-ceiling shelves, and every shelf was covered with books, folders filled with papers, ledgers, and clippings from newspapers. Some of the papers were neatly shelved, but others were in danger of falling off at the slightest breeze. A small armchair sat in one corner, a step stool next to it, and Reverend Allen's desk was across from the door. Stacks of books and papers lined the sides and nestled around a large computer, and a printer sat on a cart next to the desk.

"Wow," Mary said, looking around at the overwhelming amount of paper. Reverend Allen had been truthful when he said his office had a lot of papers!

"Yes, I think First Congregational Church has a history of pastors who are pack rats, myself included," the pastor said.

"But you never know when an old paper might just come in handy," Mary said, still gazing around the crammed room.

"Right you are," he said, easing down to look at a shelf crammed with books and papers. "Despite how chaotic it appears, it's actually quite well organized. This is everything we have from 1925, and you're welcome to browse."

This was more than Mary had even hoped for. "Thank you, Reverend Allen," she said.

He waved off her thanks, but Mary saw the twinkle in his eye as he sat down at his desk and quietly began flipping through his Bible.

Mary picked up a file, settled in the comfortable armchair, and began to look carefully through the old papers. The file contained bills, order forms, and other documents that were interesting but not related to Mary's search. A second folder yielded the same results. A third folder had a bunch of yellowing newspaper articles that featured any mention of the church or its pastor, but there was nothing about David.

Feeling discouraged, Mary picked up the last folder on the shelf, this one thinner than the others. She began to flip through and then felt her heart quicken with the excitement of a potential discovery. This folder had a list of church members. Mary read each page carefully, and about halfway through, she was rewarded. There was a list of Woodrows who were members of the church, and David was one of them. So despite his turn to crime, he had maintained his ties to the church once he reached adulthood. Which meant that there might be something else that linked to him here in this room.

Mary set the folder back and looked at the books on the shelf. There was a hymnal with a cracked spine, a book of prayer, and an old Bible that appeared to be stuffed with small papers. Curious, Mary pulled the leather-bound book out and opened it. Now that she had it in her hands, she could see that the papers were small scraps with the same small, neat script on it. Mary picked up the first one and read, *M came in to discuss problems with mother-in-law. I advised her to ask the Lord for patience and to ask her mother-in-law to share a baking secret so that they might learn to work together on something, rather than apart.*

Excitement flowed through Mary as she realized that this pastor had written notes about every parishioner visit he had. Was there any chance it was the same pastor who would have been here in David's time? Could there be a note in here about David? She turned the page, reaching eagerly for the next scrap of paper.

"Don't touch that."

Mary jumped at Reverend Allen's sharp words. He came over and took the Bible from her. "I'm sorry, but that's one document I can't let you look at," he said, setting the Bible on his desk.

Mary was taken aback by this sudden turn and bitterly disappointed to have the Bible taken from her now that she knew what it contained. "I'll be very careful with it,"

Mary promised.

But Reverend Allen shook his head, his face firm. "I'm sorry, but I can't allow it," he said. "And if you don't mind, I'll need to ask you to leave now. I have a lot of work to do."

For one moment, Mary stared longingly at the Bible. Then she heeded the pastor's request and slowly left his office. "Are you sure I can't just take a peek at it?" she asked as they walked back down the hall.

His pace was fast, as though he were eager for her to leave as quickly as possible. "No," he said shortly.

They reached the door of the church. Mary felt completely bewildered by the abrupt change in the pastor's attitude.

"Good day to you," Reverend Allen said crisply. This time Mary did not find his gruffness the least bit charming. But she did her best to smile in a courteous manner.

He stood by the door, waiting for Mary to pass through. When she had, he closed it firmly behind him.

Her thoughts were jumbled as she headed for her car, the misty air clinging to her hair in droplets, a few sliding down her face. She got in, and once the door was shut, looked up at the church, a swirl of fog covering the steeple.

She let out a long sigh. Yes, she had made a small discovery, but it had led to the tantalizing possibility of more. And then the door had shut, taking away that possibility.

She sighed as she turned the key in the ignition, and her silver Impala purred to life. But as she pulled the car to the edge of the parking lot, she decided that Reverend Allen had not seen the last of her. She'd just have to find a way to convince him to let her look at that Bible.

As she turned right on Bayberry Lane, she got a prickly feeling at the back of her neck, as though someone was watching as she drove away from First Congregational Church.

Seventeen

Rain beat down on the roof that afternoon as Mary and Rebecca stocked shelves, placed an order, and did some tidying up. Mary was thankful that Kip had fixed the leak so that the rain merely drummed on the roof but stayed outside where it belonged. Ashley, who had been dropped off by Russell right after school ended, was curled up in the carpeted bathtub in the children's nook with a Nancy Drew mystery, and as Mary walked past her, she stopped to smooth the hair that was falling free of her headband.

"Is that a good one?" Mary asked.

Ashley looked up with a smile. "It's super good," she said enthusiastically. "Nancy is so smart, and nothing ever scares her."

"She's pretty good at getting out of scrapes, isn't she?" Ashley's eyes were already drifting back to the page, and Mary gave her cheek a soft pat before leaving her.

The little girl's love of reading reminded Mary of her own childhood, spending rainy days lost in the pages of a good mystery.

Mary was feeling relaxed when the door chime rang out around four. She looked up with a smile and was pleasantly surprised to see Annie walk in.

"It's really coming down out there," Annie said, setting her blue umbrella printed with ducks in the canister Mary set out by the door on rainy days. Mary noticed that Annie's umbrella matched her tall rain boots, which were dripping from the rain.

"So nice to see you," Mary said, then introduced Annie to Rebecca.

"I'm always glad to meet a friend of Mary's," Rebecca said with a friendly smile. "Mary, I'll take over up front so you two can chat."

"That would be lovely. Thanks, Rebecca," Mary said.

Mary led the way to the back of the store and poured steaming cups of tea for each of them. Annie accepted hers with a grateful smile, took a careful sip, and closed her eyes. "That really hits the spot."

"There's nothing like a warm drink on a cold, wet afternoon," Mary said.

"This is a day for staying home on the sofa with a good mystery," Annie said.

Mary nodded, then cocked her head. "So what brings you out in the rain today?"

"A wedding errand," Annie said cheerfully. "An old friend of mine owns the stationery store here in town and insisted on giving us a discount on Kate's wedding invitations. I just went by and picked up a few samples, and I'd love to get your opinion on them." She set down her teacup to rifle through her bag. She pulled out a manila envelope, opened it, and took out three stiff cards.

Mary remembered that feeling of excitement when she and Lizzie were choosing invitations. Lizzie wanted pink to go with the theme of wild roses, but Chad had wanted something a bit more masculine. Lizzie called Mary in to consult, and they had come up with the perfect solution: a deep cream card with pink printing and chocolate brown trim.

Now Mary accepted the cards from Annie, one ecru with cornflower-blue edging and lettering, the second a eggshell-white with pink edging, and the last a pearl card with lacy, scalloped edges and plain black print.

"They're all pretty," Mary said, looking through them again.

"Honestly, they all just look white to me,"

Annie said with a laugh. "But Katie got very concerned about pearl versus eggshell."

Mary laughed. "A few years ago, I would have said the same," she said. "But between my sister's interest in interior design and having done invitations with my daughter, I can see quite a difference between ecru and eggshell."

Annie grinned. "Then I'm asking just the right person."

"I think my vote would go with this one," Mary said, holding up the pearl card, and enjoying how comfortable and easygoing Annie was.

"Oh, I like that one too," Annie said happily. "And I bet Katie will like it as well."

"Is her fiancé going to have any say?" Mary teased.

"He was happy to pass this part of the planning off to me and Kate," Annie said with a smile. "But he's doing his share of the work, doing research on photographers and bands."

"Sounds like the basis of a good partnership," Mary said.

Annie looked happy. "I think she's found a wonderful mate in Roger." She carefully put the invitations back in her bag.

Once again, Mary thought how meaningful it would be if Kate was wearing her family's ring. For a moment, she was tempted to tell Annie of the things she had learned since their last meeting, but since none of them had led to a direct clue about the ring, Mary decided to wait. It seemed unfair to get Annie's hopes up if it all led to nothing.

"So," Annie said, rubbing her hands together. "I'm ready for some books. Where do we start?"

The rain had stopped when Mary left the store an hour later, though it was still gray and cold, so Mary hurried to her car. Back at the house, they were running low on staples like cereal and bread, so Mary decided to make a quick stop at Meeting House Grocers, her favorite market in town, on the way home.

She didn't want to take too much time at the store — it was far too easy to get caught up in browsing the shop's many specialty items — so she headed directly for the dairy aisle, where she stocked up on milk, cheese, and yogurt. Crackers were next, then cereal, and Mary realized they were also low on apple juice, Luke's favorite. She was turning into the juice aisle just as another cart was coming out, and Mary had to stop short to avoid a crash.

"I'm sorry," the woman pushing the cart said. "It's so heavy it gets away from me."

Mary smiled and then realized she was looking at Deborah Taylor, the woman who lived in David Woodrow's old house.

"That's okay," Mary said, hoping to have a positive encounter. "They should really make these carts with brakes."

As soon as Mary spoke, Deborah appeared to recognize her. Her eyes narrowed and she started pushing her cart away before Mary had even finished speaking. As she passed, Mary couldn't help glancing into Deborah's cart and was surprised to see five economy-sized bottles of apple juice.

When she looked up, Deborah caught her eye and gave Mary a look so poisonous it took Mary's breath away. Yes, Mary had looked in the cart, but really what was the harm? But apparently, Deborah saw it as some kind of slight, that or she hadn't wanted Mary to see the apple juice. Whatever the reason, she practically ran to the checkout line, almost bumping into two other people with her cart as she fled.

Mary looked after her for a moment, baffled by her strong reaction. Then she slowly pushed her cart forward, taking down a bottle of apple juice and trying to figure out what was going on with Deborah Taylor.

But even after she'd paid for her groceries and was back in her car, the interaction proved undecipherable. So, reluctantly, Mary added Deborah to the list of people behaving as though they had something to hide.

"Please pass the squash," Mary said as cheerfully as she could later that evening. It was an effort, with Emma slouching in the chair across from her, a scowl on her face and refusing to engage in conversation.

"Here you are, Mother," Lizzie said, casting a sharp look at her daughter, who sat up straight and erased the scowl but still managed to radiate hostility.

Mary helped herself to a spoonful of roasted squash that she didn't especially feel like eating. It was painful to have Emma so angry at her, and worse, she knew it was causing a strain on everyone, bringing a cloud over the previously joyful visit. The dinner Betty had put effort into making — the pork chops perfectly tender, the squash dusted with cinnamon, and the salad fresh — felt marred. Even Luke was quieter than usual.

"So how was the bike ride?" Mary asked.

Lizzie had rented bikes and taken the kids on a ride along an old railroad line that had been repurposed into a beautiful wooded bike trail. Mary directed the question to Emma, but her granddaughter avoided her gaze.

But Luke perked up. "We saw a dead bird on the trail, and I poked it with a stick," he said happily.

"Yes, that was a high point," Lizzie said, a mixture of amusement and exasperation on her face. Mary imagined it had been no small feat to lure Luke away from that bird. "What else did we do, Luke?" she asked, giving up on Emma for the moment.

Luke considered as he stuffed five pieces of the pork chop his mother had sliced for him into his mouth at once.

"Luke, one at a time," Lizzie said.

Luke tried to answer, and Lizzie held up a hand. "No talking with a full mouth," she said. Then she smiled at her son. "Lots of rules to remember, right, buddy?"

Luke's eyes lit up at his mother's understanding words, and Mary felt a flicker of pride seeing what a wonderful, patient mother Lizzie was, even after a long day that had no doubt been tiring for everyone.

Mary turned back to Emma, ready to try

again. "Emma, did you enjoy the bike ride today?"

"It was fine," Emma said flatly. Her gaze flitted toward her mother, and Mary could see that Emma had only answered at all to avoid getting in trouble.

"What did you see?" Mary pressed.

Emma shrugged, then caught a look from her mother. "A lot of trees," she said in the same flat tone. "Mom, I'm done. May I be excused?"

"Yes," Lizzie said with a sigh, watching with a concerned look as her daughter went upstairs, her back stiff.

Lizzie shook her head, turned to Mary, and started to speak, then glanced at Luke. Mary knew Lizzie would never discuss Emma's behavior in front of the little boy, as it would be unfair to both of them. So Mary leaned forward, smiling at Luke. "Tell me more about the bike ride," she said.

Luke had managed to swallow all his food and was able to reply. "We rode fifteen miles," he said proudly. "And I wasn't even tired!"

"Not even a little?" Mary asked.

Luke frowned. "Even superheroes get a little tired sometimes, right, Grandma?"

Her heart melted at the concern on his face.

"Why, of course they do," she said, reaching over to pat his hand.

Luke nodded seriously, then continued to tell them about his day. The tension coiled at the base of Mary's neck loosened as she listened to her grandson's chatter, but the pain in her heart at Emma's anger still hurt.

Later that evening Mary sat on the sofa reading her Bible while Lizzie bathed Luke and Emma was holed up in her room reading. Mary was having trouble concentrating on her own reading and so was happy to have Betty come in and sit down next to her.

"Am I interrupting you?" Betty asked.

"Not at all," Mary said, slipping her leather bookmark into her Bible.

"Good, because I've been worried about you," Betty said, the concern shining in her eyes. "What's wrong?"

"Nothing. I'm fine," Mary said as convincingly as she could.

But Betty cocked her head, making it clear she saw right through Mary.

Mary leaned back with a sigh. "It's Emma," she confessed.

Betty's face was immediately sympathetic. "What happened to get her so riled up?" she asked.

Mary told Betty about the story and her well-meaning advice that had erupted into the current mess. Betty nodded and made sympathetic murmurs as she spoke.

"It's hard to hear any critique of your work," Betty said when Mary had finished. "Especially something artistic. But you did nothing wrong."

"I should have chosen my words more carefully," Mary said. "Or not pointed out the weaknesses at all, just praised the good parts."

Betty smiled, but she was shaking her head. "That would not have helped Emma," she said. "The child asked for your help, and you gave it. All you wanted was to support her writing, and if she's serious about it, she'll need to learn to take criticism. This is a good lesson for her."

Mary hadn't thought about it that way, but her sister had a point.

"Think how her teacher or an editor at the school paper will react when she hands in work," Betty went on. "I'm guessing none of them will be as gentle as her grandma. This is a good way for her to start learning how to be edited."

Mary knew in her heart that Betty spoke the truth. "You're a wise big sister," Mary said, smiling. "Thank you."

Betty waved it off with a smile.

"It still hurts, though," Mary said.

Betty squeezed her hand. "Ask God to bear that pain with you," she said. "He's always there to help us through the hard parts, big and small."

Mary nodded. "I've been praying, but maybe I'll take a bit longer with it tonight," she said.

"And do some Bible reading," Betty advised, tapping the Bible in Mary's lap gently. "That always helps me."

She stood up and headed out. Mary took her sister's advice and opened her Bible back up. And this time she was able to concentrate.

EIGHTEEN

The next day, Mary awoke to sunshine pouring in through her bedroom window and David Woodrow on her mind. Between the roadblocks from Deborah Taylor and Reverend Allen, and the apparent lie from Chief McArthur, she was feeling stymied, so she decided to fall back on the one place that hadn't let her down: the Ivy Bay Public Library. Lizzie was in the kitchen, but the children were still asleep. After checking on Betty — who was much better — eating breakfast, and making a quick stop by the bookshop to open up and hold down the fort until Rebecca arrived, Mary headed to the library to see if she could learn more about First Congregational Church from some old-fashioned research.

The town of Ivy Bay seemed to sparkle after its soaking the day before, and Mary admired the beautiful, well-kept buildings as she turned left at the corner and walked down Meeting House Road. A number of the buildings were historic landmarks, with small plaques marking them, each one unique in the piece of Ivy Bay history it held. Yet again, Mary was struck by how lovely her hometown was, and how lucky she was to live here. She gave a quick prayer of thanks as she walked the path to the library and headed inside.

Several people were browsing the stacks near the door, and two women were sitting at the wooden table near the circulation desk. Victoria was checking in a stack of books, and she smiled when she saw Mary. "Hello, Mary," she said. "More Prohibition research today? Or maps?"

"What a good memory you have," Mary said. She could remember her days as a librarian and how much it meant to people when she remembered their favorite authors or genres.

"I try," Victoria said. Her tone was friendly, but Mary could see sadness in her eyes. "How can I help you today? I need a good distraction."

"I'm happy to help distract," Mary said. "But I'd also be happy to hear what's troubling you."

"Oh, it's nothing new," Victoria said. "Just these budget cuts. I have to get a list of programs in to the board — a list of programs to cut — and I've been putting it off as long as possible."

"I can understand that," Mary said compassionately. What a tough thing to have to do. Mary remembered her own work to create and cultivate programs, and to cut even one would have been extremely difficult.

"Yes," Victoria sighed. "I'm praying for guidance on this one."

"God will help you find a way," Mary said, glad to hear that Victoria was leaning on the Lord through this time.

"Yes," Victoria agreed. "But don't let me take up your time with this. Tell me what you're looking for today."

"I'm interested in finding out more about First Congregational Church," Mary said.

Victoria looked thoughtful. "I think we go back to the Ivy Bay history section for this one," she said, leading the way. As they passed the computer room, Mary saw Connor typing away, his back to them. She didn't want to interrupt his work or delay Victoria, but she made a note to stop by and say hello on her way out.

Victoria walked to the far nook that housed the collection of Ivy Bay history books and scanned the shelves while Mary waited quietly.

"I think this will be a good starting point," Victoria said, pulling a large binder off the shelf. "It's town documents for nongovernment buildings. Government documents are in the county clerk's office, though you already know that," she said with a smile. "There are a lot of useless things, like information about water tanks, but dig a little and I think you might find something."

"Great, thanks," Mary said, accepting the binder when Victoria passed it over. It was heavy, and when she set it down on the table, it hit with a bit of a thud. "Sorry about that," Mary said, hoping she hadn't damaged it.

Victoria smiled. "That old book has survived much worse," she said. "I'll get back to the desk, but let me know if you need anything else."

"Thanks," Mary said. She sat down, pulled her reading glasses out of her purse, and dug into the binder.

An hour later, Mary had discovered a few things, one of which was that even water tanks were rather interesting when you considered them in the context of early zoning board laws. The problem with this type of research was that each paper in the binder was compelling in its own way, and Mary couldn't help peeking at each one to see what insight it gave her to early Ivy Bay.

But she'd stayed on track enough to find a few papers about the church, one being the architectural drawing of the building, which was interesting, though not especially useful. The other thing she'd found was an obituary of the Reverend Edward Montgomery, who passed away in 1931. He must have been the man, according to the article on David's disappearance, whom David had talked with right before he fled. According to the write-up in the paper, Reverend Montgomery had studied religion at a divinity school in his hometown of Philadelphia and had been a pastor there for fifteen years before being selected by the board to serve as minister of First Congregational Church, which he did for twenty-three years, until he retired. He was remembered as a beloved member of the community, a sincere church leader, and a friend to all who stepped into his church. And since one of those people was David Woodrow, Mary was that much more eager to get her hands on the Bible in Reverend Allen's office.

She checked her watch and realized it was time to get back to the bookshop. She closed the binder and put it back on the shelf, then went to peek in the computer room. Connor was still there, so Mary walked in, making her footsteps purpose-fully loud so that she wasn't sneaking up on him.

He swiveled around in his chair, his face breaking into a smile when he saw her. "Mary, hello," he said, standing up. "How are you?"

"Good, thank you," she said. "How is your research going?"

A cloud seemed to pass over him, but then he smiled again, this time in a way that didn't seem quite as genuine. "Well, thanks," he said. "I've been following leads, hoping to find out some new information."

Mary waited to see if he might say more about his leads, but he stayed quiet. "It can take time before you hit on something use-ful," she finally said.

Connor started to say something, then stopped and started again. "Well, if I could find some answers there, I'd have a great centerpiece for my dissertation."

"It is a compelling story," Mary agreed.

"Have you had any luck with it?" he asked eagerly.

"Not really," she said. "Mostly some dead ends." For a moment, she wondered if she should tell him about the map and the dead end she had reached there. But what if the map let him know about the ring? He had made it clear he was hiding things from her, so Mary decided it made the most sense to stay quiet about the map. "I thought I'd found something in the police records, but it turned out to be a false lead."

"I've stumbled on a few of those myself," Connor said, running a hand through his messy hair. Mary resisted her maternal instinct to smooth it down. "I wonder if —" He stopped.

Mary realized there was something slightly off about how he was acting. This was the second time he'd decided against telling her something. Was there more that he knew, that he was keeping to himself?

"What do you wonder?" she asked gently.

Connor scowled for a moment. "There are a lot of good hiding places in Ivy Bay," he said.

Mary felt a shiver run down her spine. She had suspected Connor was looking to find the money David had supposedly left behind, but hearing him confirm it was troubling. Of course, he could have plans to return it to the rightful owner, so Mary cautioned herself not to judge too fast.

"You mean for the money David may have left," Mary said.

Connor shot her a furtive look. "There are a lot of things he probably left behind,"

Connor said, and Mary felt her heart clench up. It was possible he had already learned of the ring. And what if he was searching for it too?

"And anything he left would shed light on his story, and I need as much light shed on it as I can get," he said with a smile that looked a touch forced.

Mary wondered if he was being honest with her. Was his interest in the things David left behind simply about learning more, or did he have other ideas? The one thing she did know was that she wanted to uncover the ring before Connor did.

"I should go," Mary said. "But it's nice to see you."

"You too," Connor said. "Thanks for stopping in to say hello. And let me know if you manage to get past any of those dead ends in the case."

"You do the same," Mary said with a smile. Then she walked out. In the hall, there was a figure in front of her, walking very quickly. He was in shadow, but his speedy movement caught Mary's attention, and as he turned the corner, he came into the light. With a start, Mary realized it was Chief McArthur. She glanced back at the computer room and realized that it was entirely possible he'd seen her talking to

Connor.

Had he been listening in on her conversation with Connor? It seemed absurd. And yet he was walking away so quickly, as though he wanted to slip away before she could see the fact that he'd been lurking. It could only mean one thing.

Chief McArthur had been eavesdropping.

NINETEEN

Mary walked out of the library, waving absently to Victoria, who was checking out books for a man Mary recognized vaguely from church. They exchanged smiles, and then Mary stepped outside into the bright sun that made her blink for a moment. When her eyes were adjusted, she walked toward the bookshop, lost in thought about Chief McArthur. It was hard to imagine the chief of police actually eavesdropping, though of course, it was probably a tool of the trade. And he had acted so secretive about David, at the same time as he made his interest in her discoveries clear. But still, was it possible?

And then something else caught Mary's attention. Reverend Allen was walking into the Black & White Diner. If he was here on Main Street, sitting down for lunch, that meant this might be the perfect time to go back to First Congregational Church. Of course, chances were it was locked in his absence, but a big church like that would surely have a lot of volunteers, and if it was anything like Grace Church, those volunteers stopped by to do work during the week. Mary felt a twinge of hesitation. Reverend Allen clearly hadn't wanted Mary to look at the Bible, and she didn't want to disrespect his authority. But at the same time, the Bible was church property, not his. And anyway, if something in there could shed light on this generations-old mystery, it would be worth the small amount of rationalization it had required.

She headed for her car at the same time she dug her cell phone out of her purse. She made a quick call to Rebecca, who said the store wasn't busy at the moment, and then Mary was on her way to First Congregational.

As she pulled into the lot, she saw a red car parked right in front. So sure enough, someone was inside the church, someone who would hopefully be willing to help.

The sun warmed her face and shoulders as she walked up the steps of the church, then walked inside its cool interior. "Hello," she called.

"I'm back here," was the faint reply coming from the back of the church. It was a woman's voice, and she sounded friendly.

Mary headed toward the voice, through the utility room. Coming out of the back hall was a woman who appeared to be in her early sixties. She wore a casual dress with brown boots, and her silver hair was cut in a short, stylish do.

"Good morning," she said cheerfully to Mary. "I'm Patrice Hayes. Are you a member of the congregation?"

Mary shook her hand. "Mary Fisher, and no, I'm actually here because I have an interest in local history."

"There's a lot to be interested in," Patrice said amiably, clearly happy to have someone wander in the church and chat.

"Yes, there's a lot of fascinating history in Ivy Bay," Mary agreed.

"And a lot to love now," Patrice said. "We moved here ten years ago when my husband retired, and I still feel lucky waking up every morning and knowing I live in this beautiful town."

"I feel exactly the same," Mary said, happy to find a kindred spirit in this regard. Though she supposed most Ivy Bay residents counted themselves lucky.

"How long have you lived here?" Patrice asked.

"I used to visit Ivy Bay as a child," Mary

said. "And I moved here full-time recently, after my husband passed away."

"I'm sorry for your loss," Patrice said, reaching out a hand and patting Mary's arm. Her face was filled with sympathy.

"Thank you," Mary said. "It helps to be a part of the community here in Ivy Bay." She did not want to lay her burdens on a person she had just met, nice as Patrice was. "That and prayer."

"God is there for us," Patrice agreed. "Where do you worship, if you don't mind my asking?"

"Not at all," Mary said. "Grace Church."

Patrice nodded. "That one's a beauty," she said.

"It is," Mary agreed.

"I could chat all day," Patrice said with a smile. "My husband says I could talk the ears off a brass monkey. But I imagine you came here for something besides conversation. What brings you to our church today?"

Mary chose her words carefully. "A good friend has an ancestor who was a parishioner here back in the 1920s. My friend is very interested in his family history, so I'm here to see if I can do a little digging to find out something about his relative."

"How nice of you," Patrice said. "I'm sorry to say that our pastor Reverend Allen stepped out for lunch, but I think I can help you. I've been a member of this congregation since we moved here, and I've done what I can to get at least some of the papers in the office organized. Come on into the church office."

The words were music to Mary's ears, and her step was light as she followed Patrice back to the pastor's office. She flipped on the light and waved Mary in. "As you can see, we keep everything around here."

Mary laughed.

"Can you tell me more about what you're looking for so I can help you figure out where to start?" Patrice asked.

"I was hoping to get a look at a Bible," Mary said. "The one that was used in 1925."

Patrice cocked her head. "Funny you should ask for that," she said. "The board of the church is always urging Reverend Allen to keep that Bible locked up. You see, it's not just a precious document but an incredible social history of our church. The pastor at that time, Reverend Montgomery, was a bit of a legend for all the notes he took. And most of them are stuffed in his Bible."

"I can see why the board would want to keep it safe," Mary said.

"Yes, but Reverend Allen feels differently," Patrice said. "He insists that such a vital piece of church history should be accessible to anyone who wants to see it."

Mary was surprised by this, given her own experience trying to look at the Bible with Reverend Allen. "Really?" she asked.

"Yes," Patrice said. She was crouching down by the low shelf that stored the documents and books from 1925. "And I must say I agree with him. What good does it do locked away? It needs to be available for people like you."

She turned with a grin, and Mary grinned back. "I certainly appreciate it," Mary said, her fingers now itching to get that Bible.

"The papers in here are more or less in chronological order," Patrice said, standing up, the Bible in her hand. "Because the pastor started sticking them into Genesis and then kept moving forward. And anyone who takes out a paper tends to put it right back where they found it."

"That sounds like the perfect place for me to start," Mary said.

"Yes," Patrice said with satisfaction. She passed Mary the Bible.

Mary held it for a moment and was just about to open it when she heard footsteps behind her. She turned and there was

Reverend Allen, a smile on his face that quickly dissolved when he saw Mary.

"Hello, Reverend," Patrice said. Her voice had a hint of a question in it; clearly she had noticed the pastor's sharp change in demeanor. "This is —"

"Yes, I know who it is," Reverend Allen said in a clipped voice as he turned to Mary and held out his hand. "I'll take that."

With a wave of disappointment, Mary saw that he meant the Bible.

"Reverend?" Patrice asked, her brows knit together in confusion.

But the pastor ignored her, his full attention on Mary and the Bible. "I believe I told you that this is off-limits."

Mary was loath to part with the Bible, which she just knew had something about David in it. "Reverend Allen, I'm sorry if I've overstepped, but I mean no harm," she said. "I simply want to find out about my friend's ancestor."

"I'm sorry we can't be of more help," Reverend Allen said.

There was nothing to be done. Mary regretfully relinquished the Bible into his open hand, looking at it longingly as the pastor took it from her and put it deep inside a drawer in his desk.

"And now, I think you should be on your

way," Reverend Allen said.

"Reverend, I don't understand," Patrice said, looking between him and Mary, her friendly face a mask of confusion.

"I'm sorry," Mary said to her. She hated that she had put kindhearted Patrice in such an awkward position. "I'll be going now," she said, glancing at the pastor who nodded.

Mary gave one last look at the drawer where the Bible was, now even farther from her reach, then left the church. She could hear Patrice's questioning voice behind her, and the pastor's quiet reply, and she wondered how he would explain what had happened.

Back at her car, Mary sank into the seat and let out a long sigh. What a frustrating afternoon this had been. To be so tantalizingly close to a document that she felt sure had answers and to have it snatched away was maddening. The Bible had been bursting with papers, and she was certain that at least one of them would have something about David. So as she started up her car and pulled out of the lot, she vowed that somehow she would be back and this time she would manage to get a look at that Bible.

TWENTY

It was a slow afternoon, and Mary's mind was churning through the leads she had, all of which were either blocked off or unclear. She felt certain that Reverend Montgomery's Bible held clues, but there was no way to know until she'd managed to see it. She believed that Connor was also searching for things David might have left behind, though she wasn't sure how much he really knew. Chief McArthur also knew something he wasn't telling Mary, and there was the house on Cook Street that was also still impenetrable. Then there was David himself and the mysterious visit to the church in his final hours in Ivy Bay.

"Is everything okay?" Rebecca asked, looking up from the inventory work she was doing on the computer, her brows scrunched together in concern. Mary realized she must have been frowning.

"I'm sorry, I just have a lot on my mind,"

Mary said.

"I know how that can be," Rebecca said. She glanced outside where sun splashed across the sidewalk. Gus was lounging in a patch of sunlight that slanted in through the front window. "You know I can take care of things here if you want to go out."

Mary smiled warmly at her assistant. How lucky she was to have found Rebecca, who was not only kind but also so well mannered. And Mary realized she really did want to do a bit of research. Chief McArthur's strange behavior had been niggling at the back of her mind for days, and this morning's sighting had prompted an idea. A far-fetched idea, but at this point, that was better than any other leads she had.

"Are you sure you don't mind?"

"Not at all," Rebecca said.

"I suppose I'm not doing much good here, anyway," Mary said with a rueful smile. "I will go out, just for an hour or so."

"Take however long you want," Rebecca said.

Mary pulled her purse from the cubby behind the counter and walked toward the door.

"Don't work too hard, Gus," she said. The cat opened his eyes and looked at her, and then closed them and rested his head on his paws.

"Lazy cat," Mary said, laughing, and then stepped out into the beautiful day. As she walked down Meeting House Road a perfect red leaf fluttered down in front of her to rest on the sidewalk. She stopped to chat briefly with a few women from church and then headed back to the library.

Victoria was busy with other patrons, so Mary just waved to her and walked down the hall to the area where the microfilm was kept. Mary slid open the drawer that contained newspapers from the 1920s. She wasn't certain exactly what she was looking for, so she took a few spools, and she settled down at one of the terminals. She threaded the film through the machine and scrolled as she tried to figure out how to find what she was looking for.

Seeing Chief McArthur in the library, with her head still in the history of Ivy Bay, had reminded Mary of a small line in Connor's book — the one about David's crime possibly being committed by more than one person. Henry wasn't the only one whose family went back generations in Ivy Bay; Chief McArthur's did too. Of course, Mary wasn't sure how far back, but what if Chief

McArthur had an ancestor around in the 1920s?

Mary narrowed her eyes and tried to focus on the fuzzy type as it zoomed by on the screen. She could hear children laughing and shrieking and assumed it must be story time in the children's area. Story time had always been one of Mary's favorite parts of working in a library. Getting kids excited about reading was a lifelong investment in their education, and Mary had always felt honored to be a part of it. Plus, they were so darn cute.

By the time she'd gotten to the end of the first roll, she was beginning to doubt the wisdom of this plan. How would she ever find anything this way? She glanced at the clock. She had only been here for a half hour. She could spare a little more time. She'd try one more roll. She carefully took the first roll out and replaced the canister in the drawer, and then threaded the new one into the machine carefully. This was the same roll she'd looked at the other day, and she hadn't seen anything about the McArthur family on it, but then, she hadn't been looking. It was unlikely, but it was worth a shot.

She scrolled through the early years on the film. She smiled at the amount of attention that the Boston Red Sox had received in the *Ivy Bay Bugle*. John, a die-hard Sox fan, would have thought that was appropriate. There were mentions of new buildings being planned in Boston and a series of arrests made in connection with the discovery of a Chatham speakeasy. Then, she saw something else. She gasped. There was a headline that read, Ned McArthur to Serve Ten Years in Prison.

It seemed Chief McArthur did have an ancestor who lived in Ivy Bay from David's era, an ancestor who had also committed a crime. She'd finally hit on something. There was no obvious connection to David, but she had a gut feeling that somehow she would find one.

Mary scanned through the article. It turned out that Ned had run a tobacco shop on Main Street and used it as a cover for an illegal arms-trading business. An anonymous tip had led to a sting operation, and Ned was caught red-handed. Apparently, Ned didn't accept his punishment with grace, taking every opportunity available to yell streams of curse words at any lawyer or law-enforcement official who came along. He readily admitted guilt, to the dismay of his mother, and seemed proud of what he had done.

Mary stopped to consider this. So there was a black sheep in Chief McArthur's family too. But that didn't seem enough to warrant Chief McArthur's secrecy. Everyone had a skeleton or two in their closet; this was ancient family history. There had to be something more he wanted to hide.

The next day's paper had a follow-up story, and Mary read it eagerly. It started with an overview of Ned's life, as well as the case. About halfway through, she saw something that made her sit up straight and catch her breath. She read it again: "Ned had planned to open the tobacco shop with childhood friend David Woodrow, but a falling-out between the young men left Ned on his own, and a silent partner stepped in with funds to open the shop." So there was a connection between David and Ned! It was right there, plain as day.

Mary leaned back, feeling almost breathless at having finally found something substantial. Though what did it mean? Was it possible that Ned had helped David with his crime? And what would that mean for the money and the ring? Or did it mean something else entirely? Could David have sold the ring to fund the store? But the partnership had ended before the store opened, so what might have become of the ring? Mary went back and checked the dates on the articles. Sure enough, the tobacco shop had opened in 1925, meaning the falling-out must have happened that year. What could the men have fought about?

Mary spent the next half hour looking through the paper, trying to discover what had happened but failed to turn up anything. And there was nothing that led her any closer to knowing if the ring or stolen money was tied to the store.

"Hello in there," Victoria said, pulling Mary back to reality.

"Hey, Victoria," she said, shaking it off.

"I'm sorry to disturb you when you're obviously so engrossed," Victoria said. "But we're closing at three o'clock, thanks to budget cuts." She frowned as she said the words.

"Oh, I didn't know, and I'm sorry to hear it," Mary said, standing up and gathering her belongings that had somehow gotten spread out when she started taking notes on all she had learned.

"Yes, I hate to have to throw people out of the library," Victoria said with a sigh.

"Well, I was about done here, anyway," Mary said. She had put the microfilm canister back in the drawer and got everything packed up. "And I found what I was looking for."

"That's always nice to hear," Victoria said. "I just need to go to the children's area before I start locking up. You can wait for me at the desk if there's anything you'd like to check out."

"I'm all set, thanks," Mary said. "See you soon."

She gave her friend a brief hug, then headed out of the library and started down Meeting House Road — her thoughts swirling through the 1920s and the story of Chief McArthur's ancestor. There were still so many unanswered questions, and she could only think of one person who might be able to answer them: Chief McArthur himself.

Mary still wasn't sure why the chief of police had been so secretive about Ned. Of course, it was possible that he was ashamed of his ancestor's actions, but it had happened a long time ago, and a black sheep in the past didn't really seem like something to hide. That said, now that the cat was out of the bag, it was possible he'd be more forthcoming about what he knew about David. There was no time now, however, as she needed to get back to the bookshop. But she knew that Chief McArthur often started his day with a cup of coffee at the

Black & White Diner, and she decided that would be her first stop tomorrow morning.

That evening after dinner, Mary, Betty, and Lizzie and her clan strolled into town for ice cream at Bailey's. The sun had just set, leaving fading pink and periwinkle strips of sky, and the streetlights were just going on, making downtown Ivy Bay feel homey and warm despite the cool fall wind. Their feet crunched through fallen leaves, and Luke stopped to scuffle leaves in the gutter at every opportunity. Emma walked silently next to her mother, a sullen look on her face. Mary tried not to notice. She still wasn't sure when and how to approach her granddaughter.

When they arrived at the ice-cream shop, there was a long line despite the cool weather.

"It's never too cold for ice cream, I guess," Mary said to Lizzie and Betty.

Luke looked up at his grandmother, shock in his eyes. "Of course not, Grandma," he said with great seriousness. "You can eat ice cream even when it's snowing outside."

"Yes, you're absolutely right," Mary said reassuringly.

Betty reached over and ruffled Luke's hair, a smile dancing in her eyes. "This one here is wise," she told Lizzie, who laughed.

"Well, if it isn't Mary and Betty," a voice behind them said.

Mary turned and saw the smiling face of Cynthia McArthur Jones.

"We have to stop meeting like this," Cynthia said jokingly.

"Actually, I can't think of a better place to keep meeting," Betty said with a smile.

"Good point," Cynthia said. She smiled down at Luke. "How are you today, young man?" she asked.

"I'm here for ice cream," Luke told her importantly.

"Do you know what kind you're getting?" Cynthia asked.

"Grandma's flavor," Luke said. "Because my grandma helps make the ice cream here."

"And she's quite good at it," Cynthia said.

"I can only take credit for the recipe," Mary said quickly. "I think it's the ingredients they get and how carefully they mix it that makes the ice cream here truly special."

"I'd say it's all the above," Cynthia said. "And I'm getting your grandma's flavor too," she told Luke.

Cynthia turned to Lizzie and Emma, and they began chatting about their day at the pumpkin patch in Barnstable. Mary tried to pay attention, but she couldn't help thinking about Ned, the coarse criminal who was somehow related to this friendly, stylish pillar of the Ivy Bay community. She wondered if Ned was a grandfather or a great-uncle, but she decided to wait to speak to Chief McArthur about it, not wanting to change the tone of the pleasant evening.

Cynthia chatted with Lizzie and a now-animated Emma, something Mary hadn't failed to notice, until it was time for them to place their order. Everyone in Mary's family except for Emma ordered Mary's strawberry almond fudge ice cream. Emma took her cone of coffee heath bar crunch without looking at Mary.

They walked home slowly, licking their cones, and Mary made her way closer to Emma. "How is it?" she asked.

"Same as it always is," Emma said, not looking at Mary.

"Maybe you could get something new next time, to spice things up," Mary said.

"I *like* coffee heath bar crunch," Emma said almost accusingly, as though Mary had insulted the flavor. "It's my favorite."

"Emma, I didn't mean —"

"Whatever." Emma picked up her pace and caught up with her mom, who was walking several steps ahead of them. Mary watched her go. She didn't know what to do. How could she get through to her granddaughter? Things couldn't go on like this. She had to figure out a way to make things right with Emma.

TWENTY-ONE

Friday morning brought another perfect crisp fall day. Mary had eaten a quick bowl of cereal with Betty and was now heading out to catch Chief McArthur at the Black & White Diner.

Her walk over was invigorating, though she was glad she'd put on her thick green-and-yellow knit sweater to keep her warm. Mary could feel the healthy color in her cheeks as she opened the door to the bustling diner. The diner was busy, as usual. The restaurant was famous for its chocolate-chip pancakes, and visitors came from all over the Cape to sample the breakfast treat.

"Hey there, Mary," Nicole Hancock said from behind the counter. Her blonde hair was swept up into a messy bun, and her gold earrings sparkled in the sunlight that streamed in through the big front window. "Take a seat anywhere you like."

"Thanks!" Mary said, and looked around

the crowded room. Mary spotted Pastor Miles and his wife Tricia in a booth toward the back and waved at them. Then she scanned the counter and saw Chief McArthur, who was nursing a cup of coffee and reading the newspaper.

Mary made her way over, trying not to get distracted by the scent of fresh pancakes and maple syrup that perfumed the air. Her stomach rumbled even though she'd just finished her own meal, but she made a note to try and come back one morning with Lizzie and her kids so they could all enjoy the pancakes together.

Chief McArthur looked up as Mary sat down on the stool next to him. Mary had never seen the chief look quite so uncomfortable.

"Morning, Chief McArthur," she said.

"Mary, nice to see you," he said. He folded his paper and then folded it again, looking at the page without seeming to really see it. He gulped his coffee and raised his hand to get his check.

Nicole appeared before them, coffeepot in hand, and dropped the check by the chief's plate. "Can I get you anything?" she asked Mary as she refilled Chief McArthur's mug.

"Actually, we're just leaving," Chief McArthur said. He stood up, slipped a five-dollar bill out of his wallet, and tucked it under his saucer. "See you tomorrow," he said to Nicole, then turned toward the door and headed out. Mary followed close behind.

It seemed the chief wanted to lose her, but she was determined to follow him until he gave her answers. But when they got to the door, Chief McArthur paused and held it open so she could go out first. His manners were, as always, impeccable. Mary stepped back into the sunny day, then turned to Chief McArthur with a questioning look.

"I need to get to the office," Chief McArthur said, his eyes not quite meeting Mary's.

"Chief McArthur, I found out about Ned," Mary said quietly, figuring there was no sense beating around the bush.

Chief McArthur let out a breath. "That didn't take you long, did it?" he said ruefully. "I knew once you had the information from the police file, you'd put it together."

"It was all right there in the library," Mary said, deflecting what for Chief McArthur was a compliment.

"That student you were speaking with yesterday has been in the library a lot, and he hasn't discovered anything about it,"

Chief McArthur said. "So my compliment stands."

Jill Sanderson's sons raced past, and a moment later came Jill, a frantic but happy expression on her face. She waved at them and then was gone in hot pursuit of her boys. The sight made Mary smile but also made her aware of where they were.

"If you have time, I would like to ask you a few questions about him," Mary said. "But maybe we could go somewhere a bit more private."

Chief McArthur nodded. "Let's do that," he said.

"My store isn't open for another hour," Mary said, starting down the block. "We will have complete privacy there."

The sun sparkled off the windows of her shop, and the wooden sign out front blew gently in the breeze as Mary unlocked the door, then ushered Chief McArthur inside. Mary started brewing coffee and tea while Chief McArthur browsed through some books. And five minutes later, they were sitting by the fieldstone hearth with steaming mugs, ready for a discussion Mary had long been waiting for.

"I'm sorry I misled you before," Chief McArthur said quietly.

Mary was touched that he was willing to

apologize. "I understand your reticence," she said kindly. "I'm not sure I'd want to air my family's dirty laundry to people either. But I suspect there's more to it than that," she prodded, thinking of the connection between David and Ned.

"You're right," Chief McArthur said with a sigh. "And you'll probably put it all together pretty quickly now that you know about Ned, if you haven't already, so I might as well just tell you myself."

Mary was intrigued.

Chief McArthur took a sip of coffee, then began. "Well, of course, I wasn't thrilled at the idea of Ned's crimes coming to light," he said. "But if it was just that, I would have told you. I'm not proud of my great-uncle, but all I can do is live my own life in a way that honors our community and God, and I've strived to do that."

"Succeeded, I'd say," Mary said.

"Thank you for that, but we're all imperfect creatures doing out best to follow God's laws," he said humbly.

Mary nodded at the truth of the words.

"I suspect you may have already discovered that Ned knew David Woodrow," he said. "That and the fact that they were good friends at one time."

Mary nodded in affirmation. "Yes, it was

in one of the articles I read." She took a sip of coffee and waited for Chief McArthur to continue.

"I think that friendship was fairly public knowledge," Chief McArthur said. "They got in a few scrapes as kids, just the usual high jinks some high school boys get involved with, though maybe coming a bit closer to the law than most. One story I've heard is that they took Ned's father's car out and somehow got it stuck in the creek."

"Kind of like boys today getting into fender benders with their father's cars," Mary said with a small smile. Lucky for her, her son Jack had been an instinctively cautious driver, but a number of her friends in Boston had not been so lucky with their sons, who had their share of scrapes and speeding tickets.

Chief McArthur smiled. "I suppose a run-in with the creek is safer," he said. Then the smile fell from his face. "But they caused some real damage to the car, and my great-grandfather's family was strapped for money, so it was a big deal to them. That and the fact that Ned didn't actually ask to borrow the car; he just took it."

Mary shook her head sympathetically.

"And as they got older," Chief McArthur went on, "the crimes got more serious, though you probably know this too." Mary nodded. "My great-grandfather's family was thrilled when Ned wanted to do something responsible and start that store with David."

Mary nodded, listening intently.

"And then there was the falling-out, and Ned acquired a silent partner for the shop," Chief McArthur said with a sigh. "And you know the rest of that story." He picked up his coffee and took a sip.

Mary did know how it ended, but she had questions about what happened before then. "Do you know the cause of the falling-out?"

"No, but I have a suspicion," Chief McArthur said, hunching over a bit as he spoke. "And this is the part I'd prefer not get out, though it is just a theory on my part. Still . . ." His voice petered out for a moment. Then he sat up, as though resolved to finally tell Mary his true concern. "David was accused of stealing money, money that was never found. My suspicion is that Ned stole that money together with David and somehow managed to pin all the blame on David." He looked at Mary. "As I know you learned, the police thought it was possible David might have had an accomplice in the theft. If he did, Ned seems the obvious choice. And if Ned managed to escape blame and David leaves town, then no one is ever any the wiser."

Mary sat still, absorbing what Chief McArthur had said and all its many implications, the most important one being that if this were true, David had not disappeared with the money at all.

"Ned was a thief, after all," Chief McArthur said heavily. "And who knows what kind of grudge he might have held against David after their argument. This would be the perfect revenge, and the perfect way to fund his business."

Mary suddenly realized something from earlier in Chief McArthur's story. "You said Ned's family had money problems," Mary said. "And David's did too. How do you suppose those boys planned to open a shop?"

"A loan, I'd imagine," Chief McArthur said, his forehead crinkling. "To be honest with you, I never thought about it."

"I wonder," Mary said slowly, "if that falling-out might have been about money."

Chief McArthur nodded. "It's definitely possible. There's certainly reason to suspect that Ned wanted to finance the store with illegal funds."

"While David might have balked at the idea," Mary said, finishing out the thought.

Chief McArthur was nodding, though now he looked sad. "It would explain the falling-out," he said quietly. He let out a long breath. "But here's the thing, Mary. Even that part becoming public knowledge wouldn't bother me if it weren't for Cynthia."

Mary was momentarily confused, but then it clicked. "Her project to get your family building named a landmark," she said.

"Exactly," he said. "You see, she's been working for two years. There's all kinds of red tape with these things, but she's kept at it." His voice was admiring. "It's supposed to be made official next week, and Cynthia has a big party planned for two weeks after that. She had the invitations printed and everything. And if it comes out that Ned might have built that store with stolen money and illegally sold guns, it starts a whole bureaucratic chain that could mean another year before the building is officially approved. Which it will be, because the statute of limitations has long run out on this crime."

"But they would still need to do the investigation," Mary said, now fully understanding Chief McArthur's concern. "Which would be such a disappointment to Cynthia."

"And I would hate to see that happen," Chief McArthur said, glancing at his watch and then standing up. "I truly do need to get to the office now," he said, and this time his smile was comfortable.

"I can understand why you didn't want me to uncover this," Mary said as she walked him to the door.

"There's never an excuse for lying," Chief McArthur said. "Though I appreciate your understanding. And I know you have to share this with Henry."

Mary did want to tell Henry the latest turn in the mystery, but her heart ached at the thought of Cynthia's pet project being destroyed. "I'll keep looking into it," she said to Chief McArthur. "Maybe there's something else, some other aspect of the story we don't know."

Chief McArthur shook his head. "That's kind of you to say, but I was wrong to hide it."

Mary smiled.

"So you tell whomever you need to," he said. "Even that whippersnapper student. And let the chips fall where they may."

He saluted Mary and then headed down the sidewalk. Mary watched him go, admiration for his truthfulness and commitment to what was right making her proud of their hometown police chief. She turned back to her store, her mind running over all she had learned, certain it was bringing them closer to unraveling the mystery of the ring.

Twenty-Two

"So what's this news you have for me?" Henry asked cheerfully, coming up to Mary where she was sitting in the gazebo at Albert Paddington Park. After her talk with Chief McArthur, Mary had called Henry, who had agreed to meet her in the late morning, after he finished up with an early-morning fishing trip.

Now Mary shielded her eyes to look up at Henry, who was standing in the sun. "You'll want to sit down for this," she said with a smile.

Henry sat, and she passed him a paper bag with a strawberry scone in it. "I thought you might be hungry."

Henry smiled. "Starved," he said. "Thank you."

Mary took her own scone out of the bag and took a bite. Crumbs rained down on her sweater, and she brushed them off with a laugh. "Good thing I got a lot of napkins," she said.

A group of women from church strolled by, and Mary waved. The pretty park was crisscrossed with stone paths lined with wooden benches and dotted with trees, flowers, and bushes. A few of the other benches were occupied on this beautiful fall day, but Mary had chosen one that gave her and Henry a bit of privacy so that she could tell him all about her revealing conversation with Chief McArthur.

Henry polished off his scone in three bites, then sat back on the bench, waiting for Mary to tell him the news, which she did, giving him all the details of the articles about Ned in addition to sharing Chief McArthur's theory about Ned being the true thief.

When she had finished, Henry gave a low whistle. "That's a lot to digest," he said. "If any of it is true."

"That's what we would need to find out," Mary said.

"Yes," Henry agreed. "Though I'd hate to upset that project of Cynthia's."

Mary had prayed over this after her talk with Chief McArthur. "I know. Me too. But the truth should come out," Mary said. "It's what's right, and I suspect Cynthia would be the first person to say it."

Henry nodded. Then he looked at Mary. "There are more twists in this story than I think even Annie could have imagined. But do you think it brings us closer to the ring? I mean, I want to find out the truth about David, but I can't stop thinking about Annie's face if we were able to give her that ring."

The same thing had been in Mary's thoughts as well. "I do think it brings us closer," she said. "I think the more answers we have, the more we understand David. And the more we understand David, the closer we come to figuring out what he did in those last days. If it's true he didn't steal the money, it makes me even more convinced that he didn't sell the ring. But the question is still, where is it? It wasn't at the spot he'd marked on the map."

Henry cocked his head. "But why would he have left the ring behind?" he asked.

Mary had been thinking about this since she had learned that David's final visit had been to the church. "What if David was hoping to change his ways?" she asked.

Henry looked surprised. "I suppose anything's possible," he said. "God's grace can save us in our darkest hour."

Mary nodded. "So if David was trying to turn over some kind of new leaf, he'd want his family to have the ring back."

Henry nodded slowly, then smiled. "It's possible," he said. "But if that's true, where is it? If he had the ring and he wanted his family to have it back, why would his map lead us to a dead end?"

Mary shook her head, wishing she had an answer.

"And if David was framed," Henry went on, "Ned did a bang-up job of it, and no evidence was ever found to prove otherwise."

"Though no one was looking for evidence of his innocence," Mary mused.

"That's a good point," Henry said. "So where do you think we should start looking for that evidence?"

"I think the two most promising places are the church and David's old house," Mary said.

Henry gave her a skeptical look. "It hasn't gone so well at either of those spots," he said.

"No," Mary agreed, dejected. "But there's no harm in trying again," she said, trying to stay positive.

"So which place first?" Henry asked, just as the chimes in a nearby church began to ring, signaling that the noon hour had arrived.

"The house," Mary said. "I can go by this afternoon." She smiled. "And afterward, I'll call with the good news of what I find."

Henry was laughing as he stood up to go back to work. "I like your attitude," he said.

Mary stood too, and they started down the path to Main Street, where Henry had parked his beloved vintage blue-and-white Chevy Bel Air convertible. When they reached his car, Henry paused and looked at Mary intensely. "It means a lot to me, you helping out with this," he said gruffly.

Mary was touched by Henry's emotion and impulsively reached out and squeezed his hands. "We'll get to the bottom of this," she said.

Henry smiled softly. "I have no doubt," he said, his eyes holding hers.

"Hello there, Mary," a sharp voice said from behind her. Mary's heart fell as she turned to greet Dorothy Johnson, who was now smiling sweetly at Henry. "Henry, how are you today?" she asked in a much more gentle tone.

"Well, thank you, Dorothy," he said. "Though I do need to be getting off to work now. It's nice to see you." He nodded at Mary, then got into his convertible and drove away.

Dorothy rested a hand on the pearl necklace that was always adorning her neck as she stared after Henry's car. Then she turned a pointed gaze to Mary. "I hope I didn't interrupt anything important," she said.

"Just talking," Mary said as patiently as she could. Dorothy's possessiveness of Henry always grated on her. "And if you'll excuse me, I need to get back to the book-shop."

Dorothy looked as though she had more to say, but Mary just smiled and headed back to the bookshop, the sun warm on her shoulders as, for just a moment, she thought about the tender look on Henry's face.

That afternoon, Mary left Rebecca to close Mary's Mystery Bookshop and headed over to the county clerk's office to see if she could dig up anything about David's old house, 43 Cook Street. There had to be something that might explain Deborah Taylor's reluctance to speak to Mary.

She pushed open the door to the cramped office, and the musty smell of old papers wafted over her.

The room was cluttered with overflowing file cabinets and cupboards holding public records and archives dating back hundreds of years. The oldest documents were housed in the basement, their paper crumbly and yellowing but carefully cared for by Bea, the county clerk, who was close to seventy and still sharp as a tack.

"How are you today, Bea?" Mary asked comfortably. Bea had overseen the notarizing of the documents that gave Mary ownership of her store when she first moved to town, and she had had a number of other occasions to visit this office to do research.

"I'm doing great," Bea said, adjusting the reading glasses that seemed to always be perched on the edge of her nose. "Another project?"

"You know me." Mary laughed. "I wanted to see if there were any papers filed or requests made from an address in town."

"What address would that be?" Bea stood up and started to walk around the counter. Mary had to smile. Bea didn't even know what she was looking for yet, but she was ready to go.

"It's 43 Cook Street," Mary said.

She walked to a filing cabinet and slid out a drawer, then rifled through the files and finally pulled out a thick manila folder. "Take a look," she said.

And so Mary did.

Her visit to the office had been fruitful, and

Mary drove to 43 Cook Street confident that, this time, she would finally be allowed inside. Once again, the street was surprisingly crowded with cars, and Mary had to park down the block from the sea-foam-blue Victorian house. She walked up the path and rang the bell, ready to convince Deborah to let her inside.

The door opened suddenly, and a small toddler in a pink dress raced out, nearly tripping over Mary before barreling down the path. A tired-looking man in his forties raced after her as he called a quick thank-you over his shoulder. Moments later, two more parents emerged, each with a toddler in their arms. They were followed by Deborah Taylor, who was chatting pleasantly with them. As soon as she saw Mary, her face fell.

"Say bye-bye to Miss Deborah," one of the moms was saying to her little boy, but he was much more interested in a plastic truck gripped in his hands than in pleasantries.

"Bye-bye, Walter," Deborah said to the little boy, reaching out to tousle his hair.

"Thanks, Deborah, and we'll see you tomorrow," the other mom said as the four headed down the path toward the cars parked at the curb.

Deborah stood in the doorway of her home, a defeated slump to her shoulders. "I see you're not giving up," she said in a downcast voice. "So I suppose you're here to turn me down."

"Not at all," Mary said easily. She was fairly certain she knew why Deborah was so anxious and hoped to be as reassuring as possible.

Deborah cocked her head, her shoulders suddenly not quite as slumped. "You're the social worker they sent to investigate me, aren't you?" she asked.

Mary shook her head. "No, I own a mystery bookshop in town," she said. "I have nothing to do with your business venture."

"I thought —" Deborah began, and she shook her head, as though ridding it of her earlier misconceptions. "Well, you must have thought me the rudest person in the world," she said. "Come in so I can explain myself. And then you can tell me why you're really here."

And just like that, Mary was ushered into David's old house and led to the kitchen, where she was served a cup of tea. After setting out honey and milk, Deborah sat down across from her.

"So you're starting a day care," Mary said.

Deborah nodded. "Last spring, my daughter moved from Ivy Bay to California for her husband's job," she began. "And I was so sad to see my grandbabies move across the country that my husband suggested I find a way to work with kids. Not that they could replace my grandbabies, of course," she said, as Mary nodded. "But because I love children so much. So I decided to start my own day care right here at home."

"What a good idea," Mary said, taking a sip of tea. She glanced around at the cozy kitchen painted a soft yellow. There was a childproof gate at the doorway. Through the glass doors on the pantry, she could see stacks of animal crackers and cheese cracker boxes, as well as a shelf of economy-sized apple juice bottles.

"Yes, but I got ahead of myself," Deborah said, turning her teacup around in her hands as she spoke. "I started telling people what I was planning to do before I looked into the process of getting a license."

Mary could guess what happened next.

"So to make a long story short, I made promises to parents about when I could start the school before I realized how long it was going to take to get approved to have a school in my home," she said.

"It must have been very stressful to know that people were counting on you," Mary said sympathetically.

"Yes, they really were," Deborah said. "And I'd been through all the hoops, and I knew the house was ready. And I was certified. It was just a question of waiting for the license to arrive. So it wasn't putting the children in danger to start the day care a bit early."

"It just put your day care in danger if someone from the licensing bureau found out you opened before you were official," Mary said.

"Exactly," Deborah said with a sigh. "And when you showed up at my door on the very first day I opened the day care, I was sure you were someone from social services who'd heard what I was doing and was out to catch me in the act. I kept thinking that if I could put you off the trail by making sure you didn't come in, that maybe I'd buy a bit more time." She smiled sheepishly. "I'm sorry I was so rude trying to get rid of you like that."

It all made sense, and knowing for sure that this was the cause of Deborah's strange attitude was a huge relief. Mary was glad to know that this friendly woman wasn't harboring secrets about David.

"I hope you can forgive me," Deborah said.

Mary laughed. "I completely understand now that I know the whole story," she said. "Consider it water under the bridge."

"Thank you for being so gracious," Deborah said. "And now, tell me the real reason you came to my door."

"A good friend's ancestor lived here," Mary said, deciding to keep it brief. "My friend thinks the ancestor may have left something here, something that might shed some light on some things he did back in the 1920s."

"It sounds intriguing," Deborah said. "And I'd like to help you, particularly after almost slamming the door in your face last week. But I'm afraid that last year, we did major renovations on the house, gutting it almost completely. If any evidence was left here, it must have been destroyed."

Disappointment pressed on Mary's chest. She had a gut feeling that David's mother had known more than her family knew about what had happened to David. Even if he had been a thief, he couldn't have left his mother without any clue about his whereabouts. But now any chance of finding her old journal or a telegram from David was lost in a pile of debris taken to the town dump months ago.

"Well, thank you anyway," Mary said,

standing up, trying not to show how discouraged she felt by this development.

"Wait," Deborah said, new vivacity in her voice. "We didn't renovate the basement. It's possible that there's something down there."

"Sure, it's possible," Mary said.

"And there are so many old boxes down there that I'm not sure we've ever gone through them all."

Mary could feel her excitement start to build. There was actually a very good chance that David's mother would have hidden anything related to her son in the basement. "Do you think I might take a look?" she asked Deborah.

"Of course," Deborah said, leading the way back to the kitchen. "Let's go." She led the way down the narrow staircase to the basement below, turning on the light as she reached the bottom. Light spilled across the low-ceilinged space. It had cement floors, brick walls, and boxes piled against all the walls, except the one in the back where there stood a washer and dryer and a rack for air-drying clothes. "Let's start looking," Deborah said, rolling up the sleeves of her shirt.

At first, Mary felt uncomfortable poking around Deborah's home, but Deborah herself was so enthusiastic, moving boxes and checking behind pipes, that Mary soon lost her reserve and started hunting for clues in earnest.

But a half hour later, all they had turned up were a bunch of dust balls and a few spiders.

"I do need to do some cleaning down here," Deborah said, wiping a cobweb off her face.

"I haven't cleaned my basement in a while either," Mary commiserated. "Somehow, when I have time for housecleaning, it always falls to the last priority."

Above them a door opened and heavy footsteps sounded.

"Oh, that's Don," Deborah said. "Let me go up and tell him what we're doing."

"Do you mind if I keep looking?" Mary asked. She hated the thought of leaving now, after she'd waited so long to get here. They still hadn't looked in the small back room of the basement, but Deborah had to be tired after a long day of caring for kids and eager to get started on dinner.

"No, not at all," Deborah said. "We eat late, and there's still that back room to investigate. You get started there, and I'll be back down in a few minutes. Don always likes to relax with the paper when he gets home, anyway."

"If you're sure, that would be great," Mary said, relieved she could continue her search.

"I'm sure," Deborah said, starting up the stairs.

The back room of the basement was dimly lit, and the old floor was uneven. A few stones were loose in the wall, and there was just one pile of boxes labeled Kids' Artwork. Mary checked the loose stones to see if anything was hidden behind them and then took the small step stool Deborah had taken out and patted down every inch of the ceiling to see if anything had been tucked in over one of the low beams. But there was nothing there, save for an offended spider who raced off into a crack in the wall.

It looked like this might turn out to be a dead end. But there was one last place: behind the boxes. Mary carefully stacked them against a different wall, then looked at the newly empty space. The floor was even, and there were no loose stones. Mary moved the step stool under this last patch of ceiling and began feeling around. The first section of beam was empty, but as soon as she reached up to the second one, her fingers brushed on something. Mary stood on tiptoe, trying to see what was there, but then almost toppled off the stool.

Reminding herself that a broken hip would help no one, she regained her balance and felt carefully above her head. It seemed to be a pile of papers, and Mary carefully slid them off the beam. She was worried they'd fly across the room once she freed them, but it turned out they were bound by a string. Mary sat on the step stool and when she saw what she held in her hand, she gasped.

"Strike gold?" Deborah asked, walking into the back room.

Mary was so engrossed in her discovery that she hadn't heard her come in. "I did," she said, looking up at Deborah, a grin spreading across her face.

"What is it?" Deborah asked eagerly.

"Letters," Mary said, holding up the precious packet. Deborah bent over to look at the faded envelopes, all addressed to Mrs. Sarah Woodrow, all without a return address. But Mary had a hunch she knew exactly who had sent these letters.

"I'm so glad," Deborah said, her face alight with pleasure.

"Thank you," Mary said, her heart filled with gratitude for this kind woman who had opened her home to Mary. "I can't tell you what this will mean to my friend."

"I'm so happy to hear it," Deborah said.

They walked up the steps of the cellar, Mary clutching the letters in one hand and brushing dust off her sweater with the other. She had definitely gotten dirty, but it was more than worth it. This packet of letters might hold the key they'd been looking for: the key to finding the ring.

She thanked Deborah again and then stepped out into the cool of twilight, filled with excitement about the papers in her hand, hoping that they might hold all the answers they were looking for.

TWENTY-THREE

Mary was late to meet her family for dinner, so there was no time to call Henry. She hurried home and rushed into the house, where she found everyone just sitting down to eat. She hurried over, full of apologies that were quickly brushed off. Everyone seemed in high spirits, though when Mary smiled at Emma, she averted her eyes, giving Mary a pang of sadness.

"We're having a seafood feast," Lizzie said.

"We went by Sam's Seafood and got lobster and clams," Betty added. "And I whipped up a batch of coleslaw."

"Perfect," Mary said. "I worked up quite an appetite today."

"Busy day at the store?" Lizzie asked after grace had been said. Steaming platters of clams and lobster began to make their way around the table, as well as Betty's savory coleslaw.

"Actually, I was doing a bit of sleuthing

this afternoon," she said, still tingling with delight at what she had uncovered. Lizzie and Betty knew a bit about her search into David's past, and she quickly reviewed the outline of the story for Emma, who tried but failed to mask her interest.

"So what did you find today?" Lizzie asked, her eyes dancing with pleasure as she saw Emma lean forward, eager to hear as well.

Mary piled food on her plate and began to tell them about the discovery of the letters, making the summary as dramatic as possible for her grandchildren, both of whom were drawn into the story.

"Grandma, will you tie my bib?" Luke asked, handing her the plastic bib with a large tap-dancing lobster printed on it.

"It would be my pleasure," Mary said, securing it around his neck and then tying on her own. With the spray that came from cracking open the lobster, not to mention the butter dip, Sam's Seafood always included bibs with its lobster.

"Can I pass you some lemonade?" Lizzie asked Mary, holding up a big pitcher, the scent of fresh lemons wafting into the air.

"Yes, and let me get you the clams," Mary said, reaching for the large platter of hot clams.

"Grandma, what happened next?" Emma asked impatiently.

It was the first time her granddaughter had spoken to her without prompting or asked a direct question in days, and Mary's heart leapt with joy.

"Of course, darling, where was I?" Mary asked.

"You just got into the basement," Luke said. His face was already half covered in a sheen of butter.

"Right," Mary said. She finished the story with as much flair as she could.

"So what's in the letters?" Betty asked. Mary was amused at how interested her sister was in the find, after all her earlier skepticism.

"I don't know yet," Mary said, breaking a lobster claw with the nutcracker.

"You didn't even peek?" Lizzie asked. She was trying to wipe some of the butter off Luke.

"I thought I should wait to open them with Henry," Mary said.

"Of course, that's the right thing to do," Lizzie agreed, while Betty nodded.

Emma sat back, and to Mary's dismay, the mask of coldness reappeared on her face.

"I'll tell you all as soon as I know," Mary

said, but Emma didn't look up, and Mary sighed softly to herself.

"Does Henry know you've found the letters?" Lizzie asked.

"No," Mary said, and some of her excitement rekindled at the thought of his face when he found out. "He is leading an evening boating trip and won't be back until eight or so."

"Why don't you go and surprise him with them?" Betty asked.

"Oh, that's a good idea," Lizzie agreed.

Mary had to admit it was an appealing idea. She herself was eager to see what the letters might reveal, and waiting until tomorrow would be hard. "You wouldn't mind if I went out tonight?" she asked.

Lizzie shook her head. "The kids are tuckered out. Luke is going to have his bath and get right on into bed soon." Luke groaned, but his eyes had the hazy look of an exhausted child. "And I think Emma just wants to read tonight."

"And if you go, I have a chance at winning Scrabble tonight," Betty said with a smile. "At least until you get back."

"If you're sure, then I think I will," Mary said, imagining how fun it was going to be to show Henry the letters.

"We're sure," Betty said, checking her

watch. "And you should go now so you can catch him after work."

It was decided.

But Mary hesitated, taking one last stab with Emma. "Em, if you want, I can come by your room and show you the letters when I get back, if it's not too late."

There was a flicker of interest on Emma's face, but she snuffed it out. "That's okay, I'm tired too. I'm going to go to sleep pretty early."

Lizzie put a gentle hand on Mary's. "You might also want to leave the letters with Henry."

That was true, Mary realized. "Well, I'll tell you all about them tomorrow," Mary said to Emma, who nodded, her face cool.

Betty reached over and patted her hand in commiseration, but Mary still felt sad as she watched her granddaughter slide back into her hard shell. Clearly, it would take more for Emma to forgive her, but they were running out of time. Lizzie and her family would be going home to Boston soon. And Mary hated the thought of Emma leaving with this grudge still lodged in her heart.

Mary took a last sip of lemonade, kissed Luke, said good night to a once-again unresponsive Emma, and headed out to discover what secrets the letters held.

It was dark by the time Mary pulled in front
of Henry's house, which was right on the
bay. Steps built into the gently sloping dune
led from Henry's cozy home to a small
dock. Waves were lapping softly on the shore
and a cool, salty breeze was blowing as
Mary walked to the house, the letters
clutched in her hand, then rang the bell.
The door was made of thick wood with
heavy panes of glass on top, and as Mary
knocked, she couldn't help noticing that the
glass could use a good cleaning. Being so
close to the water meant salt and sand
buildup, and Mary and Betty had to clean
their windows once a week. She didn't think
Henry was very likely to do that.

Henry glanced through the cloudy window
and smiled when he saw who it was.

"Mary, hello," he said, opening the door
and ushering her in. The large living room
had a maroon sectional sofa, matching love
seat, and a wall of windows looking out on
the water. The walls were decorated with
paintings of the Cape done by local artists,
and there was a fireplace against the back
wall. Mary knew that Misty, Henry's wife,
had taken great pleasure in decorating their
home, and Henry had left it just as she had

created it, with a few small touches added here and there, like the leather recliner set in front of the flat-screen TV.

"How are you this evening?" Henry asked. Then he stopped and frowned. "Is everything okay?"

"More than okay," Mary said, bubbling over. "Wait till you see what I have."

Henry smiled and gestured for her to sit, which she did, settling into the love seat. "I'm ready," he said, spreading his arms open wide.

"This afternoon I paid another visit to 43 Cook Street," Mary began.

Henry raised his eyebrows. "And you weren't thrown out again?"

Mary quickly filled him in on Deborah Taylor's day care.

By the end of the story, Henry was laughing. "That explains it," he said. "I knew it had to be something like that. You're the most likable person I know, so there had to be some other reason for her rudeness. And now we know what it was."

Mary flushed at Henry's kind words.

"So you finally got into the house," Henry said intently. "And so I'm guessing what brings you here now is that you found something."

In response, Mary took out the packet of

letters, still bound with the old string, and passed them to Henry. He took them carefully, a look of wonder coming over his face as he looked at them. Then he looked up at Mary, his eyes shining. "You really think these could be from David?" he asked softly.

"Only one way to find out," Mary said. But she knew in her bones that they were.

Henry carefully untied the knotted string, his thick fingers nimble after years of doing knots for boating. When it was free, he set it carefully on the oak coffee table. Then he picked up the top letter, a frown coming across his features.

The letter was sealed.

"My great-grandmother never read this," he said.

Mary gently sifted through the four other letters. They were all unopened.

"Why do you think she never read them?" Henry asked, puzzled.

Mary shook her head. "I can only guess that she didn't want to know what the sender had to say," she said. "But she saved them, so maybe she thought one day she'd change her mind."

"And since she didn't, I think we get to be the first readers," Henry said. Mary could see in his face that he, like she, was hopeful that the letters were indeed from David.

A thought suddenly occurred to Mary. "Do you think we should wait and open these with Annie?"

Henry paused to consider this, then shook his head. "What if the content is upsetting?" he asked. "Annie doesn't need any more disappointments, not when this is a time she should be happy planning her daughter's wedding." Henry's voice was protective. "Of course, I'll show them to her regardless. But if it is bad news, I think it's better if I can cushion it for her."

The words made sense to Mary, who was touched by Henry's thoughtfulness toward his cousin. "All right, then let's see what they say," she said, eager to learn what David had wanted to say to his mother.

"How should we do this?" Henry asked Mary, looking overwhelmed by all the possibility he held in his hands.

"I think chronologically," Mary said.

Henry looked at the postmarks, which were from places as close as Pennsylvania and as far as San Francisco, and discerned that the earlier letters were on the bottom of the packet. With trembling fingers, he selected the first envelope, pulled out the thin sheet of paper, and unfolded it with great care. Then he gestured to Mary to move closer so she could read it too.

The first thing she looked at was the signature at the bottom. Sure enough, it was from David.

Henry had seen it too, and he turned to Mary, grinning. "It's him," he said. "I can't believe you found these." He reached over and squeezed her arm. "Thank you."

"Never mind thanks," Mary said buoyantly. "Let's see what he has to say!"

The letter began with memories: the Fourth of July church picnic when he had lost his first tooth and Christmas Eve services at the church. David was obviously homesick for Ivy Bay and his family.

Henry was reading ahead, and he burst out laughing.

"What?" Mary asked.

Henry pointed to a passage at the bottom of the letter. "David mentions hiding in his sister's closet and jumping out and scaring her after she'd turned out the lights. I did the same thing to my sister, and I'm not sure she's ever forgiven me."

Mary laughed, amused at the thought of Henry doing such a thing, though easily able to imagine it having known what a mischievous boy he was.

The letter closed with an address in

Virginia where David said he'd be for the next few months, and a line that puzzled Mary: *I hope by now you have heard from Reverend Montgomery.*

What could that mean? Had he left some kind of message with the reverend for his mother? And if so, had the reverend passed it on? And then another thought occurred to Mary. Was it possible that, at the last minute, David had left the money and the ring with the pastor? If that had been the case, it would certainly explain why Reverend Allen had been so secretive about his church records.

The next letter began with David saying he had not heard from his mother, but that he hoped she would write soon. Mary and Henry exchanged a look, and Mary felt a pang of sadness for David, who had not heard from his mother again, despite his hopes.

This letter contained more memories, all fondly told, and the news that David would be moving out west but would be in touch with his new address when he had it. There was also a similar mention of the reverend.

The third letter was dated a few months later and contained just a few lines, starting with David's address in California and ending with another mention of the reverend that further piqued Mary's curiosity:

By now, I am confident you will have gotten the news from Reverend Montgomery, and I eagerly await your response.

"What do you suppose that means?" Henry asked.

"Maybe there's a clue in the next letter," Mary said. With a pang, she realized the envelope in Henry's hand was the final letter.

Henry unfolded the last paper, and they both leaned in to read it.

My dear mother,

This shall be my last letter, as I fear you have not forgiven me as I had hoped, and I do not want to burden you as I so often have. By now, I hope you know that I confessed my final crime, the damage I did with my own two hands and no other, and that my conscience is clean. I hid the money and ring, cleaning my hands of the past, and left a message for the one person who can make my wrong a right. I know he will do this and return the money and ring where they belong.

Know that God guides me and comforts me; with Him, I am never alone. Pray for me, as I will pray for you.

Your son,
David

Mary could feel her heart thumping in her chest as she finished reading. This was more than she had even hoped for!

"So he really did leave the money and the ring behind," Henry said in disbelief. "And he confessed to his crime. He wanted to be absolved."

"That must have been why he went to the church right before he left," Mary agreed. "To confess." Her thoughts were racing.

Henry nodded. "But then what happened to that person David trusted, the one he thought could make things right? Because we would know if someone he trusted had found the ring and money."

Mary thought back to all the clues they had discovered so far, going back to the map itself on the lighthouse wall. The map that had been drawn in haste. "David was in a hurry," Mary said, the thoughts forming as she spoke. "He was in a rush to get away. You can see that in the map, by how quickly it was drawn."

Henry nodded.

"So maybe the message he left wasn't enough for this person to figure things out," she said. "I suspect he means the map, that he drew that map to lead the one person he trusted to help find the money. But maybe that person never figured it out. Or hit a dead end, like we did."

"But why did David draw a map with a dead end?" Henry asked.

Mary rubbed her temples. "I still don't understand that," she admitted. "And I'm not sure how to figure it out."

"But you have another idea," Henry said, reading his old friend well.

"That person David left the map for . . . ," she said. "David could have left the money with his mother or left a clue for her," Mary said. "But he didn't. It's clear from the letter how much he cared about her, so I think he worried it might somehow implicate her in his crime. And, of course, it seems like she wasn't communicating with him at that point either."

"Makes sense," Henry said, leaning back and stretching a bit.

"So the person he left it for would have to be someone above suspicion," Mary said. "Someone who wouldn't get in trouble for recovering stolen funds or finding the ring, and someone who would know the just thing to do with those funds." Mary smiled. "And I think in his letters, David already told us who that person was." Something else clicked for Mary. "And we know a place he visited in his last hours in Ivy Bay."

Henry's eyes lit up with understanding.

"The pastor at his church," he said.

Mary nodded. "Exactly. Who else would you go to when things were desperate and no one else could help?"

Henry was nodding. "That's who I'd go to," he said. "That's for certain."

"I'd bet David felt the same," Mary said.

Henry rubbed his chin. "So David went, confessed, and told the reverend he left a map," he said. But then his brow furrowed. "Why not just give the reverend the ring and money right then?"

"That's just one of the things we need to find out," Mary said. "And I think the answer is in that Bible at First Congregational Church."

Henry's face fell. "But we've reached another dead end at First Congregational Church," he said. "It sounds like the pastor there plans to keep that Bible under lock and key."

It did seem that way, and it would help explain Reverend Allen's reluctance to show her the Bible. Clearly Reverend Montgomery hadn't kept the money, but if he had written what he knew of David in his Bible, that could be a reason Reverend Allen would be so protective of it.

Henry was looking at the clock on the mantel above the fireplace. "It's getting late," he said.

"Yes," Mary agreed. "I should get home."

They both stood up.

"I can't thank you enough for these letters," Henry said. "And I can't wait to share them with Annie."

Mary smiled at the thought. "We did find some good information," she said. "I think my next step is to finally get my hands on that Bible."

She could see Henry's frown of concern. "It sounds like that might be a tall order," he said.

"There has to be something more I can tell Reverend Allen, something that will persuade him to let me see that Bible," Mary said. But she didn't feel conviction in her own words. Reverend Allen had seemed very final in both his words and his actions. But Mary had to try.

Henry walked Mary to her car, then waited while she got in and put the key in the ignition. "You're okay on these back roads at night?" he asked her. She was touched by his concern.

"I'll take it slow," she said.

"Do that," he said, then stepped back and waved as Mary coasted down the drive.

As she stopped at the road, she glanced back at the ocean, which was shimmery in the moonlight. The sight of the water stretching out to the horizon calmed her as it always did, but as she signaled and turned her car on the road, her thoughts were jumping ahead. She would go to the library first. And then she would need a plan of action for her visit to First Congregational Church. These glimpses into David's life made her even more committed to finding out the truth, and if they were lucky, they just might fulfill his final wishes and get the money into just hands and the ring back to his family.

TWENTY-FOUR

Mary woke up still thinking about the letters and yesterday's discovery. She had realized another silver lining to the revelations in the letters. David had mentioned committing a crime, and it seemed clear he had committed it alone, which meant good news for Chief McArthur and his concerns about Cynthia's project. Mary decided to find him first thing and tell him.

Lizzie and the children were in the kitchen, eating cereal and planning the day, when she went downstairs. Mary smiled when she saw them.

"Good morning," she said.

Luke and Lizzie answered cheerfully, but Emma stared down at her cereal, silent.

Mary helped herself to some cereal and then sat down next to her granddaughter. "What are you up to today?" she asked.

Lizzie and Luke filled Mary in on their plans to build a huge sandcastle but Emma stayed quiet. She finished her cereal and rinsed her bowl, then headed out of the kitchen.

Mary followed. "Emma," she said, touching her granddaughter gently on the shoulder. Emma turned to look at Mary. "I'm sorry if I hurt your feelings about your story," Mary said. "I only wanted to help, and I feel terrible that I've upset you."

Emma wouldn't meet Mary's gaze. "It wasn't a good story, anyway," she said.

"Oh, but it was," Mary said quickly. "I loved it."

Emma shrugged, then started up the stairs. "It's no big deal," she said. "And I don't really want to talk about it, if you don't mind. I'm going to take a shower before we go."

Mary watched sadly as Emma headed up the stairs. Clearly, it was a big deal, but Mary didn't know what to say to convince her granddaughter of how good her writing was. She closed her eyes briefly. *God, please help me find the words to reach my granddaughter, and open her heart so she can hear them,* she prayed.

With one last glance toward the stairway, Mary headed outside. It was a cloudy day, and the air was wet. It was the kind of cold that sliced through thin layers. Mary was glad she'd worn her pink sweater with crocheted hearts. It was a thick, tightly knit wool that shielded her from the chill. But her face and ears were cold by the time she arrived in town.

As she walked down Main Street, Mary was pleased to see Lori Stone, the Realtor who had helped Mary buy her bookshop. She had her usual companion, her miniature schnauzer Bitsy, with her.

"Good morning, Mary," Lori said, catching sight of her. She was every inch the professional businesswoman, with her tailored blazer and olive-green skirt that fell at her midcalf. Every hair was in place, and Mary was suddenly aware of the way her sweater bagged in the elbows and her hair was blowing wild in the light breeze. She raised a hand to smooth it but then decided it was a lost cause on a windy day and bent down to pet Bitsy instead. The little dog wriggled happily at the attention.

"Are you going to the bookshop?" Lori asked.

"Yes, though I have a quick stop on the way," Mary said. "What brings you to town so early?"

"I wanted to get to the office a bit early to prepare for a morning meeting," Lori said.

"I hope it goes well," Mary said, straightening up.

Lori waved, then headed down the block as Mary caught sight of Chief McArthur walking out of the Black & White Diner. She hurried over to meet him.

"Morning," he said with a genuine smile. It was nice to see him so welcoming after their last few tense encounters. "How are you today, Mary?"

"Good, thanks," she said. "And I have an update for you, one that I think will make you happy."

Chief McArthur's smile froze. "About Ned?" he asked.

Mary nodded. "I found some old letters David wrote his mother," she said. "And in them, he refers to taking the money. Alone."

Chief McArthur let out a long breath. "Wow," he said after a moment. "That is a surprise. And quite a relief." He was silent again, clearly thinking about what this meant.

"I knew you'd be happy to hear it," Mary said. "This means Cynthia's project is safe. And that beautiful old building can be rightly named a historic landmark."

Chief McArthur smiled. "She will be so proud when that day comes," he said. "Thank you for letting me know. I'd really been concerned."

Mary was touched by his love for his sister. "I know," she said.

The chief tipped his hat and then headed toward the police station while Mary walked to the store.

It was a busy morning in the bookshop, and Mary and Rebecca took turns helping and ringing up customers. Just before lunch, the chimes rang and a familiar face came through the door.

"Hello, Connor," Mary said, walking up to the student, who was wearing an old pair of corduroy pants and a jacket with the elbows so worn they were almost translucent. Mary shook her head at the unusual clothing styles favored by students. Gus rubbed up against Connor's legs, and Connor reached down to scratch his head absently.

Connor ran a hand through his messy black curls. "I'm stepping up my research of David, so I'm spending more time here in Ivy Bay. I remembered you saying your store was right here in town, so I thought I'd check it out," he said, looking around and taking in the bookshelves, the inviting chairs for browsing, and the tables with displays of books. "And I'm glad I did. What a beautiful shop this is."

Mary felt a flush of pride at his words. "Thank you," she said. "It's definitely been a labor of love. But it was my dream, and I'm so glad it's here now."

He nodded. "I know about dreams," he said. "That's how I feel about my dissertation." The depth of feeling he had for his project was written all over his face as he spoke. Then he looked at Mary in a way that was almost cagey. "Now that we're speaking of it, have you found anything else out about David Woodrow?"

Mary had known he would ask at some point, and she'd been dreading it. While she'd normally be happy to tell him something about her latest discoveries, there was something in Connor's manner that didn't feel right to her. And it suddenly struck her as strange that he was in Ivy Bay so often these days. "Nothing solid," she said finally. It was true that she had learned some things, but the biggest parts of the mystery were still things she was merely guessing at, so her answer was honest.

Connor stared at her for a long moment, and Mary found herself becoming uncomfortable under his acute gaze. But then he seemed to shake it off again with a smile. "You have other customers, so don't let me keep you," he said in his usual friendly way.

"Do you want to look at any books?" Mary asked, relieved to have moved past David and wanting to be helpful in another way if she could.

Connor's face grew dark again. "Oh, I don't have the money for new books, but thank you," he said tightly.

Mary was embarrassed by his bluntness and by her own blunder. She had read his fashion choices as just that, choices, when in fact, he probably didn't have the money for new clothes. "I could recommend some titles if you want to get something out of the library," she said.

He shook his head. "I'll be okay soon," he said, and left the store.

Mary was chilled by the words. What did he mean, he'd be okay soon? Was Connor looking for more than answers for his dissertation? Could he be here looking for the money and the ring David had left behind?

A while later, things had slowed a bit, and Mary was getting ready to take her lunch break when the door to the shop opened. Lizzie walked in, wearing jeans and a fleece jacket, her hair up in a casual ponytail.

"I was hoping to catch you before you left," she said to Mary, after greeting Rebecca, who was ringing up a customer's purchase.

Mary felt the lift of joy that she always did when she saw her daughter. "What's up?" she asked.

"The kids and I were going to go to the diner for lunch, and we were hoping to steal you away for an hour or so to join us," she said. She leaned in and said more quietly, "It was Emma's idea to ask you to come along."

"I'd love to," Mary said, hoping that meant she had made some headway with her recalcitrant granddaughter. "Let me just get my purse."

"I'll meet you outside," Lizzie said. "Emma is watching Luke, but who knows what mischief he'll stumble upon."

"You hold down the fort, Gus," she said. Gus swished his tail back and forth across the floor in response.

Mary grabbed her purse and a Windbreaker she kept in the back room of the store for weather changes.

She met Lizzie on the sidewalk, and Luke came barreling toward her for a hug. Mary wrapped her arms around her grandson, who indeed seemed to have stumbled on some impishness as the knees of his brown corduroys were muddy. Emma stood off to the side, her arms folded across her chest.

Mary walked toward Emma.

"Thanks for including me," Mary said.

Emma nodded. "You have to eat too." It was a fair point, but whatever trace of goodwill had motivated her granddaughter to invite her to lunch seemed to have vanished. Still, Mary decided to count it as a step in the right direction.

"Shall we get going?" she asked Lizzie.

But her daughter was staring. Mary turned and her stomach clenched when she saw what Lizzie was looking at. Reverend Allen had just come out of the Tea Shoppe and seemed to be glaring at Mary from down the street. Mary assured herself it must be the sun making him squint, but she felt uncomfortable.

"Hello, Reverend Allen," she called.

But instead of replying, he turned abruptly and walked away.

"Mother, who is that man?" Lizzie asked in a low voice.

"Reverend Allen," Mary said. His snub felt extreme, and Mary watched as he walked away. Why was he being so hostile? It had to be about the money.

"The one from First Congregational Church, who doesn't want you to see the Bible?" Lizzie asked.

"Yes," Mary said.

"Mother, I don't like how he treated you," Lizzie said, her voice suddenly taking Mary back to the years when Lizzie had nightmares and needed to be reassured that there were no monsters under the bed.

"I don't think he meant any harm," Mary said comfortingly, though secretly the look had unsettled her as well.

Lizzie turned to her mother, the wind blowing wisps of hair out of her ponytail and around her face. "Promise me you'll be careful of him," she said pleadingly.

Mary nodded and promised that she would be careful. And this time, she also sent up a prayer to God, asking for His protection as she tried to do the right thing.

TWENTY-FIVE

That afternoon, Mary left the bookshop to make a quick run to the post office. It was a gloomy day, and Mary pulled her Windbreaker tight around her, keeping her head down to protect her face from the wind. She stood in line to get the supplies she needed, then greeted Cathy Smith, the postmistress, when she came up in line. Bob Hiller did the rounds through town, but Cathy was at the desk in the old building off Main Street every day.

"How are things at the shop?" Cathy asked as she opened up the stamp drawer. Cathy took pride in knowing all the Ivy Bay locals and kept close tabs on what everyone was up to.

"Business has been good, thanks," Mary said.

Cathy spread six sheets of stamps out. "Here are your choices," she said to Mary. "I'm partial to the roses myself."

Mary looked at the choices, and indeed the roses were lovely. "I'll take two sheets of them and a ten-pack of priority mail stamps."

"Coming right up," Cathy said, putting Mary's stamps in a small bag and ringing up her bill.

Mary was heading back to the bookshop when she heard someone call her name.

Mary looked up and was surprised to see Patrice from First Congregational Church walking toward her. She was wearing a fitted black trench coat, and her cheeks were pink from the wind.

"Hi," Mary said as she approached Patrice, who had just come out of Ivy Bay Bank & Trust. "I'm glad to run into you. I wanted to apologize for what happened at your church the other day." She ran a hand through her hair to try to smooth it, though the wind just tousled it the second she set it free.

Patrice looked surprised. "I think it's me who should apologize," she said. "I was shocked at how Reverend Allen spoke to you. I can promise you he is usually the kindest man. I've never seen him like that before, and I've known him for ten years."

Mary could see that Patrice was genuinely distressed by the pastor's curt manner with

Mary. "I suppose it was a sensitive matter," Mary said. "Though I'm confused as to what upset him so much."

Patrice's brow was furrowed. "As am I," she said. "I think I told you how strongly he felt about that Bible being available. I can't understand what changed. And he wouldn't speak of it after you left. He was quite short with me when I asked if anything was wrong."

It was obvious that this had hurt Patrice's feelings, and Mary felt terrible that she had put Patrice in that position. "I'm sorry," she said, reaching out and touching Patrice's arm. "I think maybe I should have told you when we first met that the pastor didn't want me looking at the Bible."

"But that's the thing," Patrice said, stepping to the side as two little boys rode shakily by on two-wheel bikes. Their father ran next to them, reaching out his arms like a giant bird, ready to catch them if they fell. "That Bible does not belong to Reverend Allen, and normally he'd be the first to say so. It belongs to our church, and it's public property." She looked straight on at Mary. "Reverend Allen has no right to keep you from looking at that Bible."

Mary felt a surge of hope at Patrice's words. "I really would love to see it," she said. "I think it has information that will help my friend."

A determined look came over Patrice's face. "I know for a fact that right now Reverend Allen is doing hospital visits. Let's go over to the church and get you a good look at it."

"Are you sure?" Mary asked. She was thrilled at the idea but wanted to be certain that Patrice didn't put herself in another uncomfortable situation by helping Mary.

"I'm sure," Patrice said. "You have every right to see it, and the pastor knows that, even if he can't see it just now."

She set off down the sidewalk, Mary following, impressed by the conviction Patrice was showing.

"I'm parked in the town lot," Patrice said. "Shall I just meet you over at the church?"

"Sounds good," Mary said, heading over to her own car and bubbling with excitement over finally getting to look at the Bible. She made a quick call home to let her family know she'd be running late and then started up her car.

Five minutes later, she pulled into the parking lot of First Congregational Church. Patrice had arrived before her and was already walking up the steps of the church and opening the door. Mary hurried to catch up with her.

"Follow me," Patrice said, striding through the utility room and then down the hall, turning on lights as she went.

As Mary walked through the utility room, she glanced out the window at the graveyard, which looked particularly gloomy with the backdrop of gray clouds.

"I'll just get this light," Patrice said as she flicked a light switch on the hall wall that lit up the church office.

Mary walked into the office, where Patrice was crouching down by the shelf that housed papers from over a century before.

"*Hmm,* it's not here," she said.

Mary felt a thud of disappointment in her stomach.

"We'll just have to find it," Patrice said firmly.

Mary's spirits were instantly restored. "When I was here last, he put it in his desk drawer," she said. "The top one."

Patrice opened that drawer and then the others, but there was no Bible. "Perhaps it's somewhere on his desk," she said. "I don't want to poke through his private papers, but I think I can lift a few things without violating anything."

But the Bible was not on the desk either.

Once again Mary's hopes began to

dwindle, but she was determined not to leave without seeing the Bible. "Is there any other storage space?" she asked. "Other file cabinets or closets?"

Patrice's eyes lit up. "As a matter of fact, there is," she said, heading out into the hall. "I wouldn't have thought of it because it's rarely used, but there's a closet right out here."

She already had the door of the hall closet open when Mary came out. Mary peered over her shoulder as Patrice began going through the black metal file cabinet that was wedged into the small space.

"I'd wondered where these had gotten to," she said, pulling out a big bag of plastic cups. "We all blamed poor Isabel Cane for losing track of them."

"Let me put them in the kitchen for you," Mary said, taking them.

"Thanks," Patrice said, her voice muffled as she dug deeper into the back of one of the drawers.

Mary walked into the kitchen. Out the kitchen window, she saw that the clouds were now hanging low in the sky and a thick fog was moving in. There was a damp eerie feeling to the day. She hurried back to Patrice.

"One more drawer," Patrice reported. And

301

a moment later, she gave a happy cry. "Here we go," she said, emerging with dust in her hair and the Bible in her hand.

"Wonderful," Mary said, thrilled to see the old book with its cracked leather cover.

"Let's see, why don't you sit in the sanctuary?" Patrice said, leading the way.

The sanctuary was dark, but Patrice flipped on the light switch on the wall outside, and a soft glow enveloped the room. Patrice handed Mary the Bible. "Take all the time you need with it."

"Thank you," Mary said, her pulse quickening as she wrapped her fingers around the old book that she was sure held something about David.

"I'm going to straighten a few things in the kitchen area," Patrice said. "Make yourself at home."

"Thank you," Mary said gratefully.

Patrice smiled, and then she headed out.

Mary sat down on a pew toward the middle of the room and then, finally, she opened Reverend Montgomery's Bible.

It was fairly bursting with papers, but after examining the first few, Mary could see that Patrice was right about them being more or less in chronological order. She realized how lucky it was that the pastor had dated each note; without that, she'd be lost. As it was, it was slow going. The pastor filled every millimeter with his small block letters, and he tended to use first initials when referring to congregants who came to him with private matters. Which of course made sense, but made sleuthing a lot harder. There were a number of slips of paper containing notes about a conversation with D, but after reading each one, Mary could see she had yet to find one that referred to David.

One thing that helped was that Mary knew the confession had taken place days before David fled. She focused on the visits in January 1925.

"How are you doing in here?"

Mary jumped at the sound of Patrice's voice.

Patrice laughed. "You're quite involved, I see," she said.

Mary smiled. "Yes, this Bible is really a storehouse of information."

"Reverend Montgomery didn't trust anything to his memory, that's for sure," Patrice agreed. She ran a hand through her hair, which, unlike Mary's, was still neat despite the outside wind. "Would you mind terribly if I left? It's later than I thought, and I need to get home and start dinner."

"Of course not," Mary said, gathering up

the little papers to put back in the Bible, and trying not to show her disappointment.

"No, you can stay," Patrice said quickly. "I just meant that I need to go, but you're free to stay as long as you like."

"You don't mind?" Mary asked hopefully.

Patrice smiled. "You've waited long enough to look at that Bible," she said. "The last thing I want to do is ask you to stop now."

"Thank you," Mary said. "I must admit I'd like to keep at it. I feel sure there's going to be something helpful here."

"Stay as long as you want," Patrice said. "Just turn off the lights and close up when you go. I'll come back in a bit to lock up."

"Great," Mary said as Patrice turned to leave.

But then she paused at the door. "And remember, the light switch for the sanctuary is out here."

"Got it," Mary said.

Patrice left, and Mary could hear her muffled footsteps grow quieter as she walked down the hall through the utility room, then the dull click of the latch of the front door of the church. For a moment, Mary looked at the shadows that were thrown across the wall and she shivered. There was something just a bit scary about being alone in an old building next to a graveyard on a foggy day. But then Mary laughed at how her imagination was running away with her. It was only in her beloved mystery novels that such a setting meant danger.

Mary went back to the Bible, which had flipped to the end. On the very back pages, Mary was shocked to see a brown stain that had soaked through, rendering several of the notes illegible and damaging the thin pages of the Bible. She investigated carefully and noticed that the stain spread through about an eighth of the whole book. When she brought it to her nose, she could smell coffee coming up from the pages. She paused, thinking about it for a moment, but then realized she needed to get back to her research.

She flipped back to her earlier place and began looking at each paper once more and going through several notes from October 1924 that revolved around a land dispute between congregants. It was hard not to get caught up in that story, and as she plucked up a folded sheet dated January 7, 1925, she couldn't help thinking that this Bible would be a great place for a writer to browse for story ideas. There were tons of drama galore in this old book.

The small paper she had unfolded was covered on both the front and back, and Mary noticed that the back was dated a week later. Curious, she took a look, and her breath caught in her throat when she saw that this paper were about a D.

D came in today, seemed very agitated. Said he needed to confess to a crime but could not say what, only that it had hurt people and he was unable to live with himself for it. He told me that his sin was great and he needed to ask God's forgiveness. We prayed together, asking for God's mercy. This seemed to calm him. As he left, he said he would be back and that I would know more when the truth comes out. But the police showed up moments later, searching for him, and I have not seen him since.

Mary's heart was thumping, and her hands were shaky. This was it! This was David's confession. She turned the paper over eagerly to see what had come next.

Worried I made a great mistake absolving D. His crime is much worse than I had imagined.

Mary was vaguely aware of the sound of the front door of the church opening and assumed Patrice had come back to check on her. But her attention was locked onto the paper in her hands. Why did Reverend

Montgomery have such a strong reaction? Her fear was that the person David had stolen money from was somehow especially vulnerable, and Mary's stomach tightened at the thought.

A terrible fire has been set, causing the death of two people, and I fear D is the arsonist because —

All of a sudden, the light in the sanctuary went out, and Mary was sitting in pitch black.

Twenty-Six

Mary cried out in alarm but heard nothing in response. Now her heart was pounding in fear. She stood up, trying desperately to make her way to the aisle. And that was when she heard the footsteps.

Her heart was in her throat as she felt her way to the wall, the Bible forgotten behind her. She stumbled slightly over the edge of the pew, but once she was at the wall, she was able to feel her way to the door. She could hear her breath coming in short gasps and beyond that, the footsteps.

Once she was in the hall, there was faint light from the windows in the utility room, though Mary still kept a hand on the wall to stay oriented, as well as to find the light switch. Behind her the footsteps were louder, and Mary made the split-second decision to run toward the front door.

The room was heavily shadowed but light enough that she could move through quickly without fear of tripping over anything. Mary was panting as she reached the front door of the church, which she wrenched open, only to see a surprised Patrice walking up the steps.

"Mary, are you okay?" she asked, her eyes widening in concern.

"I was reading the Bible, and the lights went out," Mary said, gasping a bit as she spoke.

Patrice frowned. "You mean there was some kind of power outage?"

"I heard footsteps," Mary said. Patrice's presence was comforting, but Mary's fear was still smoldering in her chest, making it hard to explain what had happened. Patrice's eyebrows were scrunched together as she waited for Mary to continue. "After the lights went out, I heard footsteps," Mary clarified. "I think someone was there, someone who turned off the light."

"Who would do such a thing?" Patrice asked, upset by the thought.

Mary had a sobering hunch, but she didn't want to make accusations.

"Let's take a look," Patrice said, striding past Mary into the church and flicking on the lights as she headed toward the back office. The dark building was quickly lit up, and as Mary followed behind, the place that had seemed so ominous was once again cozy and peaceful, making Mary wonder if her hearing had somehow played a trick on her, and she had imagined the sound of footsteps. But then how had the lights gone out?

"There was no power outage or blown fuse," Patrice said after she turned on the light in the office. "I don't understand what happened."

Mary was still in the utility room, and a movement outside the window caught her eye. "Do you know anyone who drives a black Impala?" Mary asked, as she watched the car that matched her own, save for the color, drive out of the back parking lot of the church.

"Why, yes," Patrice said, coming into the utility room and looking puzzled. "That's the car Reverend Allen drives."

That night, after a late dinner with her family, Mary read Luke his bedtime story, then headed into her bedroom and closed the door. She held her purse as she walked toward the rocking chair by the window, but a soft yowl outside her door stopped her before she reached the chair. She smiled as she went back to let Gus in. He twined around her ankles, waited for her to sit, and then settled in her lap with an air of great entitlement. Mary rubbed his ears for a moment before reaching into her purse for the paper she had put into it hours ago.

The paper from Reverend Montgomery's Bible.

At first, she had felt too shaky from her scare to think about what she had read, and back home, she had focused on her family and the talk of what Lizzie and the kids wanted to do in the last days of their visit. But as she had finished up Luke's bedtime story, her thoughts had returned to David and her dismay at what Reverend Montgomery seemed to have thought David had done. She hoped fervently that the pastor was mistaken, because arson that resulted in the death of two people — well, that was a loathsome crime.

Her stomach was in knots as she carefully unfolded the old piece of paper that felt slight in her hands. Then she began to read.

Worried I made a great mistake absolving D. His crime is much worse than I had imagined. A terrible fire has been set, causing the death of two people, and I fear D is the arsonist because of his reference to a crime that had hurt people. Had I known of the fire, I never would have absolved him so quickly. I am convinced D committed this crime, and those deaths weigh on me. I will not return to the lighthouse, and I will pray for God's forgiveness.

Mary sat back, a nauseous feeling creeping into her belly. Was it truly possible that David had set this fire? If so, Mary was not looking forward to telling Henry. Theft was bad enough, but to cause the death of two people? The thought made her heart ache, especially when she thought of Henry, his face alive with joy as he read David's letters. And Annie — this was not the kind of news they were looking to share with Annie.

Gus butted her hand gently with his silky head, and Mary set aside Reverend Montgomery's note so that she could pet him. As she ran her hand across his fur, she decided that it didn't make sense to tell Henry about this just yet. It was entirely possible that Reverend Montgomery was wrong, and until she had more evidence, it didn't seem right to worry Henry. But the sick feeling stayed in her stomach.

There was a knock at her door, and Lizzie poked her head in. "Want to join me for a cup of tea?" she asked.

"I'd love to," Mary said, happy to put aside her disturbing thoughts and enjoy some time with her daughter. She set Gus on the chair and followed Lizzie down to the kitchen, where they saw Emma filling a plate with fruit.

"Still hungry?" Lizzie asked Emma, who had her back to Lizzie and Mary.

"I'm going to work on my story, and I wanted a snack," Emma said cheerfully.

"That's good brain food," Lizzie said.

Emma turned, plate in hand, a smile on her face. But as soon as she saw Mary, the smile slid from her lips and her face hardened.

"I hope your writing is going well," Mary said.

Emma made a huffy sound as she sailed out of the room. Mary felt her shoulders slump at yet another brush-off from her granddaughter. When she looked up, she saw Lizzie smiling sympathetically.

"She's twelve," Lizzie said, as though it explained everything. And perhaps it did. "She's at that place where part of her wants to be a kid and part of her wants to be a grown-up, and those parts don't always work together so neatly."

Mary thought of Emma acting so mature in some moments, then suddenly acting like a child again in others.

"Remember when I was twelve, I gave Dad the silent treatment for a week after he laughed at my new perm?" Lizzie said as she put on the kettle for tea.

Mary laughed. She hadn't thought of that in years. "It wasn't your best look," she said. "But you were very sensitive about it."

Lizzie laughed. "I was," she said. And then she turned serious eyes to her mother. "Just like Emma is sensitive about her writing. You did the right thing being honest with her, and somewhere inside that twelve-year-old mind, she knows it."

"I just wish I knew the right thing to do to get her to forgive me," Mary said, reaching into the cabinet for matching blue teacups with roses on them.

"I'm not sure there's anything you can do. She might just need more time."

"But do you think she'll forgive me before you leave for home?" Mary asked.

Lizzie looked slightly anxious. "I hope so," she said.

Sunday was swallowed up by church and a picnic following, where a gang of kids ran around playing hide-and-seek while the adults feasted on barbeque from the large grills manned by Pastor Miles, Henry, and several other men from the congregation. After everyone had eaten their fill, a spirited game of softball was played. Mary and her family returned home late in the day, tired but happy. By the time the kids were bathed, Gus was fed, and Luke was in bed, Mary was so exhausted she fell into bed, all thoughts of the mystery wiped out by the need for a good night's sleep.

The next morning, Mary got out of bed as the sun was just peeking up over the horizon, spilling golden rays into the big windows that faced an ocean. The beauty of the day slowed her thinking, and as Mary washed up, she prayed. *Lord, please guide me in this search, leading me in Your wisdom. I want to do all I can to help Henry, but it's You I lean on to show me the way.* As always, the prayer soothed her, and in that calm state, she allowed her thoughts to return to the note from Reverend Montgomery.

As she ran through all she had learned, she realized that she couldn't swallow this new information. It simply didn't fit with the rest of what she had learned about David, whose heartfelt letters to his mother made no mention of such a crime and who had wanted to make right the crimes he had committed, like the return of the ring. The ring! With a start, Mary realized something else.

She retrieved the paper from Reverend Montgomery and smoothed it out to read again. Sure enough, it was just as she had remembered: The words that convinced Reverend Montgomery that David had set the fire were, "his reference to a crime that had hurt people." What if David hadn't been referring to the fire at all? What if he had been referring to the ring?

Mary was invigorated by the thought. It made sense. David's theft of the ring had hurt people, the people who meant the most to him: his family. And he would want forgiveness for that more than anything.

Her family was still asleep, so she grabbed a piece of toast for the road and settled in behind the wheel. A few minutes later, she was pulling into the lot of the public library.

"Hi, Mary," Victoria said. She was standing at the front of the building, keys in hand. "You're here early today."

"I am," Mary agreed, walking up with a smile.

"And you drove," Victoria observed as she unlocked the door and stepped inside the cool building.

"I have to make a stop outside town," Mary said, following Victoria. "But there's something I need to check first."

"In the newspapers again?" Victoria asked.

"Yes," Mary said.

"When you go back there, would you

mind turning all the machines on?" Victoria asked. "That will free me up to get things set up here."

"I'd be happy to," Mary said, heading toward the microfilm drawers. Once she was there, she switched on each of the units, then waited impatiently for one to warm up. When it was ready, she scanned back to the middle of January, where she'd initially seen the article about the fire at the hardware store. She reread the article. She'd remembered correctly. There was no mention of arson, and no mention of any deaths. Mary moved the film back a few days, scanning the headlines, and stopped at the front page of the paper for January 11. A fire had broken out in an old warehouse the previous evening, and two workers had died. Police were investigating, but so far there were no suspects. There was no other mention of the fire or anyone ever being arrested for setting it.

Satisfied, Mary returned the film and headed out into the sunny day. She had the information she needed, and now she was ready for her next stop.

She headed back to Main Street, to where she'd parked her car, and noticed three very familiar figures coming out of the Black & White Diner.

"Liz, Emma, Luke!" she called, walking over happily.

Her daughter smiled as she came up and Luke hugged his grandmother, but Emma looked away.

"I'm headed to the lighthouse to do a bit of investigating about David," Mary said. She watched Emma and saw that she couldn't hide her interest at Mary's words. "There were some old papers there I'd like to look through. And I thought I'd take another look at the map." She took a deep breath. "Emma, would you like to come with me?"

She could see two conflicting emotions battle in her granddaughter's eyes as her curiosity fought with her desire to stay aloof.

Lizzie set a hand on her daughter's shoulder. "Go with your grandmother," she said quietly. Her voice was kind but firm.

"Do I have to?" Emma whined.

Lizzie looked calmly at Emma, until Emma's cheeks flushed. "Sorry, okay, yeah, I'll go, Grandma."

"Can I go too?" Luke asked, bouncing up and down.

"Not this time, buddy," Lizzie said with a smile. "You and I are going to see if we can find any more shells for your collection."

"And, Grandma, I can show you when

you get home," Luke said.

"Wonderful," Mary said, smiling her thanks at Lizzie. "The car's right over here," she said to Emma. Emma headed toward it, and Mary followed. "See you later," she called to Lizzie.

"Can we at least put on music?" Emma asked, once they were settled into the car.

"I don't have any CDs with me, but we can see what's on the radio," Mary said. She reached down and turned on the radio, which was set to a Christian station. "We Are Marching in the Light of God" was being sung by a choir. "I think this is the best I can do." She glanced back at Emma who shrugged, but her face was peaceful as she stared out the window.

Mary let the music and the beauty of the day wash over her as they drove. She rolled down her window to inhale the salty ocean smell as they drew close. As she pulled the car into the lighthouse parking lot, she heard Emma's intake of breath and turned to see her granddaughter's radiant smile.

"It's so pretty," Emma said.

Mary grinned. "It is," she said, stepping out of the car. The sun was warm on her face, and she said a quick, silent prayer, asking God to be with her and Emma in this moment, to help heal the rift between them.

When Emma got out of the car, she didn't say anything, just started for the lighthouse. But she couldn't keep the sour expression on her face when they walked up the steps to the lighthouse and Mary led her to the map.

"Wow," Emma said softly, her eyes taking in the old map.

For a moment, the two of them just stared at it. Then Emma raised a hand and traced a finger along it.

"Amazing to think it was here all this time, hidden under the paint," Mary said.

Emma nodded. "Can we go up to the top?" she asked after another minute of looking at the map.

"Absolutely," Mary said. She pointed up the stairs. "You lead the way."

Emma rushed up the stairs, and Mary heard her cry of delight when she reached the top. "It's amazing up here," she said, beaming as Mary came through the door.

Mary looked around, the majestic view taking her breath away even a second time. She walked in a slow circle, taking in the endless stretch of beach with the crashing waves of high tide. The water glistened as if jewels sparkled just below the surface. The grass and vegetation on the dunes blew in the breeze that danced off the water, refreshing Mary's warm cheeks. On the other side was a bird's-eye view of Ivy Bay, and that was what Emma was now looking at.

"Can you find our house?" Mary asked.

Emma considered, then pointed to the dollhouse-sized home near the bay, just outside town. Mary couldn't resist wrapping an arm around Emma and squeezing her.

Emma stayed stiff but didn't move away.

"Are you ready to go look at the papers?"

Emma nodded and led the way down the stairs. They spent a few minutes wandering through the rooms of the small house next to the lighthouse, then went into the study, where Mary pulled open the drawers of the file cabinet, carefully taking out the log and the pile of papers and setting them on top.

"What are they?" Emma asked, looking curiously over Mary's shoulder.

"The log lists weather patterns and boats that passed and anyone who visited the lighthouse. That's where we're going to start." She opened the cover of the old book, its pages stiff and yellowed with age.

"What are we looking for?" Emma asked.

"Well, I turned up some information that said David might be guilty of another crime, a serious one," Mary said.

"What?" Emma asked, completely absorbed in Mary's words.

"Arson," Mary said. "A fire that caused the death of two people. But I don't think he did it."

Emma's brows scrunched together. "What makes you think he's innocent?"

"The letters I found," Mary said. She was finding it helpful to explain things to her granddaughter, as though saying it out loud helped her organize her thoughts about it more effectively. "He wrote to his mother that he had confessed his crimes, and I think if he had actually been responsible for someone's death, he would have mentioned wanting to atone for it. He was so honest in the letter, so wanting of her forgiveness. I think he would have owned up to causing someone's death if he really had."

Emma nodded, taking in her words. "That makes sense," she said. But then she frowned. "That's not really proof, though," she said. "That's just your hunch."

"Yes," Mary said. "But I'm hoping there might be some proof in here. David often came to the lighthouse, and whenever he did, it was recorded in this log." Mary rested a hand on the old book.

"So if he came on the night of the fire, then we'd know he didn't set it," Emma said, putting it together. "When was the fire?"

"It was set sometime in the early evening of January 10, 1925," she said, stepping back so that Emma could do the looking.

Emma bent her head over the old book. "It starts in 1924," she said.

"I guess the earlier ones were lost," Mary said.

"Oh, David was here on September 12, 1924," Emma said excitedly. "And again on October 1. He really did come here a lot!"

Mary could feel her heart rate pick up in anticipation, but she held back from turning the pages of the book to the right date, wanting to let Emma have her moment of discovery. Mary sent up a quick prayer that they might discover good news.

"Okay, 1925 starts on this page," Emma said, running her finger down the page. "Here's an entry for January 10 and — Oh, look, he was here!"

Mary looked to where Emma was pointing, and sure enough, on January 10, 1925, David had been at the lighthouse from 5:00 PM until 8:00 PM. She laughed with pleasure and was thrilled to hear her granddaughter's laughter peal out as well.

"We did it, Grandma! We proved he's innocent!" Emma exclaimed joyfully. In her exuberance, she threw her arms around Mary, who pulled her close, thankful for the discovery about David, but much more thankful to have her granddaughter's arms around her again.

TWENTY-SEVEN

Mary drove back home and dropped off a bubbly Emma, who rushed inside to tell her mother of their morning's adventures. Then Mary walked into town, planning to make a quick stop at the pharmacy before going into the store. She needed to pick up a prescription for Betty and thought to get it done early. She was still feeling the flush of her discoveries and her moment of connection with Emma as she walked down Meeting House Road and noticed a small group of people gathered in front of Cape Cod Togs. As she walked up, Mary saw that one of the people was Cynthia, and she realized what was going on. This was her family's building, the one she had been working to get named a historic landmark.

"Mary, hello," Cynthia said when she saw Mary. Cynthia was always enthusiastic, but today she seemed to be bubbling over and her eyes twinkled. "I have exciting news."

Mary smiled, ready to share in her friend's joy.

"These good people are from the historical society, and as of five minutes ago, they have officially confirmed that our family's building is a historic landmark," Cynthia said, sounding for all the world like a teenage girl just asked out on her first date.

"How wonderful," Mary said. "Congratulations."

"I'm just thrilled," Cynthia gushed.

"It's quite an honor," Mary agreed. "And I know you've worked hard to make it happen."

"Yes, though it's been a labor of love," Cynthia said. "At this point, I could tell you every scrap of history this building has ever had. For example," she said, turning to the small group of men and women from the historical society, "it had a brush with danger in 1925."

Mary grinned. That was the night of the hardware store fire next door. She knew there was more to this story than Cynthia probably guessed. She headed to her shop, happy that her friend's dream of making the family building a historic landmark was coming true at last.

The first thing Mary did when she arrived

at her store after her stop at the pharmacy was to call Henry. She quickly updated him on her latest discoveries, starting with the Bible and ending with David's innocence in the arson case. When she had finished, Henry let out a deep breath.

"I guess all this explains why David left the money and ring behind," he said. "And that he went to the church on the night he left town to tell Reverend Montgomery where to find the map that led to the treasures he had buried. We also know they were never found because Reverend Montgomery never returned to the lighthouse. But there's one thing we still don't know. Why does the map lead to a dead end?"

"That's the million-dollar question," Mary agreed. "All I can think is that we must be missing something. I think we have the pieces of the puzzle; it's just a question of fitting them together."

And after saying good-bye to Henry and hanging up the phone, Mary vowed to do just that.

That night Mary couldn't sleep. She was keyed up from the excitement of the day's discoveries but also frustrated that the ring was still missing. She ran through it all again in her mind, but Mary could not fit the puzzle pieces together. Gus was fast asleep at the foot of her bed, a strip of moonlight shining across his body. But even his deep slumber couldn't help lull Mary. Finally, she decided that what she needed was a cup of hot cocoa, and she headed quietly down to the kitchen.

Right outside the door of the kitchen, she paused and listened. Sure enough, there was the sound of something being set on the counter, and then footsteps. Mary's guard was up as she walked as silently as she could into the dark room. A figure spun around and shrieked in surprise.

"Grandma, you scared me," Emma said, squinting as Mary flipped on the light with a chuckle.

"You gave me a bit of a fright as well," Mary said. Then she cocked her head to one side. "What has you up so late?"

Emma sighed like a world-weary traveler, and Mary bit back her smile. She did not want to seem in any way condescending to Emma, who was clearly in adult mode. "I couldn't sleep," Emma said.

"Me neither," Mary said. "I was going to make myself a cup of cocoa. Can I interest you in a cup?"

She fully expected the cold shoulder she was sadly becoming accustomed to from

Emma, but to her surprise, Emma pulled out one of the chairs at the kitchen table and sank down into it. "Thanks, Grandma, I'd like that," she said.

Her heart full, Mary bustled about heating up milk, adding cocoa powder, salt and vanilla, and stirring. The kitchen filled with the heavenly scent of chocolate as she poured them each mugs.

Emma took a sip. "*Mmm,* that is so good," she said contentedly.

"There's nothing like a good cup of cocoa to soothe the soul," Mary said.

Emma nodded, then turned to Mary with a smile. "It's pretty cool how we found out that David Woodrow didn't start that fire," she said. "I think we're as good as the detectives on *CSI.*"

Mary laughed. "Yes, I think we could give that bunch a run for their money."

But then Emma's smile faded. "But we didn't solve the real mystery," she said.

"Not yet," Mary said, taking a sip of her cocoa.

Gus padded in and went to investigate his food dish.

"You really want to find the ring for Henry and his cousin, don't you?" Emma said softly.

Mary nodded. "I think it would mean a

great deal to them."

"Then I'm going to help you do it," Emma said with determination. "What's our next step?"

Mary smiled with utter delight. "Well, I'm not sure," she said.

Emma's brow crinkled. "What's weird is how the star on the map didn't lead anywhere."

Mary nodded. "Yes, it's quite odd."

"I think we should start there," Emma said, taking a sip of her cocoa.

Mary felt as though she had missed a step in her granddaughter's thinking. "Where?"

"With a map," Emma said. She had a bit of a cocoa mustache on her upper lip. "We should get an atlas out of the library and see if you were looking in just the right place."

Mary didn't want to tell Emma that she had already done that, not when Emma was so enthusiastic and they were finally talking again. "That sounds like a good idea," Mary said.

Emma smiled, pleased. "We can go first thing in the morning."

"I'd love that," Mary said.

Emma got up to put her empty mug in the sink, and when she was done, she said something too softly for Mary to hear.

"What was that?" Mary asked.

"I said I'm sorry," Emma said, her voice still muffled. "You were right about my story, and I shouldn't have gotten so angry."

"Oh, hon, I understand," Mary said. "That story meant a lot to you, and it hurt to hear criticism."

"I have to get used to that if I'm going to be a real author, though, right?" Emma asked.

"I think so," Mary said.

"Tomorrow, I'm going to make some changes to my story," Emma said. "I want to use some parts from the mystery."

"That's a wonderful idea," Mary said.

Emma looked at her shyly. "When I'm done, would you read it and tell me what you really think?" she asked.

"Only if you promise no silent treatment afterward," Mary teased.

Emma laughed, then kissed her grandmother good night and went upstairs.

Mary took the last sip of her cocoa. It was now cold, but it was still good. Her heart was light after the conversation with Emma. Mary rinsed out the mugs and headed up to bed. She was finally drowsy enough to sleep.

The next morning, Mary, Emma, and Gus,

who was nestled in Mary's bag, headed into town. It was an overcast day with just a glint of light near the horizon that hinted the sun might appear later on. The air was cool, and Emma pulled her jacket close around her narrow shoulders as they walked down Main Street.

Mary opened up the shop and set Gus down as soon as they were inside. The little gray cat scampered off to explore the shelves, and Mary went behind the counter to turn on the computer while Emma turned on the lights in the store.

"Grandma, do you have an atlas here?" Emma asked. "If you do we don't have to wait to go to the library to look at the map again."

"I'm afraid not," Mary said. "The only thing I have here is a modern map" — she pointed to the shelf where she featured maps and tour books for visitors to Ivy Bay — "and a couple of old decorative ones from well before David's time. But we can go to the library as soon as Rebecca gets here."

Emma frowned. "Well, maybe I can start with the modern map," she said.

Mary smiled at her eagerness. "In that case, let me get it for you," she said. She pulled a map down from the shelf, and

Emma took it to the back, where she sat on one of the armchairs and unfolded it. Mary bit back the urge to tell her how to orient it, knowing it was good for Emma to figure it out herself.

Mary settled on the stool behind the counter and looked at the computer, debating what to search to bring her closer to the ring.

"Grandma, do you have a copy of the map from the lighthouse?" Emma asked.

Mary tore her eyes away from the computer. "Yes, let me see if I have it with me." She checked in her purse and, sure enough, it was there. "Here you are," she said, walking back and handing it to Emma.

"Thanks," Emma said.

Mary settled back at the computer once more. Perhaps if she —

"Grandma," Emma interrupted again. "I found something weird."

With a sigh, Mary stood up. Clearly, she wasn't going to be able to do any of her own research this morning. But as she walked back to Emma once more, she reminded herself how precious this time with Emma was, and she kissed her granddaughter's head when she got to the back of the small shop. "What is it, sweetie?" she asked.

"Look," Emma said, pointing to a spot on

the map of Ivy Bay and then moving her finger to the copy of the map from the lighthouse.

At first, Mary wasn't sure what Emma meant. But when she realized, she sucked in her breath, her heart starting to beat faster.

"I found something, didn't I?" Emma asked.

"Yes," Mary said excitedly. "You really did!"

TWENTY-EIGHT

As soon as Rebecca arrived, Mary and Emma explained they had an important errand and left the store in Rebecca's capable hands, and they raced for the lighthouse. Mary had called Henry earlier, and he was waiting as they pulled up and parked next to his convertible.

"So what's the big news?" Henry asked, walking over, a smile on his face.

"Just wait until you see what my granddaughter discovered," Mary said. She had the modern map in her hands, and Emma was holding the map from the lighthouse. "Let's go over to the beach, and we'll show you."

The sun was peeking out from behind the thick white clouds as they walked, and the salty breeze off the water blew through their hair. Mary stopped when they reached the sand and turned to the colorful new map. Then she smiled at Emma. "You show him what you discovered," she said, pride in her voice.

Emma held David's map up to the lighthouse and turned shyly to Henry. "Well, I was looking at the two maps, and I saw that there's something different about them."

Henry looked at Mary, clearly thinking that Emma had seen what they had already discovered about the changes to the town. But when he looked back, he saw that Emma wasn't pointing to Ivy Bay, she was pointing to the lighthouse outside Ivy Bay. "It moved," she said. "Sometime between when David drew the map and now, the lighthouse got moved."

Henry stepped up to take a closer look.

"We did some research while we were waiting at the store," Mary said. "And this happened to a couple of lighthouses around the Cape. Decades of storms eroded the cliffs, and eventually enough of the cliffs were washed into the sea that the lighthouses had to be physically moved inland, or else they would have fallen away."

"They actually picked up and moved entire lighthouses?"

"Wouldn't you have loved to see that?" Mary said, laughing. "It sounds crazy, but what other choice did they have? The other option was losing the only thing that kept ships safe along these shores. Here" — she held out a page they'd printed off the Internet — "the same thing happened to the Nauset Lighthouse."

"But if the lighthouse had been moved, wouldn't someone have known about it?" Henry asked, shaking his head.

"No one has done anything about this lighthouse in decades," Mary said. "It would have happened long before it fell into disrepair, and everyone forgot about it."

Henry looked up at the lighthouse and back down at Mary, his eyes shining.

"Well, I'll be," he said.

"And you know what it means, right?" Emma asked.

Henry grinned. "Why don't you tell me?"

"That you and Grandma were looking in the wrong place for the treasure!" Emma crowed.

Henry's eyes met Mary's. "Indeed we were," he said.

"So now that we know, we can follow the right map and find the star," Emma said.

Henry laughed happily, but Mary, who had been studying the map, looked up in dismay.

"I believe we have a problem." She pointed to the spot where the red star would have been. It was now a hundred feet out into the bay. "The spot marked on the map is underwater," she said, all her high hopes thudding to the ground.

"Oh no," Emma wailed.

But to her surprise, Henry's grin just widened. "It's a lucky thing," he said, heading back toward the parking lot, "that I have a boat."

They looked at him in confusion. "But even with a boat, how are we going to get to something that's under all that water?" Emma asked.

"I know some good divers." He grinned at their confusion. "Over the summer, I hired some kids to help me get some old traps from a boat that sank off the coast a while back. They'll be happy to be part of a treasure hunt. I'll just give them a call."

A few hours later, as Mary, Emma, and Henry stood on the deck of the gently swaying *Misty Horizon,* there came a yell from the water.

"I think we've found something," a diver shouted to Henry, who gave them a thumbs-up. Another diver went off the side of the boat, holding digging equipment, and the pair of them slipped back under the sea, which was lit up a brilliant blue with pink tinges from the sun that was just beginning to set. The breeze was cool on the water, but Mary was warmed by the adrenaline coursing through her body because it was possible that, at this very moment, they were about to finish what David had started so many years before. Next to her, Emma was staring eagerly at the water.

Minutes passed, and Mary and Emma stood silent next to Henry, who checked the instruments on the boat. The first diver came up splashing, a package held in her hands.

"I think this is it," Henry said joyfully.

Emma squealed and rushed over to the edge of the boat. Mary was beaming as she watched the diver make her way to the boat. Henry leaned down to take the package from her. She and her partner were grinning broadly as they came back aboard the boat.

Henry, Emma, and Mary knelt down on either side of the bundle. It was about the size of a shoe box and wrapped in oilskin. Henry held a knife in his hand. He looked at Mary. "Ready?" he asked.

Mary nodded, putting one arm around Emma as the boat swayed gently under them. Henry gently sliced the package open. Beneath the layers of oilskin, there was a pile of bills. And hidden in the exact center was a small metal box. Henry tried to lift up the lid, but it was rusted shut. He scraped at the rust with his knife. After working at it for several minutes, he pried it open and carefully lifted the lid. He reached in and then pulled out a glittering sapphire ring.

Mary gasped, then felt her eyes tear up as she looked at the ring, sparkling in the setting sun. Emma squealed again.

"We did it!" she cried. "We found the ring!"

Mary turned to Henry and saw that he, too, had tears in his eyes.

"We did it," Mary said, echoing her granddaughter's words.

Henry smiled. "You did it," he said. "And I can never thank you enough."

The first stars were appearing in the darkening blue sky as the boat made its way back to the marina. Henry had wrapped the money up, planning to bring it to the police station as soon as the boat docked. The ring was tucked safely in his shirt pocket. Mary was staring out at the ocean when suddenly Henry stiffened next to her.

"Who is that?" he asked in a low voice.

Mary turned to look at the shore and a sudden chill blanketed her. Someone was standing on the dock, hidden in shadow, facing the boat. Instinctively, she glanced at Emma, who was sitting near the secured package of money, writing in her journal. She had not noticed the figure standing on the dock.

"I don't know," Mary said, fear building in her throat.

"Don't worry," Henry said as he steered the boat into its slip. He hopped onto the deck, and his hands worked quickly, tying up the boat, but his eyes were sharply focused on the man standing down the dock, who began to walk toward them. His hands were shoved into his pockets, and Mary wondered if he was hiding something.

The man passed under a lamppost, and a yellow light washed over him. Mary drew in a breath. "It's Connor," she said.

Henry looked at her questioningly.

"The graduate student I told you about," she said. "The one who was just a bit too interested in the money David left behind."

Henry's fists clenched at her words. "Why don't you wait here for a moment?" he said, walking toward the walkway off the boat.

Mary went and stood near Emma, blocking her granddaughter from view. The divers stood in front of Mary protectively.

Connor was rushing toward her now, his

face alight in a grin, his hands empty, his old coat flapping in the wind. "Mary, did you find it?" he asked excitedly.

Henry strode off the boat. "What we did or didn't find is no concern of yours," he said roughly.

Connor suddenly looked like a three-year-old who had been scolded for making a mess. "I'm sorry," he said. "I came down to the marina this afternoon hoping to catch Mr. Woodrow." He glanced at Henry. "I wanted to interview someone from David's family for my dissertation. The boat was gone, but a man told me you'd all come here in a rush and were headed for the lighthouse. I knew that could only mean one thing. Did you find it?"

Mary had figured out that much. She looked at Emma, who was now staring at the student, her eyes wide. Mary turned back to Connor. "Connor, David's money is not up for grabs. Even if you had found it, the money's not yours."

Connor looked confused and lowered his head. "Mrs. Fisher, I wouldn't dream of taking the money."

Now Mary was confused. But the shy and perplexed look on Connor's face gave her new insight. She thought back over her interactions with him, and how he alluded to needing money, and that he was working hard on his dissertation. Often, dissertations could provide financially, whether through publication or —

Connor peeled his gaze from the dock and looked up at Mary. "I've applied for a grant, is all. And if I can figure out David's story, I think I'm a shoo-in for it. And the grant will be enough to live off for a year of working on my dissertation."

So that was what Connor meant when he had muttered about money. And why he was so pushy about David. He really did have a lot riding on it. But one piece still didn't fit. "But what about the book you hid from me?" she asked.

Connor's eyebrows came together in another honest expression of confusion. "What do you mean?" he asked.

"The book, the one about unsolved crimes in New England," Mary said, the wind tousling her hair as she spoke.

For another moment, Connor continued to look confused, but then his face lit up with a smile. "Oh, you mean the first day we met?" he asked. "I was planning to read that one that evening, so I just took it with me. I didn't realize you'd notice me putting it in my bag, but now I know better," he said, grinning graciously. "You notice everything."

Mary laughed, and Henry seemed to stand down. Emma had gone back to scribbling in her journal.

Mary looked at Connor, then to Henry. "I'd say it's a good thing this young man is so interested in David. He can tell David's story in his dissertation — his whole story — and I think David would like that, don't you?"

Henry nodded slowly, then smiled at Connor, who still looked intimidated by the bigger man. "I think David would like that a lot," he said. Then Henry grinned at Mary. "And Detective Mary here can tell you all about it. But not right now. Now we have to make a long overdue trip to the police station." His face was full of emotion as he looked at Mary. "At long last, we're going to make this right."

TWENTY-NINE

Henry dropped Mary and Emma off in front of the police station, then drove around to park in the lot behind the simple, modern building. Emma sat down on a bench outside the station and began writing in her journal with light from a nearby streetlamp. Mary stood a few feet away and watched as families strolled down Water Street, their conversation and laughter soft in the night air. Stars shone above, and the yellow streetlamps cast a gentle glow over everything. Mary closed her eyes and took a moment to thank God for the goodness of this night and the joy that came from having righted a wrong committed long ago. None of this discovery would have been possible without God's mercy and grace, and for this Mary felt deep gratitude.

"Mary."

Mary opened her eyes and was surprised to see Reverend Allen standing in front of her. And then, with a flood of guilt, she remembered that she had taken a paper from the Bible. She had intended to return it, but it still hadn't been the right thing to do.

"Hello, Reverend," Mary said, stepping forward. "I owe you an apology."

The reverend raised his eyebrows.

"A few days ago, Patrice let me into the church to look at the Bible," she said. She paused to see if he would refer to having turned out the lights, but the pastor simply looked surprised. "I want to apologize for going against your wishes, though I also wanted to ask you about something strange that happened while I was there."

The pastor looked puzzled. "What was that?"

"When I was sitting in the sanctuary, the lights went out," she said, looking to see what his reaction might be.

But instead of looking guilty, the reverend just looked perplexed. "Was there some kind of power outage?" he asked.

"No," Mary said. "Someone deliberately turned off the lights, and afterward I saw your car leaving the lot."

"Wait," Reverend Allen said. "Was it on Saturday, around five?"

Mary nodded.

The pastor gasped. "Oh no," he said. "I had no idea anyone was in the sanctuary. I came into the church to put away some kitchen supplies, and I thought Patrice had just forgotten to turn the lights out. I didn't even think to check if anyone was in there."

This made sense except for one thing. "I called out when the lights went out," she said.

At this, the reverend looked regretful. He turned to the side and pointed into his left ear, where Mary saw a tiny hearing aid nestled.

"I'm nearly deaf in my left ear," he said. "And when I have the hearing aid off, it skews the hearing in my right. Someone can be yelling, and if they're in the wrong place, I won't hear a thing."

"Well, that explains it," Mary said, relieved. She remembered the time the pastor had snubbed her on the street and realized that that, too, would have been related to his hearing.

Reverend Allen looked concerned. "It must have given you quite a fright."

"It did," Mary said with a smile. "But now I understand. And I also think I understand the reason you were reluctant to allow me to see the Bible."

The pastor's cheeks flushed.

"You spilled coffee on it," Mary said softly, remembering the dark stain at the back of the old book.

The pastor's cheeks were now flaming as he nodded, ashamed. "It was such a careless mistake on my part," he said. "Especially after I kept telling the board that the Bible was safe out in the open, available to everyone. I couldn't let anyone look at it, not until I figured out how to fix it." He turned an earnest gaze toward Mary. "I hope you'll forgive me for letting the sin of pride get the best of me."

"Of course," Mary said. "And I can point you to a book restorer to help you get that coffee out."

The pastor's face lit up. "Really?"

Mary nodded, smiling. "I sometimes buy rare books and first editions, and often they are sold by restorers. They buy them at bargain prices when they are damaged, and they fix them up and resell them at a profit. Some of them do quite masterful work."

"That would be wonderful," the pastor said. "I'll be thanking God in my prayers tonight that He sent you to me. Thank you for keeping your heart open to me despite my earlier attitude."

Mary smiled, knowing that she, too, had much to thank God for.

That night over fried chicken, peas, and biscuits, Mary and Emma filled everyone in on the discoveries of the day.

"I can't believe that old map really led you to the money," Betty said, helping herself to a second piece of chicken. "And the ring! What a treasure to have uncovered."

"I'm proud of you for figuring out that the lighthouse had moved," Lizzie said, reaching over and affectionately tousling Emma's hair.

Emma quickly smoothed her hair, but there was no mistaking her pleasure at her mother's compliment. "Grandma and I are a good team," she said, grinning at Mary. "We should open our own detective agency."

Mary's heart was full as she beamed at her granddaughter, and she caught Lizzie smiling tearfully at both of them.

"I can't believe you get to keep the money," Luke said. "Are you going to buy a castle?"

Mary smiled, amused by her grandson. On the way home from the police station, she and Henry had discussed the best way to atone for what David had done, with

Emma chiming in as well.

"We'll give half the money to Grace Church," Mary said.

Emma nodded. "That way the money can be used to help people," she explained to her brother.

Mary met Lizzie's proud smile as she gazed fondly at Emma, who had promised to show Mary her new story later that night.

"Yes, I think it's what David would have wanted," Mary said.

"What about the other half?" Lizzie asked, leaning over to prevent Luke from taking any more biscuits. He already had several being turned into a fort on his plate.

"Well, we couldn't have solved this mystery without help from the Ivy Bay Public Library," Mary said. "And they are facing big budget cuts, so it seemed the perfect time to give them a donation."

"That will help people too," Emma said.

"Yes, libraries are such an important community resource," Mary said. She was looking forward to telling Victoria the news.

Lizzie stood up to clear the dishes, and Mary and Emma began stacking plates. Betty went into the kitchen and returned with warm apple crisp. She had finally managed to use up the last of the apples they had brought back from their day of apple picking. Lizzie followed with dessert plates and a carton of vanilla ice cream from Bailey's.

As Betty began slicing the crisp, the doorbell rang. Mary was surprised, but Betty just smiled at Mary as she rose to answer it. Mary heard voices in the living room, and moments later, Betty led Henry in, followed by two women.

"Annie," Mary said happily, standing up.

"And this is Kate," Henry said, his hand resting gently on the young woman's shoulder. Kate had short brown hair, an elfin smile, and her mother's and uncle's big green eyes. She grinned at Mary. "So this is the detective who tracked down the box and the money and all those answers about our family's black sheep?" she asked.

Henry laughed as a blush spread across Mary's cheeks. "I'm not a detective," Mary said.

"I think that's what they call people who solve mysteries," Henry said, grinning.

"I had some help," Mary said, walking around the table so she could rest her hands on Emma's shoulders. "This is my granddaughter Emma. I couldn't have solved this without her."

Annie bathed Emma in her warm smile. "Then I thank you too," she said.

Emma grinned, her cheeks flushing as she ducked her head shyly.

Annie stepped up and clasped Mary's hands in hers. "And I can't tell you what it means to have this mystery solved," she said, her voice heartfelt. "I had always wondered about David, and to know that he repented and did in fact leave the money behind is better than I ever imagined." She shook her head sadly. "I wish his mother could have known. I wish she had opened those letters."

Mary squeezed her hands in sympathy, and Annie smiled again. "But you found them for us, and I can't tell you what it means to me."

Betty's voice broke in. "Please join us for dessert," she said. "I made enough for everyone."

"Thanks, Betty, we'd love to," Henry said. "But first there's something we need to do. Mary, Annie, and I will be right back," he said, then looked at Mary. "If that's okay with you."

Annie had not mentioned the ring, which meant that thoughtful Henry had waited to share the moment of its return with Mary. Her heart full, Mary followed them into the living room while Kate settled in at the table, chatting with Lizzie and Betty about her upcoming wedding.

Henry stepped closer to Mary to give her the ring to present to Annie, but Mary shook her head. "This is yours to give," she said softly. "I'm just honored to be here for it."

Henry nodded, then turned to his cousin. "Annie," he said, his voice gruff. "When Mary and I found the money, we found something else, something David wanted his family to have."

Annie looked surprised.

Henry held out his hand, the ring sparkling in the center of his palm. Annie brought both hands to her cheeks as she gasped in amazement. "It's not —" she started, her eyes filling with tears.

Henry nodded, his own eyes shining. "It is," he said. "It's the sapphire ring."

Annie was laughing and crying, her face alive with wonder as she picked up the precious family heirloom.

"It's for Kate," Henry said.

Annie wiped tears from her cheeks, then threw her arms around both Henry and Mary. Mary could feel a lump in her own throat.

Then Annie stepped back and called her daughter. Kate appeared in the doorway, and her face lit up with alarm to see her mother in tears.

"Sweetheart, these are happy tears," Annie said, trying to wipe them away, though more continued to flow. "Because tonight, Henry and Mary have given me a most precious gift. And now, with the greatest joy, I get to pass it on to you." She reached for her daughter's hand and pressed the ring into it.

Kate looked down, then sucked in her breath. "The family ring?" she asked breathlessly, looking from her mother to Henry to Mary. All three nodded.

And now, Kate's eyes were filling. "Mama, are you sure you want me to have it? I know how much this ring means to you."

"Which is why it will bring me such happiness to see it on your hand at your wedding," Annie said. She turned to Mary. "And for that, I can never thank you enough."

Mary found it hard to speak over the lump in her throat. And it was hard to find words to match the joy in her heart at seeing the ring back where it belonged. "I'm just glad it's back in your family," she said. "That's more than enough thanks for me."

"Why is everyone crying?" a little voice said from the doorway.

They all looked over at Luke.

"Did you think we ate all the apple crisp without you?" he asked, his eyes wide.

Everyone laughed, and then Mary gave thanks to God for this moment as she followed her friends back to the table, where they joined her waiting family.

It was the last morning of Lizzie's visit, and it was a clear, warm day, so Mary, Betty, Lizzie, Henry, and the kids had packed up a picnic to take to the beach before they got on the road for home.

Luke rolled up his pant legs and raced down by the surf, running into the water, then squealing and running out when the cold waves lapped at his bare toes. Emma followed, lost in thought, as she looked out over the water. Mary smiled as she looked at her, knowing that her granddaughter was thinking about the adventure they had had together.

But now she felt sadness tugging at her at the thought of her daughter and grandchildren leaving.

"It's been a good visit," Lizzie said, linking her arm with Mary's and giving it a squeeze. The sun was bright overhead, making the sand gleam and the water shimmer out to the horizon.

"It has," Mary said wistfully.

"And you got to witness the solving of a century-old mystery," Betty added. She had taken off her shoes and rolled up her khaki pants to feel the sand on her toes.

"It's not every day you get to be a witness to that," Lizzie said. "Have you told Pastor Miles and Victoria about the donations yet?"

Mary looked over at Henry, who grinned at the memory. "Pastor Miles was pleased as punch when we swung by the church office this morning," he said. "The church needs a new roof, and thanks to David, and Mary here, they're going to get it."

"And you should have seen Victoria's face when we told her," Mary said, laughing at the memory of their stop at the library after their visit to the church.

"I thought she might strangle Mary, she was hugging her so hard," Henry said.

"You did a good thing," Lizzie said, and Mary felt the distinct pleasure of having made her daughter proud.

Above them, two gulls flew low, calling out to each other. Mary looked down the shore, and way off in the distance, she could just barely make out the form of the lighthouse, towering atop the dune. It hadn't been operational in years, but it was still poised to warn ships of danger, as it had back in the days when David Woodrow was a young man.

Mary sent up a silent prayer for David's soul and then a prayer of thanks for her own life, so filled with joy and people she loved. She glanced over at Henry, who was smiling softly at her. She realized that like that young David, she, too, had her life spread out in front of her, and many new joys and mysteries yet to come.

A CONVERSATION WITH ELIZABETH MATTOX

Q: *What draws you to Mary's Mystery Bookshop as a writer?*

A: Mary's love of books mirrors my own, and the setting of Cape Cod is a place I always love to visit. But most of all, I love Mary herself, her determination and smarts, and how grounded she is in her relationships with her family and with God.

Q: *Which character in the series do you most relate to?*

A: I would have to say Rebecca since my kids are the same age as Ashley, and I find myself balancing work and being a full-time mom, the way Rebecca does. And like Rebecca, I have pursued work that brings me in constant contact with stories.

Q: *What is your favorite mystery book/author? Why?*

A: Like Mary, I love Agatha Christie. The twists in her plotting never cease to surprise and please me, and she chooses such fun and exotic settings for her books.

Q: *What spiritual inspiration do you get from Mary and her journey?*

A: I love Mary's relationship with her church community and find that, in many ways, it mirrors my own. I am moved by how strong her faith is, and writing about her relationship with God deepens my own.

Q: *Have you ever had to solve a mystery? Tell us about it!*

A: My kids call me "The Finder" because whenever a shoe goes missing or a book is lost, I can find it. Some days I have more cases than I know what to do with!

Q: *Please tell us about your family!*

A: I have two almost-eight-year-olds, a husband who is also a great dad, and a magnificent kitten named Tango that I recently taught to fetch when I probably should have been doing laundry.

STIR-FRIED CHICKEN
AND BROCCOLI

1 pound chicken breast (about 2 breasts),
  cubed
3 scallions, whites only, thinly sliced on an
  angle
2 cloves garlic, minced
1-inch piece peeled fresh ginger, minced
1 tablespoon soy sauce
2 tablespoons sugar
1 tablespoon, plus 1 teaspoon cornstarch
1 1/4 teaspoons salt
1 tablespoon dry sherry
1 tablespoon dark sesame oil
About 1/3 cup water
3 tablespoons vegetable oil
5 to 6 cups broccoli, trimmed sliced stalks
  and medium florets (keep the 2 cuts separate)
3/4 to 1 teaspoon red chili flakes, optional
1 tablespoon hoisin sauce
Garnish: toasted sesame seeds, optional

In a medium bowl, toss the chicken with the scallion whites, about half the garlic and ginger, soy sauce, sugar, one teaspoon cornstarch, one teaspoon salt, sherry, and sesame oil. Marinate at room temperature for fifteen minutes. Mix the remaining cornstarch with water.

Heat a large nonstick skillet over high heat. Add one tablespoon of oil and heat. Add broccoli stems and stir-fry for thirty seconds. Add the florets and remaining garlic, ginger, two tablespoons of water, and season with quarter teaspoon salt, and pepper. Stir-fry until the broccoli is bright green but still crisp, about two minutes. Transfer to a plate.

Get the skillet good and hot again, and then heat two more tablespoons of oil. Add the chicken and chili flakes, if using. Stir-fry until the chicken loses its raw color and gets a little brown, about three minutes. Add the hoisin sauce, return the broccoli to the pan, and toss to heat through. Stir in the reserved cornstarch mixture and bring to a boil to thicken. Add more water to thin the sauce. Taste and season with salt and pepper, if you like.

Mound the stir-fry on a serving platter or divide among four plates and garnish with sesame seeds. Serve with rice.

ABOUT THE AUTHOR

Elizabeth Mattox was born and raised in New York but spent every summer of her childhood on Cape Cod, just like Mary herself. She is a mom to two adorable seven-year-olds who keep her on her toes at all times. And when she has time, she is also an avid reader, who, like Mary, loves nothing more than getting lost in a good mystery.